Dry Water

Other novels by Robert Stead

Grain
The Smoking Flax
Neighbours
The Cow Puncher
Dennison Grant
The Homesteaders
The Copper Disc
The Bail Jumper

Dry Water

A Novel of Western Canada

by

Robert Stead

Introduction and Notes

by

Prem Varma

The Tecumseh Press
Ottawa, Canada
1983

The Publishers gratefully acknowledge the support of the Ontario Arts Council and the Canada Council.

Canadian Cataloguing in Publication Data

    Stead, Robert J.C., 1880-1959
      Dry Water

ISBN 0-919662-93-5 (bound). - ISBN 0-919662-994-3 (pbk.)

I. Title.

PS8537.T42D79 1983   C813'.52   C83-090116-7
PR9199.2S73D79 1983

The Tecumseh Press Limited
8 Mohawk Crescent
Ottawa, Canada K2H 7G6

Printed and bound in Canada

Contents

Introduction

Dry Water, later named *But Yet The Soil Remains*, is Stead's most ambitious novel. Stead was working on it in December 1932 and had completed it by May 1935.[1] His most ambitious novel, perhaps his best, it aims to be a character story,[2] and the characters are indeed sharply and distinctly drawn. As well, the prairie background comes alive, with greater authenticity than in any of his previous novels. It captures also the gambling spirit infected the west during the 1920s and shows how even the farmers were lured into speculation in the hope of making easy money. With the insight of a psychologist he portrays the feelings of hope and assurance on the one hand, doubt and misgivings on the other, of people caught by the fever of easy money. He catches, too, the tempo of the times; the ups and downs in the stock exchange, the frantic buying and selling, the fall in values and speculation profits, the busy telephone lines, the crowded banks, the indecision of people whether to hold on or to sell, the desperation of those who put up their last cent to stave off calamity, and the ruthlessness with which many were wiped out—all comes alive with a sense of immediacy. And when the botton falls out finally, Stead shows the effects of the crash and how different persons react differently. Jimmie Wayne commits suicide. After his death Ellen tells Donald:

> We wanted children, but they never came. Perhaps that is why he grew to be so absorbed in business. It was a game to him, and he played it all too strenuously. But he did not have your background. The Waynes were never as solid as the Strands.

Donald's son like the return of the prodigal, comes to his father for help, but with no intention of taking Jimmie's way out even if his father cannot help him. He has come prepared; he has stolen money from the bank and tells Donald his plan of stealing a car and crossing the border. He knows that he will get caught finally, but is defiant in his attitude.

The characterization here is as good, if not better, than that in *Grain*, while the range of characterization is much wider. In *Grain*, Gander is the one primarily subtly and psychologically conceived and portrayed, but in *Dry Water* Donald, Jimmie, Clara, and Ellen, are all equally well portrayed. Clara in particular is unique in the Stead canon; in portraying her he shows a skill and insight unmatched among early prairie writers, so that as a character in prairie fiction she stands apart. Through her Stead succeeds in showing "the change in outlook, environment, and personal philosophy"[3] that he had set out to depict.

Dissatisfied and disappointed in her marriage to Donald, Clara seeks an outlet for her pent-up emotions by indulging in a flirtation with Jimmie, and has the courage to tell Donald that she enjoyed her flirtation. When she sees that her husband is still very much in love with his cousin, Ellen, she tells him: "You're in love with Ellen. You always have been in love with Ellen", and continues:

" . . . in Winnipeg you were so absorbed with her that when I started a flirtation with Jimmie to distract your attention you couldn't see it."

"So you were flirting with Jimmie?" He was amazed at the ease of her confession.

"Why not? If one can't have love one must have—something."

"Love? But you didn't want love. You have never encouraged love. You have kept me at arm's length. Until lately—"

"Thank Jimmie for that."

"Jimmie?"

"Of course. Oh Donald, do you know so little? I found flirtation pleasant, like a healing rain after a long drought. Does it surprise you that I came to life again?"

This unusual confession for its day gives the novel a modern viewpoint. For a woman on the prairies in the 'thirties Clara's attitude towards marriage is particularly forward. What she suggests to Donald is not a divorce but "an understanding":

" . . . Oh don't you see the futility of it all? Ellen would suit you, Jimmie would suit me. Why should we continue being four fools because we made a mistake thirty years ago? We are not young now, Donald. Why not seize what happiness we can?"

Clara then tells Donald that she plans a visit to Winnipeg. But Donald, deeply entrenched in his moral upbringing, cannot see eye to eye with her and tells her: "If you go you need not come back." Although he knows that Ellen is the ideal mate for him he cannot break "the thongs of convention and of a certain moral restraint which seemed to be woven into his fibre." He thus differs from Clara and finds her attitude difficult to come to terms with.

Stead is careful to point out that Donald, even before his marriage, realized that Clara was not fitted for life on the farm. In love with Ellen, but unable to marry her because she is his cousin, he is torn between two attractions: on the one hand Clara—beautiful, delicate, and refined; on the other Hester—who would have made a good wife. The conflict is well presented, and Donald's final decision to marry Clara is based on impulse, a choice made regardless of his awareness that she is the "less certain quantity." When their marriage fails, pride makes them conceal the fact from neighbours and children; when they went out they were a "respectable and courteous couple."

Ellen is more typical of the prairie women, but though she loves Donald her strong sense that cousins should not marry makes her life a mockery; for though she denies Donald for the sake of the children who would follow, for her the children never come.

The prairie landscape serves not only as the background against which the story is told but is intricately woven into the narrative and forms an integral part of the whole. It is occasionally used to mirror the feelings and emotions of Stead's characters. To cite one example: when Ellen comes back to her old surroundings, physically it is the same landscape, but it seems to share her feelings:

> The creek where so often she had played as a child still cut its circuitous route across the corner of the farm, but its voice was silent and its shallow depression partly filled with drifted snow. Away stretched the prairies, no longer prairies but the dead aftermath of the season's cultivation, not yet blanketed in their winter shrouds but covered thinly with a dirty patchwork of snow and drifted dust. The dull sky which curtained the horizon seemed an appropriate drop-piece for the still tragedy of her life.

In *Dry Water* Stead attempts to appreciate the good points of the younger generation. Frustrated in his marriage, Donald cannot help admiring the new generation "with its amazing frankness, its willingness to face facts," and wonders if they might "perhaps escape the fog in which its more conventional elders were so hopelessly lost." There is no clash, no condemnation, rather recognition that times, attitudes, and viewpoints have changed. As Donald remarks:

> "I remember at the dances if a girl showed her ankle we thought she was bold; now if she doesn't show her knee you think she is deformed."

The story of homesteading, which forms the first part, is largely autobiographical in such details as the location of the homestead, the school at the corner of the Strand homestead, the teacher who walked six miles to and back from school and boarded with the Strands, the closing down of the school during the winter months, the strict observance of the Sabbath, ploughing virgin land, and the "Scottish strain" in Uncle Jim's ancestry. Even his description of the train and how it was an improvement on the immigrant trains of earlier days, has the realism of personal experience:

> The seats were not of wooden slats, but were covered with red plush, very luxurious in his eyes, and no one was stretched out on board wearing great coonskin or buffalo coats; some were chatting amiably and others were settling down to read the morning *Free Press*. A row of bright brass lamps hung from the roof along the centre of the car, and when the train started . . . the lamps began to rattle and jingle in a very enjoyable manner.

The third part revolves around Donald, the successful farmer, with his problems, his conflicts, and his resolutions. Though it is strong in the conflict and clash of personalities, the ending is weak, for it suggests that Jimmie's death occurs to prevent Clara from leaving Donald—with one stroke Stead saves both marriages. This weakness, common to his other novels as well, suggests a clash in Stead—between his artistic bent and his strict Presbyterian upbringing, with morality taking precedence.

In *Dry Water* Stead moves beyond his other novels. More typical of the prairies, it paints the unpleasant as well as the idyllic, and thus presents a closer realism than do his earlier novels. *Dry Water* failed to get published at the time it was written because the depression had hit the book industry. McClelland & Stewart were intially interested in publishing it, but by the time the manuscript reached them the situation had worsened and unable to get American publisher to collaborate with them, they dropped it. They did suggested that Stead put more action into the book;[4] but Stead, though he accepted the charge that *Dry Water* is not an action story, refused to comply with their request.

He defended it by pointing out:

> It may be granted at once that DRY WATER is not an "action" story. It was not designed to be, but I do not admit that for that reason it is lacking in interest. It is a character story in which the effect of prairie environment on a number of persons, particularly Donald Strand, is, I think, faithfully portrayed against an authentic background. To introduce action which is not native to that backgroung would do violence to the whole book.
>
> Perhaps I may suggest that "My Antonia", in which Willa Cather did for the American prairies what I am trying to do for the Canadian, is certainly not an action book, but it is already almost an American classic.[5]

He went on to cite many other examples of books which were lacking in action but had found favour with critics and public alike. Among them he mentioned his own *Grain* and told them:

> Before publication I was urged to put more action into "Grain", (which I did not do), and the book has established for me a literary reputation with which I cannot afford to trifle.[6]

Stead wished, on the contrary, to consolidate his literary reputation with the publication of *Dry Water*. He wrote to McClelland:

> I think both my publishers and myself should take advantage of the cumulative publicity value of my previous work by putting out something along the same tenor but of still more literary artistry.
>
> This, I think, we have in DRY WATER. I have spent four years on it; it has been written and re-written; there is not a sentence in it which was not put there for a purpose. I have the utmost confidence that when it appears it will be hailed as at least one of the outstanding books of the year.[7]

In order to get an American publisher Stead sent the manuscript to Ann Elmo of the AFG Literary Agency[8] in New York. Longmans Green became interested in the novel and wanted to know "the number of sheets or copies that . . . would be required for the Canadian market."[9] Accordingly, Stead wrote to McClelland & Stewart to find out their requirement and was even prepared to "waive the pay of one thousand dollars advance royalty and accept in its place royalties on publication" in view of the difficult times. But business was bad and the deal fell through.

Correspondence dragged; business was dull; finally on November 1, 1937, Stead asked McClelland & Stewart to release him from the contract and return his manuscript if they did not intend to publish it. When returning the manuscript John McClelland expressed his dissatisfaction with the title, and suggested to Stead that he change it since it was not a "good selling title."[10]

For nine years the manuscript lay untouched. In 1946 the creative urge in Stead sparked again; besides, times had changes. The depression was already history. So, on February 27, 1946, under the tile "Prairie Farm," Stead again tried to market the manuscript; and on June 15, terms of publication were settled with Thomas Allen. In accordance with their wishes Stead shortened the manuscript, but eventually Allen, too, returned it because he could not get an American publisher.

Stead then left it until, on retirement from government service in 1947, he revised it once more, entitling it "But Yet The Soil Remains." This revised version he sent to Lorne Pierce of the Ryerson Press. It was given a favourable comment by one "Ket" a critic for Ryerson, who recommended the book although he felt it to be flawed, but attributed its "roughness" as being "due to abridgement."[11] His report read;

> It is not common in a novel to have a successful farmer as the hero, and the treatment of farming in Western Canada is well done in favor of the farmer, and that "calling" in general. Character portrayal is good, and the development of Donald's character over the years is almost the core of the story. The author has been careful of the tiniest detail even, and has made many delightful comments that will remembered for some time. This is more especially true of the boy's early life.[12]

Despite the recommendation the novel was not published for, as Lorne Pierce explained to Stead, "we have off the press this week McCourt's Fiction Award winner, *Music at the Close* and it is a dead mate for your own. The subject is very similar."[13]

Pierce suggested that Stead submit the novel for the Ryerson Fiction Award,[14] which he did. At one stage it seemed that Stead might win the prize, and a letter to that effect was inadvertently sent to him, but this novel did not have the good fortune of his earlier ones, and close on the heels of the good news came a letter saying that Ryerson had decided not to make an award that year.

The present version of *Dry Water* is based on the final draft which Stead submitted to Ryerson under the title "But Yet The Soil Remains." I have however preferred to keep the original title as I feel that it is, in many ways, more apt and more directly related to the story.

Although there are many copies at the Public Archives (Ottawa) there are basically three versions. The original one is in folder 24, the revised original in folder 21, and the final draft in folder 26. I have used the final draft because Stead did improve his manuscript when he was asked to shorten it. His changes and deletions have made the narrative more pointed and direct. Things and events that were simply narrated at length are now presented directly or just referred to. In revising he reduced much of the of pathos and sentiment, dropped much the intrusion of the narrative voice, and culled out much of the repeated stress on Donald's sense of honour and concern with sin. Stylistically he reduced allusion and descriptive passages. The final version is thus tighten and better controlled.

Notes

1. Letter to McClelland & Stewart December 15, 1932 (Stead Papers, Public Archives of Canada, Ottawa, Vol. I folder 5). Stead says that this novel is "on more ambitious lines than anything he had previously attempted."

2. *Ibid*. In the same letter Stead described it as "a character story."

3. *Ibid*.

4. Letter from McClelland & Stewart of July 16, 1935 (Stead Papers, Vol. I folder 5).

5. Letter to John McClelland of July 22, 1935 (Stead Papers, Vol I folder 5).

6. *Ibid*.

7. *Ibid*

8. I have been able to discover what AFG stands for.

9. Letter to McClelland & Stewart April 29, 1936 (Stead Papers, Vol. I folder 5).

10. Letter from McClelland & Stewart of November 25, 1937 (Stead Papers, Vol. I, folder 5).

11. Letter to Lorne Pierce, n.d. (Lorne Pierce Papers, Douglas Library, Queen's University, Kingston, Box XVI).

12. *Ibid*.

13. Letter from Lorne Pierce of November 10, 1947 (Lorne Pierce Papers, box XVI).

14. The Ryerson Fiction Award was an annual literary prize created in 1941 (for 1942) by the Ryerson Press of Toronto "to stimulate the production of novels that are skilfully written, rich in their interpretations, and genuinely creative in their approach to life." The value of the prize was $1000.00 until 1956.

Part One

1

In the winter of 1890 the branch-line train to Alder Creek left Winnipeg before sunup.[1] The occasion for its early rising was not apparent, for, once out of the yards, it abandoned all pretence of haste and lumbered amiably along the frozen bosom of the Red River Valley[2]. But as it stood at the station in the gray morning awaiting its small quota of passengers it seemed a thing at ease, suggesting comfort and escape from the bleak wind which whirled about the platform, curving little feathers of snow around its wheels and whipping the smoke from its engine into the adjacent gloom. To the left a line of lights straggled along a broad and winding street; to the right the vague outline of box-like buildings faded quickly into mysterious darkness.

Across the space between station and train came a woman holding a small boy by the hand, with the other arm carrying a pudgy valise of the type in vogue at that period, her body bent against the sharp pressure of the wind. She exchanged a few words with the conductor, kissed the boy on the forehead, spoke some assurance in his ear, and hurried to catch her own train on another track.

The conductor helped the lad into the car and showed him to a seat. "Now make yourself comfortable," he said, "and you'll be as safe as the C.P.R. Do you know how safe that is?"

"No, sir," the boy answered, honestly.

"Well, its the safest thing between H—between here and Whoop-up." Out of deference to the youth of his passenger the conductor had made a quick change in his customary figure of speech. "Let me see-what's your name?"

"Donald." He was beginning to lose his awe of the big man with the brass buttons and the heavy gold chain across his front exposure.

"Donald what?"

"Donald Strand."

"Oh, yes. That's what the lady told me. And you're going to Alder Creek to live with your uncle and aunt. And you're ten years old, and—" He was for blundering into something else, but checked his tongue. The boy looked lonely enough without being reminded of his orphanhood. "Well, I must get along and see if the engineer has steam up in his kettle, but I'll be dropping back for a chat when I have time," and he disappeared through the door forward.[3]

Soon they were out on the prairie, and the sun was coming up over the edge of the world. Donald looked in amazement. There was not *one* sun—there were three! A round red sun in the centre, and another sun on either side. They were not quite so large and not so round, but they were very red, and, it seemed, very angry looking. As he gazed, fascinated, his friend the conductor paused beside him.

"You didn't know we had three suns in this country, did you?" he remarked.

The boy's look confessed his bewilderment. "Are they really suns?" he asked.

The answer came very solemnly. "Some people say the sun had pups during the night, but I dunno. What I know is the pups show up before a storm. Lucky you are making your trip to-day; to-morrow we'll be buckin' snow."[4]

Donald began to realize that he was at last on the prairie. He had heard much of the prairie ever since it was decided he was to come to live with his uncle and aunt, but the word had suggested no definite picture to his mind. Now he looked out across an expanse as far as his young eyes could reach, as level as the surface of a lake, undulating with gentle billows of snow which caught and flashed the light of the rising sun like a sea of crystals, broken at great intervals by the tiny islet of some settler's house and stable, itself almost engulfed in the measureless sea with which it was surrounded. He was too young to

2

react to the abysmal loneliness of the scene, but its magnitude stirred within him romantic wonder. Did Uncle Jim live in a place like that, and how ever did he find his way out, without so much as a tree or fence to guide him? But as the day wore on the picture changed; the level lake gave way to rolling country, with the blue fringe of forest occasionally cutting the sky-line; the train rocked through sharp valleys and over sudden bridges; the impatient rasp of the engine came back as its strength was put to the test in climbing heavy hills. The sun was obscured, the horizon contracted; it seemed they had passed into a new world. Donald realized that he was hungry, and dug into his valise for the provision which Mrs. Barrow had made against that contingency.

Early darkness was closing in when they reached Alder Creek.[5] The conductor helped Donald down with his fat valise and hailed the station agent. "Know anything about this kid?" he asked. "Anyone here to meet him?"

The agent shunted a truck loaded with perishable express into the waiting-room before answering.

"Yep—Old Man Strand. He's to call for him. Come on in, son and keep warm."[6] Inside the waiting-room a huge stove glowed with fire.

When Mr. James Strand, homeward bound with a load of firewood, stopped at the station he found Donald upstairs with the agent and his wife, tucking a meal under his belt. "So-ho, and you're Donal'?" he said, surveying the boy. "Bessie's son, and Fred's. You favor your mother, lad. Do you know who I am?"

The boy swallowed mightily to clear his larynx. "I guess you're Uncle Jim."

"That's just me, but I didn't know meals were included in your ticket. Very good of you, Mr. Burke, to take care of him like this. Bring the missus out to the farm some day and I'll square it with two meals for one."

"Won't you sit in yourself?" the agent's wife inquired. "There's lots more."

"I'm sure enough o' that, but I'll not be stayin' to-night, thank you just the same. It's gettin' dark, and we should be on our way. The weather ain't just you'd call promisin'."

2

Down in the waiting-room, by the red pot-bellied stove, the farmer surveyed his nephew minutely. "Yes, you take after your mother," he repeated, "though I can see your father, too. How're you clad?" The quick eye took in cloth overcoat, new leather boots, new woollen mittens, a cloth cap. "Not just the thing for a winter's night, but it's only four mile—not much more than an hour—and young blood is warm." Nevertheless he whipped from his waist a bright red sash and tied it about the boy's head, turning the overcoat collar up under it, and leaving only narrow openings at the eyes and mouth.

Outside, the farmer's team stood blanketed, tied to a post at the station platform. It was quite dark now save for the oil lamp which hung in a triangular glass box at the end of the station. Threads of frost hung like thick grey hairs from the faces of the horses, giving them a strangely human appearance, and the breath from their nostrils shone white in the lamplight. Mr. Strand drew the blankets from their backs and, folding one, laid it on top of the huge load of logs behind. "Climb up and sit on that, Donal'," he directed, "and I'll wrap the other one about you."

Donald did as he was bidden, although handicapped by his new boots and his muffled head. The logs were not big but they were piled high, and his perch on top seemed precarious enough. Mr. Strand, having made the boy as comfortable as he could between the two blankets, seated himself along side. "Come Ned, come Dick," he ordered. The horses tightened their traces, the steel runners squealed in the frosty snow, and they were underway.

The boy sat still, stooping somewhat, a trifle uneasy lest he should topple off. The load swayed on the uneven road and once or twice Mr. Strand threw an arm about him. Incredibly slow seemed

4

their progress compared with travel on the train. From time to time the yellow light from some settler's window would come into view, and it seemed ages until they drew by it. Mr. Strand drove in silence, save for an occasional inquiry whether Donald was cold, and the boy was left with his thoughts.[7]

Presently a question which was shaping in his mind found speech. "Do you ever get lost on the prairie after dark?" he asked, finding that he had to shout to make himself heard. Tales of prairie misadvantures had reached his boy's ears and were exciting misgivings which even his confidence in Uncle Jim did not entirely set at rest.

"Why, bless you, yes, but never on a night like this," Uncle Jim answered. "You ain't scared, are you?"

"No," he said, sturdily, "but it's very-dark. I can hardly see the horses' tails."

Uncle Jim threw an arm about him again. "You haven't got your prairie eyes yet. But we don't really need to see on a night like this. Old Ned and Dick would take us home even if we both went to sleep—if we didn't fall off. It is only when a blizzard comes that the horses themselves can't follow the trail, because it gets blown over, and besides the snow sticks in their eyes and sort o' blinds them. Warm enough?"

"Uh-huh."[8] But he was anxious to be entirely reassured and he returned to the subject. "It isn't going to be a blizzard to-night, is it, Uncle Jim?" he asked.

"No—not for awhile, anyway. There's a bit o' grounddrift, and the wind seems to be risin', but we'll make it all right. We're more'n half way there now. Now don' try to talk, like a good boy; you'll get your lungs full o' cold air. Jus' sit still an' keep warm."

So admonished, the boy lapsed into silence. Slowly the sleigh dragged along, creaking through the frosty snow. Donald watched the occasional points of light from settlers' windows until his eyes grew drowsy and he closed them.[9]

A sudden lurch of the sleigh and his uncle's arm tight about him wakened him with a start. His eyes seemed fastened; it was with an effort he forced them open. Everywhere was darkness. The wind pressed steadily upon his back; there was a cold moistness in the air he

5

breathed. He looked about for lights. None was in sight; everywhere just darkness, and, it seemed, a rising sound. No person, no thing; just sound.

"Where are the lights, Uncle Jim?" he shouted.

"The lights?" Uncle Jim's voice came muffled through the pressing air. "Oh, yes; the lights. Guess everybody must ha' gone to bed. Go to bed pretty early on the prairie these winter nights." But he tightened his grip on the lines. "Giddap Ned, giddap Dick," he shouted into space.

Onward they dragged. Donald supposed it was still incredibly slow, but in the utter darkness there was nothing against which to measure progress. He moved his toes and made sure they were still there. Uncle Jim had said they would not be much more than an hour; surely it must be midnight; everybody had gone to bed . . .

There was a sudden change in the swirl of sound, imperceptible to Donald's ears, but plain enough to his uncle's. "That was the bridge over Alder Creek," he shouted, pulling the boy close with his free arm. "Home in five minutes." This time he did not immediately let go, but drew the young form close, and held it.

True enough, a haze of light showed up ahead. At first it was just a grey blur in the darkness, but the blur grew brighter, took shape, because a window with a lamp placed behind it. The horses had quickened their pace without urging; they were swinging along, oh, how they were swinging along! Suddenly they came to a full stop. A door opened; another quadrangle of light beat out against the darkness. There was a figure in the door; a lantern; Uncle Jim was climbing down . . .

3

Donald found himself immediately a centre of great interest. He was unwrapped by the kitchen fire; the sash which covered his face, wet with snow and breathing, was removed; his coat was off, his mittens were off, his cap was off, and he was still blinking in the light when he felt himself enveloped in warm arms and held strong against a breast which made him think poignantly of his mother.

"Oh, let me see him!" a voice was calling. "Mother, you're smothering him! Let me see him!" Then, as his eyes became accustomed to the light, he discerned before him a girl about his own age, with smooth, olive-brown features, hair braided and hanging over her shoulders, arms urging toward him.

"This is your cousin Ellen," the motherly woman said. "She is almost as big as you an' ju' the same age; you're ten, ain't you, Donal'? And this is Lizzie—you've heard o' Lizzie?" A larger girl, Almost a young woman, slipped an arm about him. They nearly were swamping him with their numbers.

With boyish embarrassment he accepted their greetings.[10] They were very kind, but they were strangers, and he was shy among them and stiff with the cold and his long ride. The younger girl plied him with questions: "How did you like riding on the train? How did you like riding on a load of wood? Were your feet cold in those leather boots?"

"Oh, leave the boy alone!" his aunt interrupted, sensing his strangeness. "My goodness, let him get his breath. He's tired an' hungry. Sit down here, son, by the stove, an' never mind Ellen."

He felt better after that, and his eyes, becoming accustomed to the light, began to rove about the room. The walls were of logs, plastered and whitewashed; overhead bare oak joists carried the floor of the upper storey. A clock, with a beautiful lady's face on it, very much like the one which had been in his father's home, ticked complacently from its shelf on the wall. Behind him was the window a lamp in it; across the room was another window, looking out into blackness, except that somewhere out in that black gulf another dimmer lamp seemed flickering its answer. Beside him was a big stove with a kettle boiling merrily, sending up a cloud of steam, and through little transparent openings in the stove came the cheerful glow of fire. A little further away, along the wall, sat a table with a red cloth covering and a lamp with a pretty shade. On the opposite wall hung a picture which rivetted his attention; a man with a gun facing a huge bear in a forest, all done in bright colors and proclaiming the merits of a certain brand of ammunition.

He was still studying this entracing picture when the door opened, admitting a gust of wind which sent the yellow lamp flames leaping in their chimneys. Uncle Jim and a large boy with a lantern were stamping in, and at their heels came a friendly-looking dog. The boy blew out his lantern, took off his cap and outer coat, shook the snow from them and hung them up before turning attention to the newcomer.

"So you're Donald," he said, when these duties were discharged. "I'm Tom." He stretched out his arm and took the younger boy's hand in his. "I hope you'll like living with us."

"I hope I will, too," said Donald, beginning to find his tongue.

"Of course you will. Here, Hector, this is our new brother. Make yourself friendly."

The dog nosed the boy a moment; then, evidently satisfied as to his credentials and character, rose soberly on his hind legs, placed his paws on Donald's shoulders, and, if Tom had not pulled him back just at the right moment, would have saluted him with a wet tongue across his face.

"Down, Hector," he ordered. "I didn't say 'too friendly'. But that's a good sign, Donald. When Hector wants to kiss you you're one of the family. He was trying to kiss Lizzie's beau the other night."

"Oh, he never was!" the big girl contradicted. "Don't believe all Tom tells you, Donald." But she blushed as though the jest had been not altogether distasteful.

8

Meanwhile Uncle Jim had removed his outer clothing, combed the snow out of his beard, pulled off his long felt boots and substitude lighter shoes, while Aunt Annie was busy setting the table. In a lull in the chatter Donald heard the stove pipes rattled with the wind.

"I guess you ain't home any too soon," the woman said. "It seems to be blowin' up real rough. We figured you'd be late, so we went ahead with our supper, but yours'll be ready[11] in a minute."

"Well, that's the best news I've heard all day." Uncle Jim answered, settling down confortably in his armchair. "Farmin' is hungry work, eh, Donal'? As for the weather, it might be better. There's enough snow to kick up a storm if the wind keeps risin'."[12]

Aunt Annie had placed on the table two plates loaded with fried potatoes and a platter of fried eggs, but as Donald sat to his meal he was disturbed inwardly by the knowledge that he already had filled himself at the station agent's only two hours before. The fried potatoes had a wonderful smell and the eggs looked tempting, but conscience prodded him. Should he make a clean breast of it; should he say, "Aunt Annie, I've had my supper?" He was still worrying over this problem in propriety when the first forkful of potatoes melted in his mouth; soberly his eyes rested on his plate, wondering what he should do. With the second forkful the voice of conscience became less insistent. His cheeks were a little red, because of course Uncle Jim knew, but he kept on eating. When, at last, he ventured to look up, his eyes met Uncle Jim's and caught a twinkle which set conscience quite at rest. Aunt Annie brought more potatoes and he took a second helping, and when his plate was clear again she poured thick syrup into it and placed the bread and butter beside him. "Must eat plenty and grow up big," she counselled. "We need another man on the farm right away."

"Farmin' is hungry business, ain't it, Donal'?" Uncle Jim repeated. Donald was at his second slice of bread and butter. :"Yes, Uncle Jim," he agreed.

4

After supper they sar for a while enjoying the happy feeling which comes from having been hungry and being well fed, but when the hands of the clock pointed to eight Tom got up, lighted his lantern, and put on his heavy coat and cap. Hector pretended to sleep profoundly in front of the stove, but Tom stirred him gently with his foot. "Get up, you old bluffer!" he ordered. "It's eight o'clock, and time for you and me to be looking' things over." At first the dog ignored the stirring foot, but a little firmer punch brought him rectantly up on his front paws. His eyes were saying plainly that this was no night to disturb a fellow, but routine and discipline conquered, and, yawning mightily, he arose slowly to all fours.

Uncle Jim was reaching for his heavy felt boots. "Don't you bother to-night, Pa," Tom told him. "You've had a heavy day, and I can manage."[13]

The farmer settled back comfortably. "Well, all right. I guess I ain't as young as I was. But be careful, son; it's blowin' pretty strong." With another sudden blast from the storm outside Tom and Hector disappeared through the door, and the farmer felt[14] for his knife and tobacco.

Ellen came quietly to Donald's side. "Would you like to play something, or look at my book?" she asked. Donald felt too tired to play so he said he would look at her books. She brought him her school reader, and in a moment had him talking about the school he had left, and asking her questions. "We have no school here in winter," she told him. "You see, a storm might come up, and the children might get lost, but Lizzie helps me an hour each day with my lessons, and she'll help you, too, and so will I."

Before he knew it the clock was striking nine. "You don't go to bed at seven o'clock," he said, returning to a subject which was vaguely disturbing him.

"Oh, no. We have prayers at nine, and go to bed right after. What made you think we go to bed at seven?"

"Well, when we were driving home all the lights went out, and Uncle Jim said he guessed everybody had gone to bed."

Ellen laughed. "Pa must have been joking," she said. "I guess there was too much storm for you to see the lights."

Donald reflected on her answer for some moments. So that was it.

He had become conscious of a certain change in the family atmosphere. There was a slight stirring around; chairs were faced toward the table. Then he notice that Aunt Annie had placed the big family Bible on the red tablecloth; Uncle Jim's armchair was drawn up alongside, and Uncle Jim was adjusting his glasses. Then the farmer opened the book at a mark and read a chapter in a deep, resonant voice, quiet unlike his conversational speech. Uncle Jim was a good reader, deliberate and sympathetic, even though he stumbled a little on strange words. After the reading each knelt before his chair while the farmer, with deep reverence, repeated a prayer well worn from long usage. Only once did he hesitate, and his tone changed as he left the beaten track. "An' bless the new son Thou hast given us, an, grant that he may grow up to be a good man, an' never have occasion to be ashamed o' anything he has done." Donald felt the blood rushing about his face as he realized that these words applied to him. It seemed a very solemn and responsible thing to be prayed for in this way before the whole household. He lost track of the prayer and was recalled to time and place only when he heard the others resuming their seats.

For a few moments they sat in silence as though unwilling to break a spell which hung about them with something of benediction in it. Then Aunt Annie lighted another lamp which she had taken from a shelf. "Kiss everybody good night, Donal'," she said, "an' I'll show you to your bed." Donald did as he was bidden, beginning with Uncle Jim, whose whiskers were still damp, and ending with Ellen, who added a little hug to her kiss. But Tom[15] landed him a playful punch in the ribs, as much as to say that we men don't take much stock in kisses but we understand each other, don't we?

11

The lower part of the house was divided into two rooms by a stairway in the centre, up which Aunt Annie now guided her guest. To the left of the stairs lay a large room in which Mr. and Mrs. Strand slept and where, as Donald was to learn, an occasional evening hour might be spent, although the real living centre of the family was the kitchen. The upper storey, to the right, was divided into two rooms, in one of which Tom slept; at the left was one larger space, occupied by the two girls. But it was to the front part of the house, above the stairs, that Aunt Annie led him. This could hardly be called a room at all; it was just a little nook tucked in between the stair railing and the wall. There was space only for a short bed and a little box in front of it. The bed was very high, the tick having been newly stuffed with fresh straw, and homemade patchwork quilts in many colors[16] lay over it.

"This will be your bed, Donal'," his aunt was telling him. "You won't fall out, will you? It's pretty high, but it 'll soon squeeze down."

The boy's shyness was beginning to be set at rest. "I didn't fall off the load of wood, did I?" he asked, with some sense of achievement.

Aunt Annie laughed. 'That's right," she agreed, "and if you could stick on it I guess you'll be here in the mornin'." She helped him with his preparations for bed and made him kneel before her to say his prayer, burying his head in her lap while her fingers fondled his hair. He rattled through his well-known lines, but the urge of improvision was on him also. "And God bless Uncle Jim and Aunt Annie and Tom and Ellen and Lizzie." That was his unpremeditated order of precedence.

He paused. "Would it be all right to put Hector in, too?" he asked.

Aunt Annie weighed the question for a moment. "Yes, I think it would," she said.

"And Hector," he added. Then, encouraged, and without further authority, "And Ned and Dick."

With Aunt Annie's help he climbed the mountainous bed and settled down between the woollen blankets. Aunt Annie stood beside him for a moment, her hand on his cheek. "God bless you, my little boy," she whispered, and, stooding down, kissed him again. "You won't need to get up till I call you."

She carried the lamp away with her and he was left in darkness. The girls were chattering in their room and there were sounds downstairs of Uncle Jim moving about, but presently these died away. As they did so, others which he had not been noticing arose to take their place. The wind was whipping about the log house, howling around the eaves, shaking the tin chimneys as though it might be in a rage at them. Now and again the bed would tremble with its violence. But it was very warm and comfortable, and Donald was sure he was quite safe with Uncle Jim to look after everything, and Tom to help.

As he lay his thoughts began to wander back over the events of recent days and weeks. The train journey had already become a mist, but behind that mist was something which never would quite fade from his memory—the day Mrs. Barrow had help him in her arms and wept while she told him his father and mother had gone to Heaven. It seemed a strange way to go, through the ice on the Ottawa river, and the water must have been very cold. He had heard the neighbors talking about it when they didn't know he was listening; they said his father must have lost his way, as there was a fog on the river, and he drove onto thin ice. They told him God had taken his father and mother. But did God send the fog. and if his father had been able to keep on the trail, would God not have taken him? It was all very puzzling, and the water must have been very cold. He wept a little as he thought about it, but presently he fell asleep.

5

When he awoke light was shinning from somewhere. It took a few minutes to remember where he was, but soon[17] he recognized his bed and saw that daylight was coming through the open doors of the rooms along the stairs. The house was shaking even more than it had done the night before, and the wind was howling louder. It was colder, too. He could see his breath as it rose above him, but the bed was warm and he settled down again, remembering that Aunt Annie had said he need not get up until called. But it was not long until a summons came by the vivacious Ellen, who bore also the important news that a regular blizzard was blowing outside, and you bet it was lucky they got home when they did or they might have had to stay on the prairie all night. "Pa was lost on the prairie all one night, once, with a load of wood, too," she added.

Donald was interested. "Didn't he get froze?"

Ellen curled a contemtuous nose. "Froze? Humph! I guess you don't know Pa. He cut some poles from his load and drove them in the snow and made a shelter with the horse blankets and then he cut more wood and made a fire and pulled the horses round so they were kind of in the shelter too and they were all huncky-dory there all night long. But Ma and us were pretty well scared and you bet we were glad when he came next day even if he had burnt up most of his load of wood."

"I guess you were, all right," Donald agreed, wondering a little to himself what Uncle Jim would have done if his team had gone through the ice on the Ottawa.

It was warmer down stairs, and Donald ate his breakfast on the corner of the table nearest the fire. The meal was of porridge and milk, with sugar, and toast well buttered. After eating he went to a window to watch the storm, but the glass was so covered with frost he

14

could see nothing. Uncle Jim and Tom and Hector were out at the stables, so he settled down with one of Ellen's books until summoned to help bring potatoes from the cellar.[18]

Donald was given a knife and set to helping Ellen peel the potatoes, a task for which he showed no great aptitude. The blade would keep either digging in or coming out altogether. With admiration he watched Ellen's slim, nimble fingers.

It was almost noon before Uncle Jim and Tom and Hector came bouncing into the house. "Whew! That's a peeler!" said Uncle Jim, slamming the door quickly to shut out the gust of snow that followed them. "Can't see to the pump. Hello, Donal'! Good job we got home last night before the storm broke."[19]

"You sit beside Tom," Aunt Annie said, announcing dinner.[20] When they were all in place Uncle Jim leaned his head on his hand and said some words very rapidly, ending in a breathy[21] "Amen", and the next moment was busy helping himself to hot fried pork from a platter.[22] The elder Strands plied knife and fork indiscriminately, and Lizzie too was somewhat open-minded, but Tom and Ellen belonged to the new generation. They were observant, and the influence of the school teacher who boarded with them during the summer, and the preacher who occasionally shared a meal at the table, had left its mark upon their manner.[23]

6

Donald lay in the comfort of his bed thinking over the crowded events of the day. A great respect for Uncle Jim and Tom was finding birth in his heart; admiration of their skill and courage, delight in their companionship. For Ellen, too, he felt something which he later knew to be the anchoring of an affection which all the troubled years to come would not dislodge. Lizzie and Aunt Annie had not yet registered deeply upon his consciousness.

It was all very strange that God should have brought him to this home on the prairie and given him friends like this. He wished his mother and father could have been there, too. But then, if his mother and father had not broken through the ice, he probably never would have known Uncle Jim, or Tom, or Ellen, or Hector, or any of them. Did God have to send them through the ice so that he might know these new friends? It was all very confusing.[24]

The blizzard continued for three days, but the fourth morning when Donald awoke he was conscious of a change which at first he could not analyze. The house was cold and he wrapped his body and limbs closely with the warm blankets. Frost had formed along the edges exposed to his breath; its wet caress drew across his cheek as he settled himself more snugly within them. Then, with complete return of consciousness, he knew what had happened. The trembling had stopped. The bed was utterly still. The whipping about the eaves had ceased; the stove pipes no longer rattled where they rested into the tin chimneys. Such sounds as reached his ears were those of industry coming from kitchen below. With sudden resolution he threw back the blankets and clambered hurriedly into his cold clothes.

"Storm's over!" cried Ellen, when she heard his footsteps on the stairs. "Come and look out. I've melted a piece of window."

16

She had melted the frost from a corner of the windowpane by pressing a warm wet cloth against it. Donald had to stand on tiptoe to look, but the sight rewarded his effort. As far as his eye could reach lay a wilderness of purest white, sparkling under the sunlight like an ocean of gems suddenly congealed in the midst of its undulations. At two or three points in the distance the snow lay heaped in larger mounds, and from each mound a spiral of blue smoke rose lazily skywards. At a great height it flattened out in a miniature cloud, presenting somewhat the effect of a huge, crooked nail with its point resting upon the earth.

"That's Calder's," Ellen said, indicating the nearest of the smoke spirals. "Their house is almost buried with snow. And that's Mergle's and that's Sinclair's, and tha's Crisp's" she pointed out other spirals. "Everybody's all right. After a storm we always look for everybody's smoke. Pa has looked all 'round, and there's smoke from everybody's house."

Ellen's eyes were bright with joy in the neighborhood welfare. But Aunt Annie was calling Donald to breakfast. "Your porridge is gettin' cold, Donal'," she said. "and there's lots o' snow to shovel today. Always lots o' work after a blizzard."

Donald found this to be true. Although the temperature was many degress below zero he was supplied with warm mittens and a pair of Tom's felt boots and set to help with the shovelling. "Keep an eye on your ears an' cheek," Aunt Annit cautioned. "Don' let 'em freeze."

Elen laughed. "How can he keep an eye on his ears, Ma?" she questioned.

"He'll know next time, if he don't," Aunt Annie answered, refusing to see anything absurd in her remark.

7[25]

Sundown[26] schoolhouse sat on a corner of the Strand homestead, across Alder Creek. The district had been named Sundown by settlers who evidently thought that here they sat on the western rim of the world. About midday of Donald's first Sunday on the farm,[27] as the noon meal was filling the house with appetizing odors, Uncle Jim remarked that like as not, in spite of the blizzard, Reverend Mr. Mackenzie would keep his preaching appointment that afternoon, and it was his Christian duty to have the school in readiness.[28]

Through a cleared space of windowpane Donald watched him plodding across the unbroken snow to the schoolhouse. A little later a column of smoke rising from its chimney gave evidence that the good work was well in hand.

The preaching service was timed for three o'clock, and with the approach of that hour Donald and Ellen kept place at the windowpane diligently, scanning the road to the north. "He'll come down by Crisp's" Ellen explained, "and we won't dress till we see him coming." To Donald's keen eyes fell the honor of first seeing the moving speck in the distance. He pointed it out to Ellen. "He's coming, Ma! she cried, and immediately there was a rush of activity as each member of the household changed to the clothes which were worn only at the Sunday service or on other very special occasions.

The activity was not all in[29] in the Strand household. From other snowed-in settlers' homes also keen eyes had been watching the road from the north, and the apearance of the moving speck had set their families agog. Soon other specks appeared on the white prairie blanket, all bending slowly toward the schoolhouse.

Mr. Mackenzie was the first to arrive. He did not stop at the meetingplace but turned the heads of his weary horses to the Strand buildings, and the wise beast summoned new energy with the prospects of food and shelter before them. Mr. Strand, Tom, and Donald met him in the yard, Tom and Donald taking charge of the team while Mr. Strand ushered the minister into the warmth and hospitality of the house. Presently the settlers began to arrive, and each teamster, after dropping his passengers at the schoolhouse, pressed on up to Strand's. Tom met them all with a cheery cry and found room for their horses by turning some of the young stock out of the stables. To mild pretests against this action Tom averred that it would do the beast good to suffer a little for the cause of religion.

At length the whole party gathered in the schoolhouse, and it was not a large group, when all were counted. Eighteen, Donald made it, including the preacher. To the boy the experience was one of absorbing interest. It was his first glimpse of the interior of the building where he was to get such book learning as was to be his for[30] the battle of life. A square box it was, four walls and a ceiling, wainscotted to the height of his head, plastered above, with a blackboard across one end. Near the door sat a huge stove[31] from which most of the smoke was conducted through a long and wobbly range of pipes to the tin chimney over the teacher's desk. The seats were of unpainted boards, too narrow and close for the comfort of adult worshippers, particularly Mrs. Harp and Aunt Annie, who compromised by sitting sideways. The great flanks of the stove were red with heat, but near the walls and up at the desk where the minister was to preach the building was still bitterly cold. The congregation stamped their feet and rubbed their hands while they waited for the service to begin.

Two or three boys about Donald's age were included in the company. Not accustomed to meeting strangers, they held a little aloof, but Tom, as the patron of his new brother, soon broke their reserve. "This is Billie Harp,"[32] he said, drawing Donald toward a slim, fair, smooth-faced chap of eleven or twelve, whose Sunday suit was in obvious need of replacing. "And this is Gordie Crisp." Gordie stuck out a stout hand frankly, and a friendship was cemented then and there. "And this is Freddie Mergle." Freddie snickered at this intimation, made as though he would speak, but shyness overcame him and he relapsed into another snicker.

Presently a hush spread through the room, and, glancing up, Donald saw that the minister was standing at his desk. Donald looked about for a place to sit, saw a space beside Gordie Crisp and a welcoming motion of the hand, and dropped into it.

The Reverend Mr. Mackenzie was tall and spare, with a beard trained to a point, and kindly blue eyes under full brows. Someone had passed around hymn-books from a cupboard in a corner of the room, and the minister announced the opening psalm. There was no organ, no choir, no soloist. Mr. Mackenzie, his lungs still contracted from breathing air at a temperature far below zero, struck an approximate note and forged ahead. After a bar or two the settlers began to take courage and come to his support. Andy Wayne, six feet and big-chested, had a ponderous bass when he could get it in motion, and Mrs. Calder's thin treble soon was joined by Mrs. Strand. Lizzie, and Ellen, and Mrs. Harp. So they were away.

Donald did not follow the service closely; there were so many things in which to be interested. He knew that the minister spoke earnestly and gently, as among a group of friends, and once he seemed to look directly at him, and Donald fancied he smiled just a little, and Donald smiled back before he realized what he was doing. And then a wave of color moved slowly up his face and into his hair.

After the sermon Mr. Strand took up the collection in his deep fur cap. Those who could not give five cents gave nothing; when coppers appeared in the collection they were taken as evidence that someone recently from the East was in the congregation.[33] Donald learned later that the financial proceeds were forty cents.[34]

When the service was over the settlers left for their homes with as little delay as possible, as the midwinter days are short, but Mr. Mackenzie accepted an invitation to stay for supper. His had been the longest drive, and his horses would be the better for a rest; the evening promised moonlight, and, failing that, or in any case, the minister would be welcome until morning. Donald became aware, too, that the household had been increased by the presence of another guest, who, he was confidentially informed by Ellen, was Lizzie's beau. "His name is Walter Spence," she added, "and I guess he's all right, but Lizzie makes me sick, pretending she doesn't care."

"*Does* she care?" Donald asked. Ellen smiled, but Donald was too young to know that here was a matter involving the feminine instinct.[35]

The meal was quite a special occasion, with the table lengthened to accommodate Mr. Mackenzie and Walter Spence, and Mr. Mackenzie asking the blessing in a manner which placed Uncle Jim definitely at a disadvantage. Donald understood, of course, that Mr. Mackenzie was on more intimate terms with God than could be expected of any farmer, no matter how bravely he could drive a team through a blizzard. Aunt Lizzie was hot with her responsibility and her Sunday dress, but her hospitality was unbounded; there were fried eggs with potatoes and homemade cheese,[36] and a jar of preserved wild strawberries, and two kinds of cakes.

Uncle Jim and Aunt Lizzie carefully directed the conversation into channels which would not involve the minister in any embarrassment, but Donald was quick to note that the minister himself seemed disposed to widen the sphere of discussion, as, for example, when he abruptly abondoned a spiritual topic to mention the report that a grain elevator would be built at Alder Creek the following summer. "A great help it will be to the farmers, Mr. Strand, not having to wait for cars. You just dump the wheat in a hopper, and up it goes."

"Where?" Donald asked, and the next moment could have choked with confusion. The suggestion of wheat going upwards with no stated destination had tricked him into a question before he realized its impropriety.

"Donal'! You mustn' interrupt the minister," said Aunt Annie, severely. But Mr. Mackenzie laughed heartily, Sabbath Day and all. "Ho! Ho! You'll be a farmer, all right. One of the new farmers, with big machines. I can see it coming. Indeed, Andy Wayne[37] was telling me after the service he'll be buying a four-horse seeder in the spring. Think of that, Mr. Strand! Four horses to a seeder! And you're the new boy I've been hearing about, Donald?" The minister was looking straight at him with blue eyes that invited confidence. "I saw you at the service, my lad, and good attention you paid, too. Always go to the service, my boy. It's a good way to begin life—and a good way to end it.[38] But you were asking about the wheat." Mr. Mackenzie had a

21

way of returning to a subject even after he seemed to have forgotten it. "It goes up on long belts with little iron troughs on them called buckets, each full of wheat, and at the top it runs through a spout into its own bin, and never a hand to touch it. It's a great age we live in, Donald, and a wonderful time to be a boy. You boys are going to see more than any of us dreams of."

"The horseless carriage, maybe, do you think?" Tom ventured.

Mr. Mackenzie smiled and shook his head. "I wouldn't like to commit myself so far as that, Tom. But the bicycle, now that they've got those air tires—the bicycle will give us all a new estimate of distance."

"Mr. Mackenzie, is it a sin to read a newspaper on Sunday?" It was the voice of Ellen that burst the blue, and the question arose out of an established order in the Strand family.[39]

The minister steadied himself against the shock, grasping in a moment that here lay a momentous decision. No doubt the issue had been raised in the household and the consequences of his answer might be far-reaching.

"Why, Ellen," said her mother, with a nervous laugh, "you shouldn' be troublin' the minister with such a question."

"He should know," Ellen insisted, doggedly.

The moment's interruption had given Mr. Mackenzie his bearings. "I think, Ellen," he said, "it depends upon the motive. The Lord, you know, looketh upon the heart. If you read for wisdom, to learn more about His world, well I wouldn't—what would you say, Mr. Strand?"

"I'm makin' no doubt you're quite right, Mr. Mackenzie," the farmer agreed, not very sure how far the minister had led him. "But I never thought o' the Almighty as bein' like a grain elevator, you know—somethin' new-frangled all the time." Mr. Strand could not bring himself to say God even in the presence of the minister; in such matters he had a shyness which compromised on Almighty.[40]

Mr. Mackenzie took the rebuke without a quiver and executed a masterly retreat. "Now there we are in complete agreement," he said. "The eternal verities are for ever and ever. 'I am that I am.' And one of the verities—you know it, Ellen—'Honor thy father and thy mother'—and honor means obey. You won't make much mistake by following that bit of the Bible, Ellen."[41]

"My word," Mr. Mackenzie commented to himself as he drove under the white moonlight to Alder Creek. "How careful one must be not to knock out the old props until he is sure the new ones will hold! But this coming generation—I'm fearing they'll kick the props about."

8[42]

One memorable night the Crisps paid a visit, driving down in their deep, homemade jumper. Mr. Crisp was white and stern, and his wife was white and gentle; they talked with the elder Strands about the coming grain elevator and the re-opening of the school in April. Charlie Crisp, fourteen, although of undoubted parentage, had an Indian blend in his make-up; he talked with Tom about rabbit shooting and his hope that next year he could earn enough money to buy a Winchester rifle. Katie, a fair girl older than Gordon and tall for her age, sat quietly, exchanging remarks in her low voice from time to time with Elllen or Lizzie. Gordie played with Donald; one moment they held hands like sweethearts; the next, they burst into wrestling matches, which, when they became too boisterous, had to be suppressed.

When conversation slackened it became known that the boys had brought their mouth organs, and, with little urging, they filled the room with their homely music. They played rather well together and Donald thought them very gifted indeed.[43]

"Why can't we have some singin'?" Aunt Annie asked. "Katie, you sing well. Can't you sing a piece to the boy's playin'?"

Katie blushed to the roots of her fair hair and twisted her lean body in modest confusion.

Mr. Crisp had a full share of parental pride in the talents of his children. "Go ahead, Katie," he said. "Sing 'The Red River Valley'."

Katie squirmed, but made ready to sing. Her father's commands were not to be disobeyed. The boys led with their mouth organs, and Katie's clear treble followed them, diffidently at first, but gaining courage and volume as the song progressed. Gradually the others took up the air, and when she reached the chorus she was leading her choir:

24

> Then consider a while ere you leave her.
>> Do not bid her a hasty adieu.
> But remember the Red River Valley
>> And the girl that has loved you so true.

The song was followed by others, and before they realized the flight of the clock was striking ten. Mrs. Strand had found part of a tin of coffee which had been reserved for just such an occasion as this, and they feasted on coffee and slices of buttered bread. When the party broke up Donald and Ellen watched the jumper jogging into the milk-white moonlight. Their arms were about each other, and their pressure tightened with something they did not understand.

So the winter wore on. Even the shock of the tragedy which had made Donald an orphan lost its reality and hung like a vague dream on the outer edge of his consciousness.

9

Spring swept down upon them suddenly with a mild west wind and skies of deeper blue. The snow sank and sank and grew darker and darker; here and there the plowed fields showed through their warm winter blanket; water gathered in rivulets and went swirling on its way. It gathered, too, in brown patches in Alder Creek, soaking up through the deep snow that filled the little valley. The drifts held it back and it gathered higher and higher until it could force a channel; then it gurgled on, filling the depressions, mounting over the snow that blocked its passage. It fascinated Donald. At the price of wet and inflamed tonsils he explored its course daily, watching the steady-rising stream. Tom explained to him that this was just local water; the real break-up would come later. "Then, look out!" said Tom. Donald spent all his work-free hours looking out.

To the east of the Strand homestead Alder Creek flowed between substantial banks out but to the westward its course was little more than a depression in the prairie. Down this course Donald was assured the flood waters would eventually come, and, although he watched for them diligently, to Ellen fell the honor of breaking the great news. "The creek is coming; the creek is coming!" she cried, running out to the yard where Donald was piling wood. "Come; you can see it from the upstairs window." True enough, away to the westward lay a shining channel between the brown shoulders of the uncovered earth, the sunshine glistening on it like a blade of quicksilver. Ellen seized Donald's hand and held it tightly. This was a moment for emotion; this was the birth of Spring, the burial of Winter.

After a moment she released his hand, and, turning toward the sun, raised both her arms, palms foward, above her head. It was a gesture she had; it seemed to motivate itself within her at high moments.

The sun was in her eyes and the west wind was in her face. She breathed deeply and joyously, as though drinking life from its primordial sources.[44]

The water took longer[45] to come than Donald would have thought, and the afternoon was well worn when the stream flowed through the Strand farm.[46] Donald, Ellen, and Tom watched it from the banks, moving with it as it went. At the front it threaded out into mere fingers, as though to feel its way, but behind the fingers came a huge flat hand, filling the bed of the creek from side to side, and behind the hand a stout right arm, bending and twisting and lapping higher and higher. In an hour the banks were full; water rushing under the bridge and over the roadway on either side, cutting off the Strands and all settlers south of the creek from those on the north, stirring waist-high among the willows that at normal tide merely dipped their toes in the gentle pools which mirrored their slim branches. The creek was down; springtime was in the land; noisy regiments of wild geese were wedging their way northward;[47] the wet earth shook and sunned itself and stirred from its long sleep. Ho! Now to work! Now to work!

The days that followed were a steady crescendo of activity. The seed wheat had to be cleaned and blue-stoned, and Donald worked with the energy of a man at the fanning-mill and in shovelling the wheat forward from the bins in the granary. As soon as the frost was sufficiently out of the ground Tom was on the fields with the harrows, and almost before they knew it the soil was ready for the seed. The creek level had fallen and the roads were passable; Andy Wayne had driven by with his new four-horse seeder, stopping long enough for its sturdy mechanism and bright red paint to be admired by Mr. Strand and Tom and Donald.

"I'm thinkin' you'll be takin' in seedin' with yon gigantic thing," Mr. Strand said, willing to pay his neighbor's enterprises a compliment. "It's only a couple o'years since you an' me was sowin' our fields by hand, Andy."

"I'll put in my crop in half the time," said Andy, well satisfied. "And you know, Mr. Strand, every day saved in the spring means a day's less danger o'frost in the fall, an' that's the more reason I shouldn' be standin' here keepin' you from your work. Good day, Mr. Strand."

27

"Good day," they answered and waved him on his way, not knowing that Big Farming had nodded to them and, for the present, passed them by.

10[48]

The Band of Hope met at the schoolhouse Friday afternoons at four o'clock. It was conducted by Mrs. Calder, whose drunken father had made of her an enemy of alcohol in all its forms. Ellen and Tom belonged, as did most of the boys and girls of the district, although there were some scoffers. The Waynes and the Harps had broader views, and snickered their contempt of the whole movement.[49] Donald joined at the first meeting of the term. Mrs. Calder read a prayer from a little book, after which the children repeated their pledge in unison: "I hereby pledge myself to abstain from the use of alcoholic liquors, including wine, beer, and cider, as a beverage, from the use of tobacco in every from, and from all profanity." Probably none of them knew the exact meaning of the words. "Abstain" and "beverage" puzzled them all, and Donald was in his second year's membership before he discovered that he had been guilty of a slight inaccuracy in beginning his obligation. "I hear by a pledge myself." But the general import was plain enough. The members were not to drink liquor, smoke or chew tobacco, or swear.

Mrs. Calder led the reading: "Who hath woe? who hath sorrow? who hath contentions? who hath babbling? who hath wounds without cause? who hath redness of eyes?"

Children: "They that tarry long at the wine; they that go to seek mixed wine."

Mrs. Calder: "Look not thou upon the wine when it is red, when it giveth his colour in the cup, when it moveth itself aright."

Children: "At the last it biteth like a serpent, and stingeth like an adder."

Mrs. Calder: "Wine is a mocker, strong drink is raging: and whosoever is deceived thereby is not wise."

Then they sang a song to the effect that Satan profited by the use of tobacco. Donald at first interpreted this to mean that Satan was a heavy smoker. When Mrs. Calder explained that those who used tobacco were helping Satan bring evil into the world he challenged her forthwith: "My Uncle Jim smokes, and my Uncle Jim is not a bad man," he said belligerence in his eyes.

"Of course, Donald, your Uncle Jim is not a bad man," Mrs. Calder agreed. "Everybody knows he is one of the best men around Alder Creek." Mrs. Calder, notwithstanding her militancy in the warfare against alcohol and tobacco, was one of the most gentle of women. "I am sure your Uncle Jim is not a bad man," she conciliated.

"But he smokes," Donald insisted. In his ear Gordie Crisp managed to whisper, as though marshalling reinforcements: "So does Mr. Calder."

"So does Mr. Calder," Donald repeated openly. He was for giving no quarter.

"Plenty of good men smoke," Mrs. Calder answered, heartily wishing herself rid of the subject. "But I don't think they would advise their boys to smoke. You might ask your uncle what he thinks about it, Donald."

Donald did not follow this advice. It was not an easy subject to open with Uncle Jim. And besides, a new complication arose the very next day. A warm Saturday afternoon was still young when Jimmie Wayne rode into the Strand farmyard on his bay pony, Prince. Donald rushed to meet him. The boys greeted each other:

"'Lo Jim."

"'Lo Don."

Donald rubbed his hand on Prince's nose and the pony nodded affably.

"Can you stay a while, Jim?"

"Yep, if you ain't busy." Jimmie discarded his good English as soon as he was out of the schoolroom, and Donald easily surrendered to his example. "Can I turn Prince into your pasture with Jack?"[50]

"Of course. They can stay together"[51] They removed saddle and bridle and turned the beast loose, Donald meanwhile wondering the purpose of his friend's visit. "What did you come for, Jim?" he asked at length, eager to get to the bottom of it.

30

Jimmie's face betokened mystery. "Let's go down to the creek," he suggested.

They walked along the side of the creek, watching their reflections in the water. A plover ran before them in the mud; a pair of wild ducks had nested on the opposite shore. The drake sat on the water, the bright plumage of his wing glinting in the sunlight; the gentle grumblings with which he reassured his mate could be heard distincly across the pond. Jimmie plodded on.

"What is it, Jim? What did you come for?" Donald might be outraging the conventions, but he wanted to know.

For answer Jimmie tapped mysteriously the bulging pocket of his coat.

"What is it, Jim? What have you got?"

Jimmie leaned close to his friend. "Cane. Smokin' cane he whispered.

"Smokin' cane? What's it for?"

"Why, to smoke, of course."

They came to a spot where a shoulder of creek bank hid them from the house and where low willows gave protection from any casual wanderer on the other side of the stream. Here they lay down on the ground and Jimmie produced his treasure. Found a whipstalk," he said, as he revealed[52] a few pieces wood somewhat larger than a lead pencil.[53]

"Where'd you get it?" Donald asked, not yet quite understanding.

"From an old whipstalk, I said. You get it in whipstalks that is, if they ain't rawhide. You see, it has holes right through it and you can smoke it just like a cigar."

Donald handled one wonderingly.

"I got matches, too," said Jimmie. He put one of the sticks in his mouth, lit a match, and pulled vigorously. The end of the stick began to burn; smoke issued from Jimmie's mouth.

"See? It's as easy as that," he said. "Ain't you goin' to light up?"

"Why, yes," said Donald, rather doubtfully. He selected a stick and put it in his mouth; Jimmie supplied the lighted match. With his first breath Donald took a lungful of sulphur which sent him gasping.

"Aw, you got to be careful," Jimmie scolded him. Don't swallow. Just draw gentle."

31

Donald tried again with better results. The smoke came and went in a pleasant little cloud. The end of the stick glowed There was a happy sense of adventure to it. They were men, smoking together.

A sudden memory shot through Donald and stopped him "But my pledge, Jim! My band of Hope pledge!"

Jimmie laughed. "Hasn't nothin' to do with this," he said "It's all about smokin' *tobacco*. This ain't tobacco, so you're all right."

They floated again into their world of make-believe. They were Gentlemen Adventurers from England; they were Pirates camped on some palm-ringed shore of the Southern Seas.

"Got a new slang word, too," said Jimmie.

"You have? What is it?"

"Goll.[54] You can say it when you're mad, and it ain't swearin'. If you're very mad you can say goll darn."

"You can? You're sure it ain't swearin'?"

"Course I'm sure."

"Goll darn it, I'm glad of that. I needed a new word."

"For the next time you fight Freddie Mergle?" said Jimmie, pointedly.

"Aw, that's all over. But I wish I'd known that word then."

"Yep," Jimmie agreed. "It's too goll darned bad."

Again they smoked in silence, but presently it began to pall upon them. They seemed suddenly to lose enthusiasm for it. Jimmie impetuously flung his burning stick into the creek.

"Will it make you sick, Jim?" Donald whispered, with sudden misgiving. His stomach was threatening; he seemed to have lost appetite for everything.

"Naw, not if you don't take too much. Throw it away."[55]

Donald did so, and they sat together, watching the slowly-moving water as it slipped along between its grassy banks. They were barefooted, and the earth before them was soft and moist; they dug their heels into its surface, finding some elementary comfort in the contact of their skin with the source from which it was created. Their bodies relaxed on the bank. Overhead the sky was immeasurably blue and deep; wisps of feathery cloud hung motionless against it; at great height a hawk floated on outstretched wings.

32

Jimmie was the one to break the spell; "What you goin' to be when you grow up?" he asked.

"I dunno. A farmer, I guess."

"Thought you were goin' to be an engineer?"

"Oh, I thought that when I was a little kid, but I guess I'll be a farmer, and drive a new seeder, like your father bought."

"Well, I ain't," said Jimmie, decisively. "I'm goin' to be a lawyer. Pa says so. Farmers are always workin' for other people, an' have to take what they can get, but a lawyer charges what he likes. Supposin' you was a lawyer an' was pleadin' the case for a man up for murder, you could charge him"—Jimmie paused while his mind reached for an astronomical figure—"you could charge him a hundred dollars!"

"But suppose he *had* done the murder?"

"Then you could charge him two hundred. Even if you lose the case you can charge. But if you're a farmer, an' your crop gets froze, who can you charge it to? That's what Pa says."

"That's so," Donald agreed, thoughtfully. "Still, if there was no farmers, there'd be nothin' to eat."

"There'll always be lots of farmers," Jimmie assured him. "You're goin' to be one. But if you have a law suit I won't charge you nothin'."

"And if you're hungry I'll give you some wheat off my farm." That seemed a satisfactory arrangement, and the boys lay long in contemplation of it. Suddenly a rushing sound in the willows brought them erect with prickling hair. The next moment Hector pounced upon them, his eyes bright with doggish affection, his tail waggin in the delight of his discovery.

"Don't you wish a dog could speak?" Donald asked, when they had quietened Hector's enthusiasm.

"No. That's why a dog makes such a good chum. He can't give you away."

"Goll darned if you ain't goin' to be a lawyer!" Donald exclaimed, with a new respect for his friend's cleverness.

11

Hester Harp's interest in Donald became too obvious to be disregarded. Donald basked in it. It gratified his pride that Hester should have selected him in preference to all the other boys at school. She was the fastest runner among the girls and as speedy as any boy of her age. She could play third base almost as well as Gordie Crisp and she could bat like a boy. Her legs under her short skirts were long and thin and when she ran bases her hair would fly loose in the wind; she suggested a colt racing about a pasture, its mane whipped by the breeze. Her face was fair and freckled and her eyes were hard to resist.

Donald found himself often in her company. Of course, there was no privacy about the school, and they had nothing to say even had there been opportunity, but they just seemed to gravitate toward each other. They tried to be chosen on the same side when playing ball, but even when on opposing sides there was little rivalry and no enmity between them. When Hester played third base Donald's chief objective was to get that far, and there he would stand, forgetful of the game, while Hester missed many an opportunity to put him "out". Their bodies would brush each other as they passed and neither would know what it was all about. Sometimes in their sports there was an excuse for wrestling together; Hester was strong, and Donald had to put his weight into it to save his sex the disgrace of being thrown by a girl. Those were strange moments. Donald analyzed nothing; he only knew that he liked to be in Hester's presence, he liked when they clashed together.

"I wish you wouldn't play so much with Hester," Ellen said one afternoon as they walked home from school.

"Why?" said Donald. "I don't play with her much."

"Yes you do. Every chance you get." Ellen was very earnest and to the point.

"Suppose I do?" Donald challenged. "Who cares?"

"I do. I don't like Hester."

Donald paused in his stride, surprised. "You don't?" he said. "Why, you are always nice to her."

Ellen laughed. "Of course I'm nice to her. You have to be nice to a person if you don't like her. But I don't want *you* to be nice to her; that is, not too nice."

Donald turned this piece of feminine policy over in his mind. "Of course," he observed, as though to dismiss the subject "I'm going to marry you."

Ellen faced him abruptly, her eyes aglow. "Are you, Donald? Are you really?"

"Of course," he answered. Didn't you know that?"

Ellen slipped her hand into his. "I'm glad, Donald. I thought you liked Hester," she said.

Donald was going to insist that he *did* like Hester, too, but thought better of it.[56]

12

The first two weeks in July were observed as summer holidays. The school was closed and deserted; the teacher had gone to his haying, the boys and girls were helping with the work on the farms. To Donald was assigned the task of herding the cattle. The fence pasture field was cropped close and as far around its fringe as long bovine tongues could reach under the wire, but vacant land lay to the west where the herd could range in safety, provided they did not invade the neighbors' crops.

"The lad can manage it all right," Uncle Jim had stated the matter at the breakfast table. "He can take Jack an' Hector, an' the stock'll give no trouble once they're past the green crops. With two week's rest the pasture'll be good again for another month—if we get any rain."

"It's a long day for him to be out all day in the sun," Aunt Annie had protested, "an' the pony'll maybe run away, an' dear knows what'll happen, and besides, the garden needs weedin'."

As between herding cattle and weeding the garden Donald's choice was instantly made, and he sat with heart aflutter while the issue hung in the balance.

"If the pony runs away he'll jus' come home," Uncle Jim rejoined. "You won't be havin' a saddle, Donal'; I'm no wantin' ye dragged home at the end o' stirrup. Lizzie and Ellen can do the weedin'."

Safe out of range of the parental eyes Ellen made a face appropriate to the occasion. She would much rather have gone with Donald to herd the stock, but there was no good argument to that end, and she resigned herself to the long rows of onions and carrots.

"Put up a lunch for Donal'," Uncle Jim settled the question, "an' Ellen'll help get the stock across the creek. You can take some o' that copper wire, Donal', an' amuse yourself snarin' gophers, but don' let the cattle into anybody's crops. You'll know when it's time to eat by your shadow fallin' due north—"

"I'll bet Donald'll be mixed in his directions by ten o'clock," Tom put in. "Herdin' is awful hungry work."

"—an' when your shadow's fallin' due east you can start for home. Don' run the cows; give 'em plenty o'time."

Mounted on Jack, with his lunch bag over his shoulder and Hector at his heels, Donald set out in high spirits. He had been called to a man's job; he was to be a lone cowboy on the plains. Perhaps he would not see anyone all day.

Ellen helped him round up the cattle, eight milch cows, fourteen young stock, twenty-two head in all. They bunched at the creek, hesitating to take the ford, until Hector nipped a heel or two; then they plunged in, stopping in midstream to drink prodigiously, Hector was at a disadvantage in the water, but Jack knew his job; he splashed after the cattle, pinching one or two dilatory cows at the base of the tail with his strong teeth, and soon had them all in motion, although he nearly lost his rider in the scramble. Donald hooped his bare legs as best he could around the pony's body and by good luck was still on top when they climbed the other side.[57]

Soon they had passed the cultivated land, and Donald brought Jack to a standstill. Finding the pressure from behind removed, the cattle slowly began to scatter, grazing as they went.[58] The grass was rich and sweet with the flavor of manyflowers, and with the temptation of the more luscious wheat fields left safely behind the herd[59] probably would give no more trouble.

The day wore on;[60] the sun hung lazily in a cloudless sky, and heat began to shimmer over the prairie. Donald, lying on the grass with Hector at his side,[61] drew his big straw hat across his face. It was very restful here. Insects were humming, the smell of wild flowers was in the air, and high above through a break in the crown of his hat he could see two gopher hawks circling in motionless wings . . .[62]

The hours[63] seemed endless, but at length there was no doubt his shadow was falling eastward, and the distant wheat fields were taking on a deeper green from the slanting rays of the sun. Donald gathered up his things and with some difficulty mounted Jack, while Hector set the reluctant herd[64] in motion. Once on the way they gave little trouble; they were headed for home, the milch cows to the relief of their straining udders and all to water and the protection of familiar things before the fall of night.

"Well, Donal', ye made it all right?" Uncle Jim greeted him as he rode into the yard, very sunburned and very proud. "Ye'll be a cooman[65] yet, I'm thinkin' if ye're no somethin' better." The Scottish strain in Uncle Jim's ancestry peeked through his language at unexpected moments.

Donald thought of that after he went to bed. A cowman? Well, perhaps. Or an engineer.

The next day Billie Harp and Hester brought their cattle to the range, and so it continued ultil the end of the holidays. The Harps had no pony, and Hester was sent to help her brother if the stock were hard to drive. Without knowing just why, Donald could have wished that Billie might have been needed on the farm; he and Hester could manage both herds without trouble. In some unspoken way he learned or felt that Hester shared that wish. Sometimes they would wander off together while Billie snared gophers or played with Hector, and sometimes they would wrestle and roll in the grass, for Hester was strong as a boy, and often it was as much as Donald could do to throw her. Then they would lie and rest under the warm sky until the cattle began to stir or Billie came to disturb their germinating romance.[66]

13

One memorable day Uncle Jim took Donald with him on a visit to Alder Creek. The wagon rattled along cheerfully and Uncle Jim was in good spirits, for the crops held promise of heavy harvest.[67] As they rumbled along, well out of earshot of their own or neighbors' houses, the farmer burst into snatches of song welling up through memories of thirty years before.

Perhaps it was unconscious reminiscence of his own childhood, induced by the association of his song, which[68] turned him suddenly to the boy with the question, "What are ye goin' to be when ye grow up, Donal'? I'm thinkin' ye're old enough to be sometimes wonderin' about that.[69] It is a farmer ye have in mind?"

Donald was shy about discussing his plans for the future even with his uncle. They were dreams, and to put them into words might rob them of whatever substance they had; besides, he had a fear that his ambition to be an engineer would not be encouraged.

"Would you like me to be a farmer, Uncle Jim?" he asked, approaching the subject obliquely.

Mr. Strand let the horses drop back to a walk, hooked the reins about his foot, and filled his pipe before answering.

"Well, that's a question to which one might say yes and no," he said. "It's a hard life, farmin'. Long hours an' hard work an' all kinds o' weather, an' what do ye get for it? what the storekeepers an' grain buyers is willin' to give ye. Now, when we go to get your pair o' boots, who do ye think'll set the price, Donal'?"

"I suppose the storekeeper will, Uncle Jim."

"You suppose right. An' when we sell that tub o' butter in the back o' the box, who do ye think 'll set the price?"

Donald hesitated. "The storekeeper?" he ventured.

"Ye're right again. That's what us farmers don' like, Donal', but we can't help ourselves. Still, I'm not sayin' there's no good things about farmin'. It's a fine life, workin' in the earth, makin' things grow, an' if ye get out o' debt, so ye can sell when ye like an' hold when ye like, perhaps there's no better. But ye're a bright boy, Donal', if I do say it as might be spoilin' ye by it, an' I'd like to see ye make the most o' yersel'."

"Jimmie Wayne's going to be a lawyer," Donald hazarded.

"Aye, that's a great profession, an' they call it an eddicated one, but I got a letter from a lawyer once an' I couldna' read it no more than I could read the tracks o' a plover in the mud,[70] so I sent it back, for his name was printed on the corner. An' then he came to see me' an' he wasna' a bad chap at all, an' maybe some day I'll be tellin' ye more about it. But ye're no thinkin' o' being a lawyer, ' Donal'?"

"No, Uncle Jim," Now seemed the time for the great revelation. "I think I'll be an engineer," he added, boldly.

Uncle Jim failed to fall off the wagon seat, but he cheeped the horses to a trot before answering. "So it's to be an engineer?" he said at length. "Well, I'm thinkin' it's not a bad job, with hard work, an' dangerous, but good pay. Aye, there's worse jobs, Donal'—an' some better."

Donald grabbed at the concession. "Then it's all right, is it, Uncle Jim? I can be an engineer, can I?"

Uncle Jim seemed strangely solemn as he answered, "I'll be wantin' ye with me until ye're twenty-one, Donal'. Then ye can be an engineer, or whatever, if that's yer will."

They dropped into silence then. The day was hot and the sweat was beginning to mark the horses in soapy streaks along the backbands and cruppers. Slowly the elevator at Alder Creek[71] heaved its bulk a little larger across the intervening plain, and the houses and shops of the little town began to take shape.

Suddenly Donald was surprised to see something like water lying between them and the town. "Look, Uncle Jim!" he exclaimed. "Is that water? I didn't know there was a pond like that. It's right across the road!"

Uncle Jim chuckled. "That's the heat," he explained. "Don' ask me why, but it looks like water. When men are dyin' o' thirst in the desert, that's what eggs them on, promisin' water for their burnin' throats, but never givin' it. You see, it moves ahead o' us; we'll never reach it, no matter how far we drive. Dry water, I call it, Donal'."

"My father and mother could not have been drowned in water like that," Donald observed, soberly.

Then Uncle Jim made a strange remark: :"Many a man is, Donal', and' may ye never live to know what I mean!"

14

When they left for home the sun was setting,[72] not over the edge of the earth, as it usually did, but behind a bank of cloud, blue and solid as a range of mountains, slowly heaving above the western horizon. Overhead the stars came out; the broad gray band of the Milky Way, and brighter, close stars, reminding them as the wagon rumbled on through the darkness that the heavens are His firmament. To Donald the stars always suggested God. Even when he had sat in the water at the edge of the marsh while Tom and Walter talked in low whispers together he had looked at the stars and wondered if they really were the eyes of God and if they could see him so far away among the rushes and marsh grass. He would have like to ask his uncle about it, but although Mr. Strand read a chapter and conducted family prayers every night, matters of this kind were never discussed. A certain inevitableness and awe surrounded eveything relating to religion, and to try to understand its mysteries was like exploring into forbidden territory.

To save a quarter of a mile of distance the trail angled through Mr. Crisp's wheat field with complete indifference to the trampled grain. Mr. Crisp offered no objection; there was plenty of wheat, and a few bushels more or less did not justify and inconvenience to his neighbors. The wheat stalks were now tall and strong, carrying long, heavy heads well filled with milky kernels, and as the horses jogged in their slow trot the heads brushed against their sides and rustled gently against the wheels and axles of the wagon. Dew was settling, and a rich smell from the growing crop filled the nostrils of a man and boy. If one listened closely and infinite whisper seemed to fill the world; millions of wheat heads speaking gently together, touching, withdrawing, murmuring, raising a voice of magnificent prophecy. How proud they were, these stately grenadiers, their massed formations stretching everywhere into the infinity of night!

"Never saw better," Mr. Strand commented, as though they had been speaking of the crop. "Another rain or two, to help with the fillin', and we'll be threshin' forty bushels this fall, Donal', me lad. Then I'll be payin' the store bill, and' the last payment on the binder, an' the taxes, an' maybe a bit over at the end o' the year." Mr. Strand sighed contentedly. To have a little over when his bills were paid was all the wealth he coveted.

The subject was too advanced for Donald, and he made no direct reply. "Looks like we might have rain to-night, Uncle Jim," he said. "The cloud seems to be getting bigger."

A thin film of light from the departed sun still marked the outline of the cloud, certainly heaving, as Donald had suggested, into vaster proportions against the western sky. Sudden flame shot through it as they watched, but the distance was so great no rumble of thunder reached their ears.[73]

It had grown quite dark, but the horses threaded their unerring way along the well-known road. The sound of the wheels on the bridge marked their progress; Alder Creek lay like a curving plate of steel between banks that were lost in gloom. Ahead and to the right a column of light cut its broadening swath from the farmhouse window. Hector, who had been content to follow behind, now dashed forward, banking, to carry the good news of their arrival. Tom came down through the yard, his swinging lantern throwing gigantic and grotesque shadows against house and stable.

"All right, Dad; I'll take care of the horses," he said. "Well, Don, how did you like the big city?"

"It was all right," Donald said, for lack of other remark, as he clambered down over the wagonwheel.

Donald had hoped that Ellen would be up so that he might tell her of the wonders of the day, but she had gone to bed. Lizzie set bread and buttermilk and green onions on the table, and the travellers, hungry again after their long day, feasted heartily.

"Better be off to bed, Donal'," Aunt Annie urged. "There'll be no readin' the night."

Donald dragged himself upstairs, glad to free his feet from their cramping boots and his neck from its burning collar. But his heart was full of long, long thoughts. His prayer was an emotion rather than words; a feeling, a happiness, a hope, a sense of doors opening on a world ahead and of great things to come.

He was awakened by a terrific crash.[74] The house shook under a deafening[75] roar. He sprang up in bed and a wind whipped his face. There was a confused sound of rushing feet, of voices, of breaking glass. Impenetrable darkness was cut for an instant by dazzling light to close an instant later into gloom more impenetrable than before. A hand touched him; he seized it; arms clung about him.

It was Ellen. Her body, clothed only in her nightgown, trembled against his.

"What is it, Ellen?" he tried to make his voice sound brave as he shouted against the overwhelming crash of sound.

"Hail!" she cried back. "The windows are smashing in. Let's get down stairs before the house blows over!"

By a flash of lightning they found their way to the head of the stairs. A lamp of ice bounced on the floor in front of them, Water was splashing on the steps.

In the kitchen the west window had blown in, Uncle Jim and Lizzie were trying to hold a blanket over it, but the wind bellied the blanket like a sail and kept whipping corners free.[76] Aunt Annie was fussing with a lamp which was continually blowing out,[77] but Tom had more success with the lantern. All[78] were just as they had sprung from bed. Uncle Jim was fruitlessly shouting instructions against the clamor of the storm,[79] but Tom found hammer and nails and soon had the blanket securely fastened. No other window had blown in although many panes were broken, and ice and water were splashing about in all parts of the house.

In five minutes the fury of the storm was over. The roar on walls and roof sortened into the wash of a steady downspour of rain. The broken panes were covered; the wet floors were mopped up. The members of the household, wrapped in such clothing as they could find, gathered in the kitchen, clustering together for courage and comfort.

44

"Well, it[80] looks like a knock-out," said Tom.

"Looks like it," said Uncle Jim.

Aunt Annie's face began to twist into strange, pathetic lines, and Uncle Jim drew his arm about her shoulder. "Never mind, Ma," he said. "We're all here, an' that's all that matters."

"Yes, Ma; see, we're all right," said Ellen. "Here's Tom, and Lizzie, and Donald, and me."

"Yes, we're all here," Aunt Annie admitted. "An' what are we goin' to eat?"

"We'll eat all right," Uncle Jim assured her. "We've always et, an' I guess we won't be quittin' now. We'll be fightin' it out, Ma!"[81]

Aunt Annie found relief in action. "Put on the kettle,[82] Lizzie," she said. "A cup o' tea'll do us good. An' watch out for glass, with your bare feet.[83]

They grew[84] more cheerful as they ate and drank. They even laughed about the spectacle presented by Uncle Jim and Lizzie trying to hold the blanket against the window.[85]

But when Donald went back to bed he remembered they had not had family prayers that night. Perhaps that was why the storm had come?[86]

In the morning they looked out upon utter desolation. The grenadier ranks of wheat had gone down like a massacre; the fields were bare as plowed ground. Only here and there a broken stalk trembled in the sunlight.[87]

Part two

1

Donald Strand was twenty-one years old in August, 1901.[1] He took the day casually, as other days; it did not seem to mark any particular milestone in his life. For years he had been a man doing a man's work. Twenty-one meant that he would vote at the next election, but otherwise had no practical significance.

He had spent the forenoon waltzing the new binder and a four-horse team through a field of early-ripened wheat. The smell of paint was still on the machine and its bearings were not yet run smooth, but it clicked out the sheaves with masterly precision. From his high seat he watched the whole mechanism; the reel striding implacably forward into the standing crop, the glitter of knives as they sheared the yellow straw, the momentary poise of the severed stalk before it fell headlong on the canvas, the full-throated vomit of prostrate wheat as it was hurtled into the packers, the swift circle of the discharge arms and the fleeting wink of the knotter ere the sheaf was shot onto the carrier. It had become routine to him in his eleven years on the farm but a routine that never sagged into drudgery. There was music in the hum of the drive chains and poetry in the swaying wheat.

As the noon hour approached he glanced ever and again[2] houseward for the flag which would indicate it was time to stop for dinner. The horses, too, nodding prodigiously under the heavy load and exuding the pungent odor of sweat into the hot air, had an eye for the signal, and when it made its appearance summoned unsuspected energy for the last homeward sweep along the field. Donald smiled a little as the machine speeded up; a handsome, firm-lipped smile which

47

gave a glimpse of strong white teeth against a sunburned face.[3] At the end of the field he dropped from his seat, threw the trace chains over the horses' backs, and guided them through the stooks to the water trough in the yard. The windmill was clank-clanking in a slow breeze, but the trough was well filled, and the thirsty animals[4] plunged their muzzles into it, snorting with satisfaction and indelicately dripping white slavers into the trough.

Mr. Strand came down from the house. He had put on weight with the years; his body bulged over the waistband of his pants, the skin sagged about his jaws,[5] and the angle between neck and chin was flattening into a fleshy curve. The broom-like[6] beard he had formerly affected had given way to a trimmed chin-whisker revealing a swarthy, well-haired expanse of chest where his shirt hung open at the throat. But there was strength in his step and he could still upon occasion set a pace for the younger men, albeit he now was satisfied to set the pace for a short period and then find his presence needed at some less strenuous duty of the farm.

"How's she goin', Don?" he asked, as the two men stood together watching the horses drink.

"Fine as silk," Donald answered. "That eight-foot cut makes the old binder look like the barber's clippers. Whoever stooks up to that machine will have a wet shirt before night, I promise you,"

Mr. Strand put his hand on his nephew's shoulder. He had to reach up a little to do it now; his arm hung around a body tough as oak. "I guess Tom'll follow you all right—with a little help from the old man," he suggested. "Go and get yourself washed up for dinner; I'll put the horses by. You know the new school ma'am starts boardin' with us to-day an'ye'll need to get the machine oil o' yer hair."

Donald[7] laughed. "School ma'ams don't worry me, Uncle," he said. "Unless they try to be—intellectual. However, I'll hope to[8] do the family justice. Tom's not back yet?"

Mr. Strand glanced up the road toward Alder Creek Station, where the shoulders of four grain elevators cut their solid cubes against the northern sky. "Should be here any minutes," he said. "That Maggie-mare jus' eats up the road, an' Tom lets her go. A bit too fast, I tell him sometimes—an' that goes for you'[9] too, Donal', me lad. It's getting' to be the dangdest age for speed. I use' to do it with old Ned an' Dick an' the lumber wagon—well, well, them was differen' times." Mr. Strand sighed gently as though not entirely in sympathy with the new tempo. "He'll be here any minute," he repeated, returning to the matter of Tom's arrival.

"He'd better. I'm just out of twine.[10] I'm thinking he'd make time it he didn't have to pass Crisp's."

"You mean Katie?"[11]

Donald grinned. "Who wouldn't?" he shot back over his shoulder as he left on a dogtrot for the house.

Donald washed at the bench in front of the house and threw the dirty water at the surrounding hens. Before a mirror nailed to the wall he parted his hair with just a little more exactitude[12] than usual. He glanced at the finished job with some approval. School ma'ams might be[13] nothing to him, but all girls were girls.

Ellen met him in the door. Ellen was tall and slim and had an oval face and cheeks[14] that kept their schoolgirl complexion without any artificial assistance. Nature had given her skin of light olive color which resisted the ravages of sun and wind, but better still, nature had given her a cheerful spirit which gleamed in her eyes and hung in the smile[15] of her thin red lips. The curves of her body, too, slim though it was, might have been modelled by a sculptor;[16] not even familiarity could breed indifference to her charms. Donald knew this as his shoulder rubbed hers slightly when they met.

"Many happy returns, Don," she whispered, "but don't let Miss Wilson know the great day it is.[17] You'll be scheming[18] to go to school next winter and they don't take 'em over twenty."[19]

Donald gave her arm a pressure that was more caress than pinch and moved in to his place at the table.

"This is Miss Wilson, Donal'," Mrs. Strand introduced them. "Donal' is our nephew but he's lived with us ever since his parents were drownded[20] when he was a little boy, an' I'm sure he's jus' like our own son. Miss Wilson is the new school teacher, Donal'."

Donald bowed and Miss Wilson acknowledged the greeting with what seemed to her just the right degree of reserve. This was her first school, but she knew some things that were not in the curriculum; for example,[21] that a teacher must not make the mistake of being too friendly, especially with the young men. With her first glimpse of Donald she knew, too, that this principle ran some risk of being shattered. All the more need for her studied reserve.[22] Donald allowed an appraising eye to rest on her a moment. She was shorter than Ellen[23] and a little sturdier in the build; her skin was of the milk-white kind that takes freckles easily—[24] a band of them bridged her nose and flung scattered outposts well across her cheeks; and her hair, with one more dash of fire, would have been indisputably red. She was younger than Ellen, too; Donald estimated that she was not more than eighteen, and she would need all the firmness suggested by her full-length upper lip in handling the boys and girls of Sundown School.

"I hope you will like your school," he ventured.

"Oh, I know[25] I will." On that point she was quite enthusiastic.

"Tough young rascals," he assured her. "Boys are not what they used to be when I went[26] to school."

"I suppose not," she agreed, but her eyebrows had arched just a little.

"Of course, we used to put the teacher out once in a while, but we were careful not to hurt her, and we never threw her in the creek."

"Oh!" The brows had gone higher still, the upper lip was straight and firm.

"Don' pay any notice[27] to him, Miss Wilson," Mrs. Strand intervened. "The boys here ain't a bit worse than anywhere else. It's only the young men you need to be scared of."

"So I think," said Miss Wilson, cryptically.

At that moment Mr Strand came in and took his chair at the head of the table. He hurried through his blessing, a rite which seemed also to be taking on the greater speed of the age, and the business of dining was carried on with aggressive concentration. The meal was barely finished when[28] Miss Wilson asked to be excused on the ground that she had to be at her school by one o'clock. Grace and confidence were in the poise of her body, the easy sureness of her step, as she went upstairs to her room.[29]

"What do you think of her?" Ellen asked, as soon as she could get Donald alone. "Pretty, isn't she?"

"Oh, she's all right," Donald agreed, "but as for pretty—this house has more than its share of that already."

Ellen's eyes danced.[30] "You never get over it, do you, Donald?"

"I'm a heart-broken man, Ellen," he answered. "Biology, or whatever it is—you know, about cousins marrying each other—has played me a rotten trick. As for the rest of the world, I'm not interested."

"Poor Don," she mocked him. But her arm stole about his waist and they went out and leaned over the fence together.

"Tom isn't back yet," she said, to make conversation.

"No, and I'm out o' twine. I bet he's eating with Katie Crisp."

"Well, don't be so crisp about it. Walter Spence ate here for years every time he passed the door."

"You mean every time he didn't pass the door. And see what happened—now he has a wife and three kids."

"Well—are you jealous?"

He flung her round and held her face firmly between his two hands. "Quit it, you little devil, will you? If I was marrying into the Strand family you know who'd be the mother of my kids."

"Donald! How fearfully frank you are! And you swore, just like a man."[31]

"Well, what of it?" Donald returned. "Your father was saying to me before dinner that life is speeding up, and I guess that applies to language, too. Only"—more soberly—"I don't swear as a general thing."

"Only on provocation. You'd do most anything on provocation, wouldn't you? Well, which would you rather have: twenty-one thumps on the back or—?" She pursed her lips.

Color was running up through her olive skin when she drew away.[32] "That wasn't just what I call cousinly," she said.

2

Mr. Strand interrupted them, and with an upward gesture of his chin, signalled Donald toward the table. The old sod structure had given way to a frame building with ample, high-set windows and ventilation blowing through two open doors. The horses, sensing the presence of their master, vigorously attacked their empty mangers as though to indicate that the noon hour could not be nearly over,[33] but their misgivings were unwarranted, for Mr. Strand turned into the empty stall allotted to the Maggie-mare and let himself down heavily on the clean straw. Donald, a little surprised, squatted beside him.

"No use startin' until Tom gets here with the twine," Mr. Strand suggested in explanation of his behavior. "I'm thinkin' we'll be havin' a K.C. in the family before long, Donald'."

"A K.C?" Donald was puzzled.

Mr. Strand chuckled over his wit. "Katie Crisp, I'm meanin'," he explained, "You were indicatin' before dinner how the wind blows."[34]

"Wind? I'd call it a hurricane."

"Well, prepare for the worst. Tom's been talkin' it over with me. We'll be havin' to reorganize things a bit, Donal'."

"Yes?" Donald waited for his uncle to continue.

"Still hankerin' to be a train engineer, Donal'?"

Donald shrugged his shoulders. "I suppose there's a time when every boy feels the call of steam, Uncle Jim, and it still tugs me a bit, but I've got kind of fitted into this farming job. You see, Uncle Jim, I'm twenty-one to-day, and I know more about farming than anything else. But I haven't decided on anything."[35]

"That's what I was wantin' to talk to you[36] about; you're twenty-one, an' I have some things that has to be said. Do you remember your father an' mother, Donal'?"

52

"Yes, a little. I can see a red brick house with trees about it, and a garden, and trees with apples, and my father and mother—a little—but you and Aunt Annie have been father and mother to me, Uncle Jim."

"We've done our best,[37] me lad, an' it's been no hardship, but a joy. But there's some things I have to be sayin'. Before you came there was a letter from a lawyer, but I couldna' read it, such a mess—they weren't usin' them writin' machines then—so I sent it back to the name that was printed on the corner. Then came the lawyer himsel'; he sent a message, an' I met him at Alder Creek."

Donald waited, feeling that a curtain which had obscured some part of his early life was about to be lifted.

"Well, it was about you he wanted to see me. Your father an' mother, dyin' sudden as they did, left no will, an' the Court had to appoint a guardian.[38] Some friends suggested me, an' bein' your father's brother an' your own blood, so to say, there was only one answer. That's what Mr. Smart—that's the lawyer—wanted to see me about."

"And you agreed?"

"Of course. There was some papers signed, an' I was your legal guardian until you were twenty-one. That is to-day, Donal'. I've tried to bring you up like one o' me own, Donal'; not much luxury an' plenty o' hard work, but a Christian home, if I may be so bold as to say it. I've guided you so far but now it's your privilege to take the reins yoursel'. I'm hopin' you'll pull a straight furrow, Donal'."

The old man's voice had gone husky. Donald let his hand fall on his uncle's arm. There was a moment of silence between them.

"I'll try and never disgrace my bringing up, Uncle Jim," he said, as one making a vow. Then, after a pause, "Does this mean I have to get out?"

"There's no 'have to' between you an' me, Donal'. But I hav' na finished my story. You mind the brick house, with the trees and the garden? It was sold, all accordin' to law. There was some debts to pay an' the balance was put in the bank for you. It's yours today' Donal'."

Donald smiled incredulously. "Balance? Bank? You're not joking, Uncle?"

"Well, if five thousand dollars is a joke, then I'm jokin', Donal'."

"Five thousand dollars! You mean—? And you never said a word."

"I did na'[39] want to spoil you, Donal'. Many a good life goes wrong by dreamin' o' the future instead o' workin' in the present. Besides, it'd do you no good in this district for this to be known. You'd marked out as a child o' Fortune, an' all kinds o' schemes laid to help you spend your money. An' of course it wasna'[40] five thousand to start with; there's been interest for eleven years, an' interest piles up, as you'll find if ever you have to pay it. So I've kep' your secret, Donal', so you could[41] have, as you might say, an even start."

Donald got up and stirred himself, filling his chest, tensing his muscles, trying to get his new focus on life. The horses, puzzled by the long delay, stood silent in their stalls as though anxious not to attract attention.

"You have been thinking it all out," Donald said. "You have some plans for me? First, of course, I must pay you and Aunt Annie for all—no, I can't pay for all you have done, something on account."

Mr. Strand made gesture of dissent. "Not a dollar, Donal'; not a cent. You've pulled your weight an' more. An' Ma an' me is not needin' it now." Donald pressed[42] the matter but his uncle would not hear of it. "Not a dollar; not a cent," was his only answer.

"You have plans for me?" Donald repeated, when he found his uncle regarded any suggestion of payment as almost an offence.[43] "You have been thinking it all over?"

"Not plans, meanin' anythin' you must do, but suggestions, if you like. Will I be tellin' them to you?"

Donald nodded.

"Well, then, I'm pleased you're sort o' resigned to be a farmer. It's hard work, but it's work on the soil, it's work with God, if you like, Donal'—an' it's honest. In business, success often means some one else's failure, but in farmin', success helps everybody. An' if you're out o' debt it is the most independent life in the world, an' if you're in debt, too deep to see the light, it's jus' about the dangdest dog's life there is. You have a chance to start right an' to stay right. Now this is what I'm thinkin':

"Your Aunt Annie an' me is not as young as we was, Donal'.

54

Sixty-two I am, an' she's sixty. We've worked hard for fifty years, Donal'; maybe more, an' we think it's time to be lettin' down the pressure. There's three quarter sections o' land here now—'twas one quarter when you came, Donal'—an' it's all paid for, an' everythin' that's on it is paid for, even the new binder, I paid for it cash in the hand. A dozen years ago I wouldna' ha' thought it possible. And Tom is thinkin' o' gettin' married, which is natural an' proper, an, Katie is a good girl, strong an' willin' an'll make a good farmer's wife. Take an old man's advice, Donal'; pick 'em strong when you come to pick; strength o' muscle an' strength o' heart'll[44] carry you through where the flimsy ones'll go sick an' be a drag on you all your life. Well—Ma an' me has our eye on a cottage in Alder Creek; the Brown place —maybe you know it?—a snug little house wi' stablin' for a couple o' cows an' a good big garden, an' we're thinkin' o' lettin' Tom have the farm. I'll rent it to him on share, half an' half as a goin' concern, an' the rent'll keep Ma an' me confortable—"

"And Ellen?" Donald interrupted.

Mr. Strand's eyes twinkled. "Ellen'll live with us in Alder Creek, unless she marries," he said. "I'm thinkin' maybe you an' her'll be settlin' that." The old man paused, sensing a change in his nephew's mood. "I'm not tryin' to press you, Donal! but the signs have pointed that way. If I'm wrong I'm pleadin' no offence."

Donald tried to cover embarrassment with a laugh. "There's no offence, I'm sure. There could be no greater compliment.[45] Ellen and I have talked about it, but, you see, we're first cousins, and, you know—well, hang it, Uncle, you know what I mean."

Mr. Strand nodded meditatively. "Perhaps you're right, although often no harm comes of it. I'm not urgin' you, Donal'. You'll make up your own mind, an' Ellen'll have a home with us until she finds another. Now as for you—I've heard that the Farquhar farm is to be sold for debt. It's a good farm—"

"For debt?" Donald interrupted. "I thought Mr. Farquhar was a good farmer. He works hard, and he's been getting good crops—"

"So he has, so he has. But it takes more than that to make a farmer. Farquhar can't say no. Every glib salesman in the country knows that Farquhar can't turn him down. He's always buyin' new machin'ry before the old is half wore out; his house is full of falderals he don' need an' his store bills is unpaid an' the mortgage company is for seizin' his land. I'm thinkin' we need a new course in our schools to learn our boys an' girls to say no. The salesman is trained to sell, an' it's no fair to turn him[46] loose on men an' women that's never been trained to say no, an' say it wi' a good stiff jaw. If a prize fighter was to pick an issue wi' you or me they'd call him a coward, wouldna' they? Well, what's the diff'rence? Both is special trained for their job.[47] Never be gettin' into debt, Donal'. Easy credit wrecks more homes than doin' without. But that's by the by. Farquhar has a half section wi' a twelve hunder[48] dollar morgage on it, an' some interest overdue. I'm thinkin' you can buy it for fifteen hunder. If it goes to mortgage sale he'll get nothin', for his other creditors'll swoop down an' take all there is. They're like that; mighty pleasant gentleman when they're askin' your name on the dotted line, but they've hard faces[49] on collection day.

"Then there's the half alongside. That's railway land; nothin' better out o' doors; never been a plow in it, an' offered at four dollars the acre. You see, you can buy the whole thing an' set yoursel' up on a full section o' land, all paid for, wi' an outfit to work it, an' still ha' money in the bank. Not many boys gets away to a start like that, Donal'."

Dreams were taking shape[50] in the boy's brain. "A full section," he said, hoarsely, as though it were unbelievable. "Do you think a man can handle that much land?"

"I didna' use to, Donal'. I use' to think a quarter section was plenty, but that was when I sowed the wheat wi' my two fists an' walked behind two horses on a plow. But now, wi' the big machin'ry an' plenty o' horseflesh, it's all diff'rent. You new binder'll cut three hunder acres as easy as one. Look at Andy Wayne, workin' his section an' a half, wi' one man an' a little extra help at harvest, an' Jimmie in college. It's no the farmin' I was brought up to, Donal', an it's maybe time I was gettin' out, but you young fellows'll be doin' it that way."

The dog barked, and the two men emerged from the coolness of the stable into the bright sunlight. Tom was swinging up the drive, the Maggie-mare stretching herself like a thoroughbred, the sunlight flashing on her nickel-trimmed harness. She came to a stop before them, her nostrils dilating, the sweat standing like soap along her neck.

Tom dropped[51] easily from the buggy seat. He was no taller than Donald now; when the two stood together they were much of a size, and the family likeness ran strong in their blood, but Tom emphasized his superior age with a cautious mustache.

"Hope I haven't delayed you,"[52] he apologized. "Alder Creek's getting to be a regular city, and I had to wait for my twine longer than I expected."

"It's all right," his father said. "I'm thinkin' it wasna' at Alder Creek you had your big delay. But the harvest is no pushin' yet, an' Donal' an' me has jus' been havin' a bit talk. We'll be gettin' the horses out now, an' away."

Donald lined up his four horses with the ease of long practice, stuck a few balls of twine on their hames, and started for the field. There were wonderful things to think about, and the dream kept focussing more clearly and taking form all afternoon while the binder clicked its incessant stream of sheaves and the drive chains sang in the hot sun.

3

Donald worked late to make up for the long noon hour. At six o'clock Ellen brought him sandwiches and hot tea; from his high seat on the binder he saw her leave the house with his lunch pail, timing her trip to intercept him at the nearest corner of the field. She was a trim figure as she came through the stubble in her clean printed dress and with a broad straw hat saving her face from the sun. He swung the horses' heads out from the wheat, and, throwing a few sheaves into a stook, motioned her to sit beside him in the shade.

"Mighty good of you, Ellen," he said, as she laid stout sandwiches before him and filled his cup with tea. "I feel a vacancy inside me about the size of Hudson Bay. Somebody is going to draw the world's first prize when he lands you, Ellen,"

"Hush. I thought we had decided not to talk about that any more."

"So we did, but you know, I somehow feel that, no matter who you marry, you will always—sort of—belong to me."

"You mean we will always be good friends," she clarified his remark. "Of course we will, and perhaps being good friends is better than being poor husband and wife."

He patted her hand and pressed it a little. "You're quite a philosopher," he said. "When I marry-if I do—I[53] hope it will be someone who has sense and can make sandwiches that fill a gap."

For a time she watched him without comment, happy in his presence. His eyes searched her face and she dropped her lashes before them, but the curve of her lip was exquisitely tender.

"What do you think of Miss Wilson?" she challenged at length.

"Nothing. That is, I haven't been thinking about her at all. Really. Ellen, I've got bigger things to think about to-day." She raised her eyes and they met his steadily. He leaned forward a little, tightening a grip on her hand. "Ellen, how much do you know?"

"I know you are twenty-one; a great, big, powerful, dangerous man."

"Don't kid me. What else do you know? '

"Well?" she made a bewitching gesture which might mean anything or nothing.

"I mean about me. About what has—happened—to me—to-day?"

"Happened? To you? Nothing serious, I hope?"

Then he told her. While the shadow of the stook lengthened slowly to the eastward he recounted his conversation with her father, told her something of the dream which had found birth in the stable stall that noon. When he had finished he waited for her to speak.

"I congratulate you, Donald," she said, steadily. "You are away to a wonderful start. You will be a big man some day, and I will always be very proud of you."

"Ellen!"

"When you have your own farm of course you will marry. And I will still be proud of you."

"Don't Ellen! Why should I marry?"

"Why shouldn't you? Hester?" Her eyes again stole up to his.

He laughed. "Hester!"

"Why not?, You like her. No, dear, I'm not jealous—not a bit. I just want you to be happy."

"Then why not let us say to the devil with biology, and take a chance?"

She shook her head. "We've been all over that, We would never forgive ourselve if—if the chance didn't work. And now, sir," she threw all her sprightliness into her voice, "I brought you this lunch to save your time, and here you are wasting it!"

"Not wasting," he protested.

"Well—spending." She was gathering up his cup and the empty tea bottle. "That's the boy, Donald. Back to the job!"

He looped an arm about her, drew her to him. His lips sought hers, but she turned her face away. "No, Donald; not that, any more. We're grown up now. We grew up to-day." Obediently he released

59

her.[54] She turned her face toward the low-hung sun, and the glow of its red light was in her eyes. She seemed wonderfully straight and supple as she stood among the sheaves, casting her long shadow eastward. Her arms went up—an old gesture of childhood which recurred at climatic moments—her lungs were full; she stood as one in attendance upon the gods. How much she was casting out of her life in that moment of sublimation Donald could not guess.

"You are still a sun worshipper," he said.

She turned toward him, and as she did their lips met for an instant. "No; a cousin worshipper," she answered, as she broke from his grasp.

4

It rained that night; a gentle, friendly rain which did not batter the crops but wrapped them rather in a last farewell caress. Donald heard its footsteps on the roof and lay awake, planning. There would be no harvesting at least until noon and the idle half day would give him a chance to negotiate with Farquhar.

Miss Wilson, exercising a boarder's prerogative, did not rise for breakfast with the family, but Donald might scarce have seen her if she had, so occupied was he with other matters.

"I think I'll act on your tip," he said to his uncle, when the two met in the yard. "If you don't mind I'll slip over and see Farquhar this morning. Perhaps you'd like to come along?"

But Mr. Strand was too shrewd to mix in the details of the boy's affairs. "What'd you be needin' me for?" he parried. "I'm wagerin' you'll drive harder bargain than I'd have conscience for, at that. But, mind you, not more than fifteen hunder."

Donald hitched the Maggie-mare to the old topless buggy, as the new one was much too dainty to soil its wheels[55] in muddy roads when that[56] could be avoided, and took his way along the trail to Farquhar's. The old buggy sagged prodigiously to the right, and the wheels described four successions of unrelated curves in the soft earth, but despite appearances the vehicle hung together and rode joyously. It was the same trail over which he and Jack and Hector—two good pals both gone to their reward—had driven the cattle that day of his first experience as a cowboy, but a different country met his eye. The vacant section where the cows had grazed was now red with wheat; even the trail[57] had suffered from the encroachments of prosperity and was confined to a straight-laced road allowance instead of wandering care-free over the prairie. The low sod shanty of the Harp's had given place to a

61

two-storey frame box with four corners and a roof; farther north, on the Marble homestead, a bright red barn dozed under the morning sun; farther still, the four stout elevators at Alder Creek held guard over the surrounding fields like blockhouses of the invading conqueror, Wheat. The ponds that in earlier years[58] had dotted the plain were drying up; some of them had disappeared; the nesting place of wild duck, the parading grounds of snipe and plover, after a few protesting seasons had surrendered to the plow and were now meekly growing barley for the settlers' hogs. The creek[59] itself was but the shamefaced ghost of its past, a disconnected succession of stagnant pools where once brown water had rippled all summer long. But these thoughts—if he thought them—brought no melancholy to Donald.[60] The ruthlessness of Progress had not yet touched his heart. Instead he saw the growing countryside, the fields heavy with harvest, and the chance within his grasp of being the youngest and most prosperous farmer of them all.

That thought grew upon him. Somewhere, so far down in his nature that he never had recognized it, had lain for years an irritation to his self-esteem. Jimmie Wayne was to be a lawyer; under his father's instigation he had accepted glady a course that would lead to an altitude higher than that accorded to the farm. Donald, in thoughts that never had been expressed in words, had resented that assumed superiority. It was not a personal issue; his friendship with Jimme unbroken; it was a issue with his class—with any class—which made pretentions to a level higher than those who wrung their living from the land. Most unexpectedly had come to him an opportunity to vindicate his kind. Here was a chance to lay hold upon Success; to make for himself a prosperity and a name that would ensure a place of honor in his community. A seed of ambition, lying long dormant within him, now burst into sudden flower. He would show them! He would show them![61]

"In ten years I'll have the world by the tail," he promised himself. "You see if I don't. Work!" His muscles rose under his thin shirt at the suggestion of the word. "And with this!" He tapped his head. "If they put if over me they're better men than I am—and they're not!"

Mr. Farquhar and his hired man were grinding binder knives in the shade of his granary; the hired man turning the stone, which called for strength, and his employer holding the knives, which, like any de cent work of skill, was the easier job of the two. As the hoofs of the Maggie-mare sounded in the yard Farquhar looked up, and, recognizing his visitor, leaned the knives against the granary and met him with a welcoming smile.

"Well, Donal', how's she goin'?" he asked, with a hearty shake of his hand.

"Not so bad, Mr. Farquhar. Just an hour of two in the bone, account of last night's rain."

"Yep. We could ha' done without it, but we'll take it, now it's here. Will you come in?"

"Well, thanks, but I wanted to have a little talk with you, if you don't mind." With his eyes he telegraphed a suggestion that the hired man was superfluous. Mr. Farquhar disposed of him with some petty order and, resting his foot confidentially on the buggy hub, continued, "Well, lad, what's on your mind?"

Donald thought he had rehearsed his part carefully, but he suddenly became aware of[62] something tragic in the situation for which he had not made allowance. He had always liked Farquhar; indeed, there wasn't a better-liked man in the settlement,[63] a good neighbor, always ready to lend a hand, always ready to give without asking in return. And now he was to be sold out because he was sympathetic, because he could not say no, because he could not harden his heart. The boy's eyes roved over the farmyard; its accumulation of machinery told its own tale. Very well; they wouldn't get him that way. He would say no, when no was the word, with a stiff jaw, too, as his uncle had said.

He came back to earth, and his eyes, hard for his age, met the friendly face of his host. "The fact is, Mr. Farquhar—and I'll ask you to say nothing about it until it must be known—I've come in for a little money, and I'm thinking of starting a farm of my own."

"That's fine, fine." Mr. Farquhar's enthusiasm was real and spontaneous. "You're a good boy, Donal'. I'm congratulatin' you, and wishin' you all success."

"Thanks, Mr. Farquhar. And I was thinking maybe I could buy yours."

"Buy mine?" Farquhar laughed. "You're jokin'. I'm not thinkin o' sellin'."

"Maybe not, but I'm thinking I can do you a good turn as well myself. Your farm is mortgaged, Mr. Farquhar?"

The farmer's face firmed a little, but only for a moment. "Well, yes; most farms are," he agreed. "A mortgage—that's one thing grows powerful well in this country."

"And you're behind in your payments. And the mortgage company are threatening you. And they're going to sell you out if you don't come through. And I'm here offering to buy you out before they get a chance."

The smile had definitely faded from Farquhar's face; it took on a touch of hardness,[64] and yet it was gentle still; the man found it impossible to be harsh. "How do you know all this?" he said.

"The money I have come in to was left me by my parents. My uncle has been my guardian. Naturally, he had been advised by a lawyer—a Mr. Smart. Mr. Smart also acts for the mortgage company. He told my uncle there is no question that they will sell you out this fall if they don't get their money. It isn't just what you owe on the land. It's because you are in debt to everyone. They have given up hope that you will ever get on your feet; you are getting in deeper every year, so they have decided they may as well clean you up at once."

Farquhar seemed to shrink under the brutality of the attack, but he did not fight back. He was like a cowed child. "And you came to tell me this?" he said at length.

"I came to show you a way out. Listen; If they sell you out, of course it must be advertised, and all your other creditors will jump on you. They'll leave you nothing but your exemptions. You'll be on the road. But if I *buy* you out it's nobody's business. You're still a good citizen, in good standing. You can get another farm; buy railway land, or rent one, or buy on crop payments. I give you a marked check; you pay off the mortgage company; everybody says, 'Look at Farquhar. He's cleaned up his mortgage; he's away to a fresh start!' How much is it, Mr. Farquhar?"

Farquhar's smile had returned. "There is something in what you say," he agreed. "It's about thirteen under. Of course the farm is worth a lot more than that," he added, hopefully. "Twice that, I should say."

"A farm is worth just exactly what you can get for it, Mr. Farquhar. At a forced sale you won't get a dollar for yourself,[65] and if you do, your other creditors will take it from you. Now here's my offer: I'll give you fourteen hundred dollars, cash or marked check the hour the papers are signed, and nobody need know what I paid —that'll be between you and me. You can say two thousand—three thousand—anything you like. That'll help your credit. You'll get away to a new start."

Farquhar tried to bargain. "I ought to get more than fourteen hunder," he pleaded.

"Fourteen hundred is my offer, Mr. Farquhar. I can buy railway land for less, and the buildings mean nothing to me. Of course, if you're not interested, there's no harm done. I just thought i'd make you the offer before I did anything else." he lifted the reins.[66] The mare became alert.

"Let's go in and talk it over with the wife." said Farquhar.

5

Donald bought the Farquhar farm for fourteen hundred dollars, but he let his uncle think he had paid fifteen; he was not sure Mr. Strand would approve the bargain he had driven. He bought the adjoining half section of railway land for four dollars and acre—twelve hundred and eighty dollars, and he paid cash, something at that time[67] almost unknown in the experience of the railway company with settlers.

He was now the owner of a section of land, six hundred and forty acres, one square mile. It was not actually one section but two half sections, with a road allowance between them, but that, as he pointed out to his uncle, was really an advantage. The Farquhar buildings, while convenient to the road allowance, were almost in the centre of the sqare. This made for efficiency—for short hauls and short trips to any part of the farm.

On Sundays he would go over to his farm and walk the four solid miles around it, swishing his feet through the long grass, stopping often to breathe the smell of the soil and the gaze across the broad sweep of prairie or the brown stubble of Farquhar's harvested crop. With the easy gesture of one whose magnanimity costs him nothing he had agread that Farquhar might remain in possession until December. "That will give you time to dispose of your crop and to arrange for moving out," he said. "The mortgage company wouldn't have done that for you."

"No, I suppose not," Farquhar had agreed, doubtfully. The wisdom of his sale was frequently challenged in his mind. Some of his neighbors had congratulated him upon getting twenty-five hundred —the sum he had given out—but agreed that the price was none too high. And some of his creditors wanted to know, now that he made such a good sale of his farm, how about settling his little account?

So Donald walked about his farm, kicking the good soil with his heel, examining the fresh earth where it was turned up by badgers, lifting it in his hands, pressing it, tossing it in the wind. It was his.

The fact of his inheritance could not long be kept a secret, and wild guesses at the amount were running through the community. At the Sunday services at the old Sundown schoolhouse Donald, never an outsider, had become the focal point of interest. The girls with whom he had gone to school—Annie Mergle, Winnie Calder, Elsie Marble, Hester Harp, Jessie and Jennie Sinclair, Mary Orde—all the rising womanhood of the little community, had glances[68] for Donald Strand and found a new warmth in their cheeks and in their breasts when his eyes flickered back to theirs. There was even some buying of new dresses and hats and shoes[69] in the stores at Alder Creek. Not that any of the girls would have deliberately set herself to marry money, but Donald was an attractive match in his own right and the glamour of his good fortune subtracted nothing from the confident set of his head or the easy freedom of his behavior.

"Will ye think o' that, now?" said Mrs. Harp, plumper and even more amiable with the years, to Mrs. Crisp, who had grown whiter and thinner. "An' to think they never breathed a word of it. He didn't know himself till the day he was twenty-one. Twenty thousand, they say it was."

But Mrs. Crisp conservative, or perhaps through Katie she had a more accurate estimate. "I'm doubtin' if it was that much," she answered. "But he's a fine boy, and it's luck may it bring him!"

"He is that. And mind ye, our Hester—they've gone together ever since they were children at the school. Ye never can tell, can ye, Mrs. Crisp?" Over an ample diaphragm Mrs. Harp leaned toward her neighbor in anticipatory confidence.[70]

"Indeed, no," said Mrs. Crisp, whose only daughter was to marry Tom Strand as soon as the threshing could be cleared away.

Meanwhile Clara Wilson, teacher of Sundown school and member of the Strand household, was holding certain communions with her heart. Clara had no illusions about her profession. Even before she had earned her certificate she had laid it down as her scheme of life that she would teach until something better turned up, but this was her first school and she wondered if Fate had crossed her path so soon.[71] There was a young fellow in her home town whom she counted a prospect; there had been several experimental by-plays between them. Harvey Graves was going in for medicine, and a doctor's wife has social prominence, but Harvey was in debt, and might be a long while getting out of it. Anyway, it would be years before he would be in a position to marry her, and teaching was drudgery. It was worth while to cultivate Donald and see what would come of it.

6

Mr. Strand bought the Brown cottage in Alder Creek,[72] and Tom and Katie were married on a mellow afternoon in October.[73] Donald made his home with Tom and Katie until the freeze-up, but his presence was small disturbance to them, for he left early and returned late, working all day on his farm and having his midday meal at Farquhar's, for which he paid fifteen cents, although the easy-going[74] farmer protested against taking anything. He had bought a two-furrow sulky plow out of Farquhar's over-stocked yard by paying two dollars more than was still owing on it, and hired a four-horse team at a nomimal price until freeze-up.

"Why don't you buy the team?" Tom had suggested. "You'll need it in the spring."

"Yes—in the spring," Donald answered. "I'll let Farquhar feed it till then."

Donald had sat a plow on the Strand farm many a chilly October day, and never had he been indifferent to his uncle's interest, but the fascination with which he watched his own earth crumbling under the mouldboards was absolutely a new experience. With a stout duck outer coat to break the wind and a felt hat pulled low on his head he rode up and down the mile-long furrow, listening to the gentle scrape of the shares in the earth, watching the stubble bend as the friable soil broke loose before its summersault, glancing back from time to time at the long, straight, glistening black ribbons[75] that marked his progress.[76] During these days, although his eyes were on the earth, his mind was building its castles, congratulating him upon his wonderful good fortune, plunging ahead to the time when he would be—why not?—the wealthiest farmer in the Alder Creek district; sometimes linking back to the parents who had placed opportunity in his way but never would be able to share the pride of his success.

He wished they might have been able to follow his career.[77] He wondered vaguely whether or not they knew anything[78] about it. According to the belief of his childhood they had gone to Heaven (or Hell, but that was unthinkable; all one's friends and relatives, after they were dead, were assumed to have gone to Heaven, although doubtless the lower[79] destination drew a considerable population from other sources) and there they lived in perpetual bliss, walking in golden streets, playing on golden harps and singing around the Throne. But now, even in such dim recollections as he could summon from childhood, they seemed to fit rather badly into such an environment. He supposed the whole picture[80] must be allegorical—although to have openly declared[81] such a view might have stamped him an infidel—and yet there must be truth in the allegory.[82] It was all a mystery, not to be too much brooded over; but here was something solid; land; land that scraped under his own plowshare; that would lie nursed of rain and snow until another Spring; that would take his labor to its bosom and bear him a harvest as a woman bears a child.

From that point his thought proceeded into explorations of his domestic future. He had accepted as natural if not inevitable the idea that some day he should marry,[83] but he never had thought of it as a prospect for immediate consideration. But now—why not? He had a farm; when Farquhar moved he would have a house![84] The house needed repairs, but that would be much cheaper than building anew, and he had money in the bank. Indeed, yes, why not? At first he toyed with the possibility, but—why not? Nothing stood between him and marriage save the selection of the right girl, and her consent. And yet there was something; a barrier of some kind; a wall that had to be broken down. For all his semi-intimacy with Ellen he could not at once picture himself in the relationship of husband to any girl he knew. In an abstract way, yes, but not when it came down to cases. Hester Harp? He had wrestled with her on the playground at Sundown School, and in the pasture section where they herbed cows together; he remembered the touch of her warm, flecked face and the pressure and pull of her muscles as they strained together, but that was exploratory experience disguised as fun; to deliberately think of her as his wife called for a leap of the imagination that had no sure landing-place. And again, why Hester? She was a strong girl, dutiful, and accustomed to the work of the farm. She could milk cows and make butter and no doubt raise children as her mother had raised her. But any strong and willing farmer's daughter could do that. So why Hester? Why not—well, yes, hang it—why not Clara Wilson? His heart jumped a little at that thought; he twisted on his seat and shouted to his horses. It was an audacious thought, but it intrigued him. Clara for a while had regarded him with studied reserve, but she was melting now; he had known it one[85] night when they sat together on the stairs.

He shook his head as though to clear mind of the haze that enwrapped it. He tried to see clearly. Clara had no special qualification[86] to be a farmer's wife. Perhaps she could milk, or learn to milk, but she woudn't want to; she was too proud of her clean, soft hands for the dirty work about a farm. She would not want to get up at five in the morning to cook his breakfast; she generally had to rush at the last moment to reach her school at nine. She liked pretty dresses, and she wore them well; but his wife, for a few years at any rate, would have little time and money[87] for finery. The five thousand dollars with which he was starting would have to be doubled and doubled again before he would feel secure. That would take work and soiled hard hands and no time for finery. All the logic was against Clara. Yet his heart speeded up when he tried to picture Clara as his wife, and thoughts of Hester left him almost unstirred.

"No hurry, anyway," he said to himself. "Take a year or two to think about it. I'll be better on my own for a while. Wives and kids are likely to upset calculations. Look at Watt Spence. Four youngsters to feed and clothe and doctor, and Lizzie beginning to run to seed. No, thank you. Not for me."

But as he sat in the kitchen that night when Clara went up to her room he could not help appraising the trim ankles and a few inches of calf which a negligent skirt exposed on the stairs. "Good night, Donald," she called to him, with a smile, and her face was very pretty in the glow from her lamp.[88]

"Good night," he answered, but his mind was whirling absently. There were stairs like that at Farquhar's only they were against the wall, and he wondered if some night—perhaps. . . . Certainly she was very pretty when she smiled.

7

It was mid-November when the Farquhar moved.[89] Frost had put a crust on the earth, and the plowing was stopped, so Donald, having nothing better to do, walked over the fields from Tom's to lend and hand with the loading. Farquhar met him with a smile; moving to a new farm was something of an adventure, and Farquhar never had quite outgrown the optimism of childhood. "I've taken the machines over, from time to time, and the cattle," he explained, "so there's just the things in the house and a few odds and ends. It's very good of you, Donal', to come and see us off. It's just what your uncle would have done if he'd been still livin' on the old farm."

"Oh, I don't know; I'd nothing else to do," Donald replied, truthfully. Farquhar's high opinion of him always filled him with a vague disquiet. The man was so mild and unresentful; if only he would fight back, against fate, against him—Donald—against anybody! But there he stood, his long, lean form angular through his shabby clothes and a smile on his thin lips. "Can't I help you load something onto the wagon?" Donald suggested, eager for action.

"Well, I suppose," said Farquhar, who was accustomed to agreeing with suggestions. "There ain't much, but the missus is packin' some things in the house, and I suppose we could give a hand."

Donald found Mrs. Farquhar packing dishes in a barrel with the dubious assistance of her three children. The fire had been allowed to go out; the house was cold and very uninviting. The woman straightened her tired back and mustered a smile for her young neighbor.

"Don't look much like a home now, does it, Donal'?" she said, and there was a note of bitterness in her voice. "Well, I suppose one place is as good as another. We eat, we sleep, we work, we have children, and some day we die. What difference does it make?"

For lack of an answer Donald offered his help at packing dishes. Mrs. Farquhar seemed reluctant to accept, but, once he was started, she aided and abetted him. The plates were cracked and chipped; the cups were lacking handles. Kitchenware had not yet become subject to high-pressure salesmanship.

The rattle of a buggy on the frozen road came in through the open door and Farquhar went out to see who his visitor might[90] be. The three children scurried after him.

"I hope you don't feel that I am—sort of—putting you off the farm," Donald said when they were alone, giving voice to a thought that was fermenting within him. "I wouldn't like you to feel that way about it."

Mrs. Farquhar's square features held him in a firm but not unfriendly gaze. "I'm findin' no fault with you, Donal'," she said. "We'd 'a' had to get out anyway, and you'd be foolish not to take your chance. If George was as good a business man as you we would n'[91] be movin', but these agent fellows get round him with their soft speeches and he can't say no. There ought to be a law against people sellin' people things that people don' need, but I'm not blamin' you, Donal', you know that, and I wish I could leave the house better shape, but the stovepipes are down and there's no hot[92] water—"

"Don't you worry about that. The house is just fine, and I'll fix it up in a few minutes after everything is out. I've nothing else to do, anyway, now that the freeze-up has come."

Mrs. Farquhar looked about the bare walls. "It's a good house, Donal', even if it is a bit heaved and cracked. I hope you'll be very happy in it, and have a good wife and a lot o'[93] nice children—"

"Thanks, Mrs. Farquhar, but of course I don't expect that all at once. Now, what's next?"

She handed him some dishes. "We'd be all right if only George wouldn't let them talk him into buyin' things he don' need," she repeated, with the bitterness of discouragement. "If only he'd tell them to go to—to—"

"Hell," Donald suggested, in a voice that had caught some of her bitterness.

She paused with a chipped pitcher in her hand and leaned over the barrel, her square face close to Donald's her eyes boring into his. He became aware of a strange fascination in her eyes; as a younger woman she would have been hard to resist. "Donald," she said, "I'm goin' to ask you a question.[94] Do you believe in Hell?"

He straightened up slightly, resting his elbows on the barrel, mentally unsteadied by her unexpected challenge. "Why, yes, I do; that is, I guess I do," he answered.

"Well, I don' know," she said. "I use'd to, but now I wonder. The preachers don' talk about it so much and people live like there was n' any such place. If people really believed that if they did wrong they'd be burned in fire for ever and ever they wouldn' do it, would they? Mind you, I'm not sayin' I'm against Hell; I'm just wonderin', People talk and talk, but they don' say what they really mean, do they?"

"I guess not," Donald agreed. "Our ideas change. I remember one night when I was a little boy I lay in bed shaking with terror because that day I said damn. I was afraid if I went to sleep I might wake up with the flames all round me. Now I say damn, and worse things, too, and it doesn't worry me."

She seemed relieved; her tightened figure relaxed. "Thanks, Donal'," she said. "Excuse me for talkin' to you about it, but you've had a good education, and you're a good boy, and what you think is n't likely to be far out. For I've been thinkin' strange things—things I suppose I should go to Hell for, if there is a Hell."

"About people who sell things, and get you into debt?"

Her lips tightened as she nodded. "I've thought murd'rous things," she said. "My man's as gentle a soul as ever walked, and a good worker, but everybody puts it over him."

Plainly she did not intend her remark to apply to Donald, but his sense of discomfort grew within him. "Perhaps things will be better on your new farm," he said, with an attempt at cheerfulness.

But she could not be led into any false optimism. "No, they won't," she asserted. "Not as long as salesman come around with soft soap in their mouths. You know, Donal', I've been hearin' that they *train* men to do that kind of thing; have schools for it, like a college?"[95]

At that moment Farquhar's footstep sounded at the door, and the subject was dropped. Farquhar's face was drawn and colorless; the cheerfulness was gone from his lips. For a moment he watched his wife and the boy at their work; then he touched Donald on the arm. "Can I speak to you a minute?" he said.

They went out together, and Farquhar, obviously steeling himself to an unhappy task, broached his subject. "There's a collector here from the village," he said, "an' if I don' pay at least a hunder dollars on account he's for puttin' the bailiff after me. I have n' the money, Donal'; the wheat didn' turn out as well as I expected, and I don' see it in sight. If I had hunder dollars it would tide me over." He paused, as though hoping that Donald would offer a suggestion, but when the boy made no answer he plunged into his request, his voice husky with emotion: "Can you let me have a hunder dollars, Donald'? I'll pay you next harvest, with good interest or work for you next summer, or anything you like. It would be a great favor, Donal'."

Donald's impulse was to give him money. He had a check-book in his pocket; it could be done in a moment. But the scene in the house, the bitter woman thinking murderous thoughts, rose up before him. Farquhar was where he was because he could n't say no. Donald has his life before him; he was away to a good start; weakness now might mean weakness always.

"I am sorry, Mr. Farquhar," he said, "but I have only a five cents in my pocket."

"But you could fix it, Donal'; if you say you'll do it he'll take your word. Anybody would do that, Donal'. Everybody knows that you're as good as your word, Donal'." The pleading of a hungry dog was in his eyes.

But Donald had had time to bring sentiment under control. "I want my word always to be like that," he said, ; so I have to use it sparingly. And if I gave you this money it would n't get you out of debt; you would owe just as much as ever. I'm sorry, Mr. Farquhar, but I'm afraid I can't do it."

Farquhar's gaze held him for a moment; he might have been a sinking man who sees a boat deliberately pull away from him. "All right," he said, in a colorless voice, and turned toward the collector, who, huddled from the north wind in the shelter of the stable, had been awaiting the result of the interview.

When the Farquhars were gone Donald went into his house. In its utter emptiness it had the sepulchral atmostphere[96] of a dead body. The lower storey consisted of one square room,[97] with stairs at the end; the empty floor complained under his footstep. Upstairs were two rooms, bare and low-ceilinged, with blisters in the plaster where the roof had leaked. Not much of a house, but good enough until he could afford better.[98] Already he was drawing mental pictures of the fine home he would build when he had a few crops tucked away. In the meatime this would do for him—and perhaps for Clara. He looked at the two rooms, wondering which they would use, and found himself caught in a mesh of strange speculations.

The short day was closing with the rapidity which marks the onset of a winter's night when he finally dismissed his musings and loocked the door of his house. Snow was still falling thinly; the ground was almost covered with its sifted whiteness. As he stood at the door, held by some strange reluctance, the huge mound of one of Farquhar's straw stacks, like a gray hill through the gathering dusk, caught his eye and offered a suggestion. No better night to fire it than his and get it out of the way before Spring. With this purpose in mind he strode across the field, the rasp of his boots in the stubble half cushioned by the snow.

On the lee side of the stack he turned out a few armfuls of straw; struck a match; applied it. A thin tendril of flame clung for a moment to a few stalks; reached out, embraced more; reached farther, seized more; leaped, clutched its victim, roared to the top of the stack in a flood of fire. He drew back, driven by the heat and sobered by the sense of inevitable waste. As the smoke billowed and the flames roared his little drama[99] Mrs. Farquhar was re-enacted in his mind, and he remembered how as a boy the burning straw piles, for all their beauty, had conjured up the torments of Hell. Some little touch of that early terror twinged in his heart still, but it struck him less vividly now; surely one could hardly believe that souls were burned for ever in fire like this? Yet[100] it was a terrifying thought. If he really believed it he probably would have let Farquhar have the money, just to be on the safe side.

He watched the fire untils its flames were shortened and it began to sink within itself like the red glow of a rising moon. Darkness crowded closer; thin streaks of snow fell like a slow spray of sunlight between him and the fire; the heat was somewhat abated. But Hell was supposed to go on for ever and ever with no morsel of moistening for the most blistered tongue. After all Farquhar would really have been better off; it would just have been a matter of changing creditors. And one had to learn to say no.

For the second time that day he drew his mind clear of a miasma of strange speculations and, summoning his young energy, started briskly across the fields to the supper which Katie Strand would be keeping warm for him in her clean oven.

8

Winter is resting time in the prairie country, when all the world pauses to take its breath. With the coming of snow the high pressure of harvest time gives way to a lull as soft and universal as the white blanket that covers the earth. The fruitful soil[101] goes into its winter hibernation and by some strange chemistry draws from the snow and the frost qualities which re-charge its fertility for the coming year. The settlers, like the earth, draw in under their coverings except for the necessary tasks and for the dances and other social events that relieve the slow drag of the calendar from December to March.

Donald spent the winter with his aunt and uncle in Alder Creek.[102] There was no bedroom for him so he bought a contraption that could be used as a seat in the living-room during the day and could be made up as a bed at night. He consoled himself that the expenditure was not a wasted, as he would need something of this kind when he moved out to his farm. In return for his keep his helped with the few chores about the place and hauled the family firewood from the valley about ten miles distant where the settlers still got their supply of fuel. He hauled also a few loads to his own farm. The empty house lay very cold and dejected, a tiny spot on a white counterpane. Sometimes he went upstairs and looked at the two rooms and came down again with a feeling of having intruded upon some strange privacy. He would sleep on the couch. The rooms upstairs belonged to another world and another day.

Jimmie Wayne, who was pursing his law studies in Winnipeg, came home for the Christmas holidays,[103] and, on Donald's invitation, stayed overnight at the Brown cottage. Ellen insisted on turning her room over to the boys and herself adopting Donald's couch for the night. "Well—I don't see how else we can make it," she answered their protests, and the slight embarrassment of the situation sent a pleasant color to her cheeks.

"Of course, you might have married Donald in the interim," Jimmie suggested.

Ellen made an enticing grimace. "I shall never marry anyone in the interim," she answered.[104]

Donald felt that he was on the fringe of the discussion. Ever since he had greeted Jimmie at the station he had been conscious of some kind of intrusion between them. Jimmie carried himself with an ease which Donald found disturbing; he seemed to have been rubbing with the Outside and acquiring something which Donald had missed. The old inferiority of the farm again oppressed him; Jimmie's ease of manner only deepened his determination that some day he would show him; some day he would show them all!

Mrs. Strand, a little plumber than ever since her release from the heavy work of the farm, greeted the visitor almost as her own son. The relationship of the pioneers toward each other expressed itself in a sort of community parenthood of all their children—an expression which was intensified almong the old-timers as a new wave of settlers filled the vacant spaces and a period of material prosperity introduced a different sense of values. Mrs. Strand took Jimmie's face in her hands. "My, my, it seems only yesterday you were a bit of a boy runnin' 'round the farm in your bare feet, an' now you're next thing to a great lawyer. Your ma and pa'll be glad to see you, Jimmie, and proud to have such a clever son."

"I'm afraid I'm not as clever as you think," Jimmie answered, modestly. "A fellow has to go away from home to find how much he does n't know."[105]

Donald thought Jimmie might have been more tactful, but at that moment Mr. Strand came in from the post office, and there was a new series of greetings. When they were settled Jimmie fumbled in his pocket, looked uneasy for a moment, then produced his pipe.

"Do you object to smoking, Mrs. Strand?"

"Huh! An' me married to a chimney for forty years? But I did n' know you smoked, Jimmie?"

"Oh, we get that way," he said, lightly. "Have n't you taken it up, Donald?"

Donald shook his head.

"Not since the old days when we smoked whipstalks in the willows down by the creek, eh, Donald?"

"And you taught me to swear in safety by substituting goll for god?"

"Those were great days, old kid." Jimmie's fingers ran affectionately along Donald's thigh, and the gulf between them seemed to close. Donald's blood warmed to the realization that their old friendship was still unbroken.

That night the young people went to the rink, and Jimmie and Ellen skated long together. They skated well, and Ellen's light body seemed a part of his as they took their rhythmic stride. Their laughter as they rounded the corner by the waiting-room sounded clear above the crisp clangor of the skates. Donald waited, brooding. When at length he had Ellen to himself he took her to task.[106]

"Don't be silly, Don," she chided him. "You can skate with me all winter. Jimmie is here only for a day or two."

"You seem to be making the most of it," he observed.

"Well, why not?"

"Oh, its all right with me," he conceded, ungraciously.

"Of course it is," Her hand slipped along his arm. "Dont be silly, Don." He looked into her face. She was smilling; her eyes were dancing, her oval olive cheeks aglow. He had to return her smile, and his voice was good-humored again as he added, "You're too darn good for him, Ellen."

"Oh, you're miles ahead of both of us," she said. "Forget it."

"Ellen—tell me one thing," he said with sudden surmise. "Have you been writing to Jimmie?"

"And if?" she parried.

"Did you know he was coming to-day?"

For a moment she teased him with her eyes. Then: "Yes, I knew he was coming to-day; knew he had written his folks he would come to-morrow, so that they would n't be at the station to meet him; knew that he would stay at our house to-night, and sleep in my bed; that's why I changed the sheets this morning. Now see if you will be as frank with me when you have a secret."

"I suppose I should wish you great happiness?"

"Well, don't you?"

"Of course I do. But I mean—a sort of congratulation?"

"Oh, that's miles away—if ever. Come, let us skate, or he'll be snatching me right out of your arm."

It was late when Donald and Jimmie went to bed, and they talked far into the night, recalling their boyhood together, making occasional explorative plunges into the future. Suddenly Jimmie turned on his side and threw an arm over Donald's shoulder.[107]

"Sorry, old man," he said. "I've forgotten to congratulate you. I hear you are quite a man of means, with a fine farm, and all set up. You'll make a good farmer, Don. Good luck to you." His hand tightened on Donald's arm. Then, with a little betrayal of nervousness in his voice; "One of these days you'll be getting married."

Donald snorted amiably. "Nothing in sight," he said.

"Sure?"

"Quite."

"Not Ellen?"

"Don't kid me. Ellen and I grew up together."

"All the more reason."

"Besides, we're cousins."

"Plenty of cousins marry."

"I know, but it's not good—" He was going to sat "good management", but the words did not seem to quite fit the case, and he left the sentence unfinished. "Of course, I like Ellen—tremendously," he went on, "But I guess we are more like brother and sister. Anyway, we've talked it over, and that's where we stand."

Jimmie sighed gently. "Thanks, Don," he said. "I've been thinking about Ellen a good deal, and I don't want to clash with an old friend. I take it the coast is clear."

"Clear as a summer's day," said Donald. But afterwards he lay awake for a long time, wondering why he lied.

9[108]

Miss Clara Wilson stood in her northeast room combing her hair before the little framed mirror that hung on the wall. The eyes that looked back at her found a frown on her pretty face, and her lips moved in response to more that the pulling of her comb. "You are a fool, Clara," she told herself, but the declaration did not ease the trouble in her eyes. "You have made a mess of the whole thing. You should have known that a boy like Donald cannot be forced. And he is just stubborn enough to throw himself away on that Harp girl." Her lips twitched again, this time with bitterness and contempt. It would[109] be bad enough to lose Donald; to lose him to Hester Harp would be humiliation.

She shoved her hairpins into place with unnecessary vigor, and, without knowing she did so, turned her face toward Sundown School. The water of Alder Creek rippled under bright sunshine and a blue sky, for it was May again, and the scene of her educational efforts stood weather-beaten and drab against a background of green fields spotted with[110] prairie flowers. The sight of that box-like structure did nothing to restore her spirits.

When Clara had gaily returned to Alder Creek at the beginning of the term, wearing her new astrakhan coat to surprise and impress Donald, she had confidently promised herself that this was to be her last period of forcing knowledge into unwilling and unreceptive minds in Sundown or any other schoolroom. During the Christmas holidays she had decided to marry Donald Strand. It had been no part of her original plan, when she took up school teaching as a stop-gap, to become a farmer's wife, but the engagement of the young doctor whom she had regarded as her best prospect brought about a quick re-arrangement of objectives. Donald was no ordinary farm lout. He had a fair education, he spoke good English, he had a solid moral background; he was the kind of chap who, once he accepted the bonds of matrimony, would be likely to stay bonded. And he had money. The exact extent of his windfall Clara had not been clever enough to learn, but she knew it was substantial, whereas her doctor prospect would enter the matrimonial estate with little but a bag of surgical equipment and a accumulation of college debts. Do she was resigned to Donald.[111] And now it was common talk that Donald and Hester would be married in the fall.[112]

For this she had herself to blame, and she knew it. While she was at her home during the Christmas holidays Donald, for lack of other company, had taken Hester to a dance.[113] Clara set out to discipline him by developing a flirtation with Harry Long, son of the postmaster at Alder Creek. Too late, she has discovered that her attempt to drive Donald had driven him to Hester's arms, meanwhile acquiring for herself a liability in the person of Harry Long. Harry's self-esteem always had needed little encouragement, and his belief that Clata had accepted him in preference to Donald made him even more insufferable than he otherwise would have been. And she had to suffer him. To drop Harry now would be to disclose the fact that she had been playing a game deeper than he suspected and had been beaten at it. In short, she had lost Donald, whom she wanted, and she had acquired Harry, whom she did not want, and who had failed her even in the purpose for which she wanted him.

Clara hooked the neck of her dress high about her throat, drew her fingers under her eyes to relieve their heaviness, frowing again at the little bridge of freckles which was making its re-appearance with the summer sunshine,[114] and went down to breakfast.

"Good morning, Clara," Katie greeted her from the stove. "I'll have your porridge in a moment. It's a fine morning—what's left of it." Katie had already got Tom's breakfast and her own, milked three cows, fed the calves and the chickens, skimmed the milk, steamed the pans in hot water and set them out to air, and was now busy with her breakfast dishes.

"I suppose you think I'm awfully lazy," Clara sighed[115] as she took her chair at the table. "You often say 'It's a fine morning —what's left of it.'"

83

Katie paused in her dish washing and looked at her paying guest. "Land sakes, Clara, it don't annoy you, does it? Then I won't say it any more. I'm sure I don't blame you for taking life easy when you can. I wish I had your luck."

Clara adjusted the napkin—the only one used in the household—on her lap. "Do you mean it,[116] Katie?" she asked. "Would you really rather be teaching school than—what you are?"

Katie took some time for thought. "It's hard to answer that," she said at length. "It's hard to imagine you are what you ain't, and what you just naturally can't be. I haven't the education to teach school, so that's ruled out. I was brought up on a farm, and perhaps I know my job as well as the next one, if I do say it. I can milk and hoe and wash and iron and teach a calf to drink without feelin'squeamish or gettin' my fingers chewed. You see, it's what I know, and I guess we all fit in best doing what we know. But I will admit that when Tom's alarm goes off at a quarter to five I sometimes wish I had a nine-o'clock job."

"Yes, I suppose you do.[117] But it isn't all a matter of hours. Perhaps[118] my seven hour take more out of me than your fourteen or sixteen do out of you. After all, what does it matter, if you're happy? And you are happy, aren't you, Katie?"

Katie wrung her discloth dry and threw it with unerring aim against the nail where it hung. When she turned to answer there was light in her eyes.

"Yes, Clara, I am happy. I don't suppose Tom will ever be Premier or—or—postmaster," she added, with a wicked dash of mischief, "but[119] he's solid as a rock. It's a great thing to have something solid to tie up to."

Clara folded her napkin and rose from the table. "I suppose so," she said. "And you wouldn't call a postmaster a very solid rock, eh, Katie? Oh, don't waste your wit on him. I'm just using him to kill time."

"Take care you don't kill more than time."

"What do you mean?"

"Well, to put it bluntly, Harry's not in your class."

"Oh, thanks. But what am I going to kill? You said I might kill more than time."

"Chances—your own chances. As long as you are going with Harry other prospects may pass you up."

Clara laughed. "Other propects? I don't think there are any. Just what are you driving at?"

"Well, to put it bluntly again, I used to think there was a chance that maybe sometime you and me would be sort of relatives—by marriage, you know."

The blood tingled in Clara's cheeks. "But he's going to marry Hester," she said.

"Oh, is he? I hadn't heard. And I rather suspect[120] it all depends on you. But you'll have to meet Donald a little more than half way, always."

Clara walked more lightly down the well-worn path to the schoolhouse. At the bridge she stood and looked over the rail, watching suckers darting in the brown water. So that was the way of it. If Donald were really engaged to Hester Katie would be likely to know. But she would have to go half way-more than half way.

"All right," she said, speaking to her reflection in the water. "I will go half way. All the way, if necessary."

Her face smiled back at her. She leaned over until her whole figure showed in the stream. Clara was competent to appraise a figure, and she, gave her own no low rating. For some minutes she surveyed it with satisfaction, changing position slowly to show the curve of her body to best advantage, watching the ripple of the current as it toyed with her in smooth, cool intimacy.[121]

"Hester!" she laughed.

10

When school was dismissed for the day Clara asked one of the children to run up to Mrs. Strand's and say that the teacher had decided to go picking[122] wild strawberries on the prairie, and not to be concerned if she were late in getting home.[123] Clara stood in the schoolroom door,[124] for a long while seeing, but not seeing; she was not even consciouly thinking, but a process of determination was going on within her, taking form as a cloud takes form out of the stillness and emptiness about it. "I will do it," she said at length. "I will meet him more than half way. If I fail he may despise me, but if I don't try I shall despise myself. Anyway, I can't go on here. And I really like Donald."

The last words were a concession to her self-esteem.[125] Clara would not have admitted, even to herself, that her motives were unworthy. She believed that a woman should respect and honor her husband; she could respect and honor Donald, just as she could have respected and honored Dr. Graves, had fate turned the wheel a little more, or less. Between decent men there wasn't much to choose; a wife got the worst of it, unless she had the strength of character to dominate. And that was something to be settled later.[126]

At length she[127] adjusted her hat by the reflection in the little nickelled clock that stood on her desk, and, leaving the school, turned along the road that led westward—the road along which Donald had driven the cows those summer mornings when he shared the days on the range[128] with Hester and Billie Harp. She walked slowly, often turning aside to pick flowers or to toy with the grass, for she knew she might be seen from Katie's window, and she meant to give her strawberry fiction some semblance of probability.[129] After half a mile the road ascended a slight hill and dipped over it on the farther side; here she was secure from observation from the Strand homestead,[130] and she quickened her step. Donald's house—the old Farquhar house—lay only another half mile[131] ahead, and her heart speeded up[132] with her step as she saw Donald himself plowing at the far end of the railway half section which lay between. If she timed her progress rightly they should reach the end of the furrow together.

She was first to reach it. The furrow ended at the road and she stopped to look down its long, glistening surface to the point where Donald's six-horse team broke the line of vision. She was fascinated by the magnificence of their approach; there seemed something inevitable about it like the turning of the world on its axis or the succession of the seasons. It was virgin land he was plowing; land which never before, in all the ages since the world began, had felt the thrust of the shares of the cool embrace of the mouldboards as they turned it to the sun, there to enter into a disintegration which would be the beginning of new life. As the horses approached she could catch from time to time a glimpse of the driver behind, seated on his two-furrow plow, busy with his levers and the direction of his team.[133]

Donald brought his plow to a stop beside her. Surprise at her presence[134] was ricochetting back and forth in his brain, but his voice was steady: "I hope I didn't frighten you. I didn't see you for the horses."

She was silent for a moment, wondering what to say. "I suppose I was very stupid," she ventured. "Would they have run over me?"

"Perhaps. They're not cruel, but they expect people to get out of the way."

She thought they were not unlike their master, but she did not offer that comment. "I am looking for wild strawberries," she said.

"Oh." He seemed glad that she had put up a peg for conversation. "Had any luck?"

"Not yet."

"I think I saw some down the field. There is a low spot there; moist; plenty of blossoms. If you come I will show you."

With the dexterity of one bred to it he swung his team around at the end of the field, straightened up for the return furrow, dropped his plowpoints into the sod at just the right spot. She noted his movements, the ease and confidence of his control.[135] There was admiration in her voice when she said. "You are very clever, Donald."

He laughed her compliment off, but it did not displease him. "Sorry I can't offer you a ride," he said. "This bicycle isn't built for two." In a moment he felt how inane his remark had been. It called up a popular love song of the times, the theme of which was as well known to Clara as to himself. And love songs were not in his mind at the moment. What does she want? Why does she come here? he was wondering.[136]

She pretended not to have followed his thought. "Oh, I should be afraid to ride on that machine—even if I could," she said. "Will it bother[137] if I walk alongside?"

He smiled assurance in answer to her question,[138] and spoke to his horses; the traces tightened; the crackle of roots came up from the shares; two long, smooth, earthen streams began to flow back over the mouldboards. Walking in the grass beside the blackened earth[139] she suited her pace to the plow, watching the colters as they ruthlessly cut through the sod, regardless of the prairie flowers that blossomed on its breast.[140] Glancing backward she saw the moist, glazed, straight line of the furrow stretching behind, now peopled with a company of blackbirds, Indian file, hopping along in quest of worms. Then, raising her eyes a little, she looked at Donald. She had dropped a little behind and she could study him in safety; his attention was occupied by his plow and his horses. His blue overalls and shirt hung loosely about him, coated with dust, but they did not hide the lithe strength of his body or the easy movement of arm of leg as it worked the controls of his machine. When he spoke to his horses his voice was not high-pitched, but it seemed to fill all the surrounding space; it was the voice of one to be obeyed.

Presently he stopped. They had reached a little depression in the prairie where the grass was greener and more lush, and through it peered the modest[141] faces of innumerable strawberry blossoms. "You may find some here, if it's not too early," he said. She stooped low, running her fingers through the grass. "Oh, yes, there are some. Thanks, awfully. You don't mind my picking a few on your estate, Mr. Big Farmerman?"

"Of course not. But why do you call me that?"

"Because it is what you are, and, even more, what you will be." Her tongue seemed to loosen at last; something which had separated them had broken down. "As I watched you driving those great horses—your ease, your strength, your skill—suddenly I seemed to see something about farming which I never had see before. I don't know—I seemed to be seeing it from the opposite side, if you know what I mean. Always it had seemed to me that the farm drove the farmer, but here it seemed was a farmer driving the farm. Does that sound awfully stupid?"

His reserve was thawing out. "Not stupid at all, I guess. I think I know what you mean. I intend to make my farm serve me, if I can.[142] You have nothing to pick in?"

"I'll use my hat."

"Take mine." He pulled a limp felt hat from his head, releasing dark brown hair, slightly curled with perspiration, to fall about his temples. "I won't hurt it if you squash a few. I'll get it when I come back."

She found a few berries, but most of her attention was upon him as he pursued his mile-long furrow to its southern end, turned his team and started again[143] toward her. Her heart quickened its beat at his approach. What do you next? She had no course mapped out. Her one immediate purpose had been to see him; if possible, to talk with him. So far all had gone well. He had been reserved, but not cold; it was as much as she could have hoped. She must trust to her intuition guided by any mood he might disclose.

He stopped again as he came alongside,[144] and this time he got off his plow and came toward her. "Not very many," she said, holding his hat so he might see. She had put some leaves in it first and the few handfuls of berries were almost lost among them. He bent over the open hat. "It takes a great many of them to make a pound," he commented, "but they have a wonderful flavor. It's a strange thing about strawberries; most fruits are improved by cultivation, but nothing equals the wild strawberry for flavor."

"Perhaps some things can be too tame," she suggested.

He glanced at her quizzically, now frankly interested and amused.

"And people?" he led her on.

She placed a red berry between her lips and turned her face tauntingly to his. "Perhaps."

He veered away. "How can you carry[145] them home?" he asked. Then, answering his own question: "Take my hat. I won't need it."

"And leave you to catch your death of cold—if it rains? Oh dear no. I will donate them to my Big Farmer friend. You see, they are his, really. And I am holding up the work on his estate. Let me walk with you to the end of the field, and then I will run away home."

The horses tightened their traces again; the rasp came up from the shares. This time she placed her hand on an unused lever; it steadied her and aided her as she walked. Presently he said: "This will be my last round to-night. Unhitch at the end of the field."

She glanced at the sun, white as a silver dollar in the honey-colored west. "And you have still your own supper to make," she said with a little strange note of compassion in her voice.

"Oh, I don't mind. Get used to it. I say, I've some cream[146] How would you like—that is—would you care—" He stopped, colored a little, as though he had gone further than he intended.

"I'd love to. I can get supper while you are putting your horses away. It will be fun."

"You'll find things in the house pretty wild," he cautioned her. "But then, you like them that way."

For answer she leaned toward him and placed a ripe berry between his lips.

11

As Donald had predicted, Clara found the house somewhat wild. Unwashed breakfast and dinner dishes had been shoved to one end of the table, and, as doors and windows were unscreened, flies buzzed in profusion. The rusty stove bore up doubtfully under a load of kitchen utensils. The blankets on Donald's couch in a corner of the room were thrown back just as he had left them in the morning; a soiled pillow was lying on the floor. She shuddered a little at the disorder of the place, and wondered that Donald could prefer this to boarding at Tom's, which was not unduly far from his work and where he could be free of all household duties. The thought that he preffered these conditions to enforced association with Miss Clara Wilson was not flattering. But he had been courteous enough to his visitor, and she had become sure, during that last walk with her hand on his plow, that he bore her no unalterable resentment. Perhaps their little difficulty might even work out to her advantage; on the back-swing toward goodwill he might go further than he intended. . . .

For a moment she stood irresolute, wondering where to begin. But there was no time to be lost; he would be in presently, and she must make her mark on the place before he came. It was a chance to demonstrate the power of the feminine touch. So she started a fire in the stove, and then, with a little tremor of indelicacy, stripped the blankets from his bed. Deftly she replaced and smoothed them; shook the pillow out its lumpy irregularities; turned back the top of the blankets in an inviting triangle.

"When Donald came in he found her washing his accumulation of soiled dishes. "Oh, that's not in the bargain," he remonstrated. "I always leave them until after dark. Can't do anything else then, and it helps to fill in the time."

"Find something and wipe them for me," she told him, without looking up from her work. "You know, Don, you need someone to look after you, and to leave your time free for bigger things. There must be much to study about farming. Batching is all very well for those who can't do better, and you are very wise to think of getting married.

He took a wet plate from her hand. "If that's a shot in the dark," he said, "you are not a very good marksman."

"It's not a shot in the dark at all. It's common talk all around Sundown that you and Hester are to be married in the fall. I think you are very wise."

He did not answer, and she wondered if she had been driving too hard. They finished the dishes without much further conversation, and she prepared the meal, exchanging words only when it was necessary for directions. Donald watched her deft, neat hands as they set the things in place, and something of the old surge he had occasionally felt for her began beating within him again. Inevitably he compared her grace and skill with Hester's competent mobility. Something of Ellen's warning that he should choose a wife for health and good humor came back to him at that moment. Hester complied with those requirements; but here, he saw, was something more; something which he could not define, and, equally, could not escape. He supposed it might be spirit; Hester was a faithful plowhorse, but Clara had in her a dash of[147] the thoroughbred. Nevertheless, or because of that,[148] Clara had treated him shabbily, and while he would not return meanness for it, she should learn that, be it plowhorse or thoroughbred, each[149] must obey the rein of the driver.

"There, Mr. Man!" she welcomed him at last. She had chosen the best dishes, and, while there was no tablecloth to give them background, she had arranged them neatly, and had set the lamp where its light fell to advantage on their shining surfaces.[150]

Donald lauched into his meal. "It certainly is a bit of all right, Clara," he said, as she watched with satisfaction the effect of her entertainment. "I begin to think that you are going to make this place seem pretty empty after —without—that is, to-morrow."

92

She came to his side to pour his tea, and her arm, light as a feather, touched his ear as she poured. "Never mind to-morrow," she said. "Just let's be happy to-night." When she had returned to her chair at the opposite side of the table he raised his eyes to hers and was caught by the depth and glamour of them. "You are very beautiful, Clara," he said, offering her simply one of his few compliments.

The glamour of her eyes deepened, and a little wave of color flowed up from the close neck of her dress about her cheeks, smothering her freckles[151] and tingling into the hair caught backward high above her brow.[152]

"I will see you home," he said abruptly, when the meal and[153] their work was finished.

"Oh, don't bother. Get your sleep, you rise so early." But she knew she had won the round. She went first to the door, waiting for him there against the deep twilight of the summer night. He blew out the light and followed her. She had not moved. Where she stood against the door his form touched hers, and sudden fire leapt in his veins; his cheek rested against hers; their lips met. He drew her to him and for a moment they swung in ecstasy. Then he released her gently, placed her arm in his and without a word they started down the trail to Tom's. She held him tightly with the muscle of her arm, but he had no words.[154] His world had reversed itself, turned around; east was west, north was south. He was happy in the discovery, yet fearful of it, the underlying caution of his nature warning him against the illusion of the senses. If he seized this moment it meant a re-charting of his whole life. And further back than caution lay the inhibitions of his training, the glimmer of the literal[155] Hell he no longer believed in but which still hung about him like smoke from an extinguished fire; a sharp distinction between right and wrong which brooked no compromise and resisted every sophistry. But for all his caution and inhibitions, or because of them, he was supremely happy. Something new had come into his life, stirring a deep nature deeper than ever before it had been stirred, and from its depths sending up a joy higher than ever before it had attained.

At the top of the little raise in the prairie which marked the half-way point between the two farms Clara paused, as though the pace had been too fast for her, and he became aware that he had been swinging her along at a tremendous speed. "Hope I haven't been walking you too fast?" he said.

She cut right through his casual courtesy. "Angry?" she asked.

"No."

"Sorry?"

"No."

Her hands stole up his arms, her voice became a whisper. "Then kiss me again," she invited. As his arms folded about her she confessed her love, and he was aware of her confession, but his own he put not into speech. He must have time to think, to decide, to clear this sudden glorious confusion from his mind, to calm these flying pulses which made sober thought impossible.

12

On his walk back alone Donald tried to re-arrange his mind for consecutive thinking, but it was like raising some fragile structure against the pressure of the sea, which almost every moment over-whelmed it, flooding into unknown corners and lapping into caves of his being where thought thinned out and gave way to something deeper than reason. The Big Dipper glowed down through immeasurable spans arched with night;[156] the North Star, high and lonely, held its cold vigil undisturbed by the turmoil in his brain. As a child he had learned to locate the North Star as the one dependable guide to the prairie traveller in the darkness, and although he knew the trail to his house like his own palm, his eyes would turn to it as one who wishes to be convinced of that which he already knows is[157] true. At the spot on the road[158] where he and Clara had paused he paused again, but this time to look at the star, and to wonder. At a time when everything was spinning it steadied him to see its cold light pointing at him like a silver needle from infinite space. He remembered that as a boy he had marvelled how strange it was that,[159] wherever he went, the star pointed its needle straight at him. Then it had been one of God's eyes, perhaps, and not so far beyond reach; now he knew it lay across[160] im-measurable voids of space. So much had slipped away in those eight or ten years; God Himself, it seemed, had receded with the stars. With something of a pang he recalled the confident faith of his childhood and realized that if the growing doubt of later years had dulled the fear of eternal torment if had also blurred the assurance of eternal reward. Was the moral law he had learned in his Ten Commandments really the direct revelation of God, or only a code of ethics which shrewd old politicians had reinforced with superstition as a means of controlling the masses for their own good? To get down to cases, when at this very spot and hour ago for the first time in his life he had known the sweetness of proferred surrender, had he, by rejecting it, shown himself a man of strength or a frightened weakling?

He turned his eyes from the stars to the grey outline of the road and walked on toward his home, unanswered questions buzzing in his brain. As he walked and the circulation quickened in his healthy limbs confidence returned. While he weighed again the possibilities and dangers of that night Caution threw her weight on the side of Morality, and he knew that he had been strong and wise. He suddenly found himself supremely happy; it seemed as though he were moving through floods of well-being. A new fire had been fanned to life within him which warmed him pleasantly and without pain. Kisses? He smiled to himself even as he tried and failed to understand. He had known Hester's and found them placid and unresisting; but at the touch of Clara's lips a flash of sheet-lightning had enveloped his body, tingling from his toes to the roots of his hair. Its suffused warmth still hung about him.

The old Farquhar buildings loomed up through the star-shot darkness. A horse whinnied in recognition of his footstep. "I must get a dog," thought Donald; "a dog would come out barking and plunging." The house, which never had been quite friendly to him, shrank back into its own shadow as though it rather deaded this masterly man who has succeeded the weakling, its first owner; but when his hand was on the door it yielded itself and received him, reluctantly. He lit the lamp and as the glow of its rising flames gradually penetrated the gloom the light fell back from four bare and empty walls. Not knowing why,[161] he went to his cupboard and opened its doors; there, neatly piled, were the plates and cups and saucers her hands had washed—for him. He touched them with his fingers. Something of her presence still lingered about them; he was now conscious of it through all the room. He moved about in it, too irresolute to go to be, although it was long past his usual hour. He wondered if she had retired. He could picture her in that northeast room, so well known to him, perhaps standing by the window in her nightdress, looking out at the stars; perhaps kneeling to say her prayers; perhaps already between the sheets, staring into darkness, her upturned fingers about her face, thinking of him.

With something of a blow it struck him that her thoughts might be following him even as his were following her. He loosened the laces of his boots and kicked them off, revelling for a moment in the release of his tired feet; then, through the few swift motions of his undressing he was ready for bed. His couch stood in a corner of the room where the stairs led to the upper floor, a storey entirely deserted and unused, and as he approached it he saw for the first time that it had been placed in order by fingers more deft and careful than his own.[162]

The morning brought clearness of purpose. He would marry Clara. Fortunately he had made no commitment with Hester; fortunately, too, he had not pressed for privileges she might have been pliable enough to yield.[163]

But as he rode his slow course up and down the prairie field all that day the thread of his purpose again became entangled. The witchery which Clara had woven about him dissolved under sunlight, and cold Reason began again to shape his course. Reason told him he was making a mistake. Reason told him Hester would do his bidding; she was strong and healthy and used to the hard work of the farm, to early rising and scratching and digging and milking and mending; she would help him to make money and she would not be too insistent about spending it. On all these points Clara was a less certain quantity. He never had[164] know her to rise at five in the morning, he hardly could picture her milking cows and feeding pigs. Ellen's advice on the choice of a farmer's wife rang true in his ears. But Hester's kisses had stirred him mildly, while Clara's had set him on fire.[165]

As labor and the routine of the day sobered his mood he began to ask himself, Why marry at all? Ever since that fateful day when his uncle had informed him of his patrimony a vision had been taking shape in his imagination. It was a vision of property; of a farm well-tilled and fruitful, of cattle and horses and up-to-date machinery, of a large red-painted barn, and even, parhaps, his own elevator where he would store his wheat until the market would be favorable for selling. No combination of market manipulators would get him in its grip, depressing prices in the fall and expanding them the following summer after the wheat was out of the farmers' hands. He would play them at their own game, holding his wheat and selling at his convenience. And just as the buyer of wheat imposed prices and terms upon the seller, so he, as a buyer, would impose his prices and terms upon whomever would sell to him. He had done so in the case of the Farquhar farm; he had done so in the purchase of his equipment; every dealer in the country fawned upon him, knowing that he could pay cash and dictate terms. With these advantages and his skill and strength and industry there was no reason why he should not become a very rich man; not merely worth ten of fifteen thousand dollars, but twenty-five thousand dollars, perhaps even fifty thousand dollars! It was a fabulous ambition. He entrusted it to no one, not even to Ellen, but in his heart he was convinced that it lay within his possibilities.

And what had marriage to do with all this? A wife and family, of course, would be needed to round out his success, but for the present his hands were full, and family cares would be more likely to prove a hindrance than a help. At this point in his reasoning a picture of Clara washing dishes and smoothing the blankets of his bed came alluringly upon him, but he realized that this was weakness, and he was now strong and sane. Women always gained more than men by marriage; wasn't it common talk, even among the women themselves, that a boy was "caught", and that the girl "landed him"? And didn't they trust to a man's physical longings to make a fool of him, leading him into a situation from which he could not extricate himself? He supposed that he was as human as any of them but he meant that his head should rule his heart. His head told him that marriage at present was not essential, or even desirable, but if he married at all a girl like Hester would meet his requirements better than Clara.[166]

13[167]

When Donald had parted with her after her visit to the Farquhar farm Clara sat a long while in her room wrapped in a mixture of emotions which she found it hard to analyse or define. She supposed if anyone could guess that she had set out deliberately to capture Donald Strand by a little display of femininity in his own house, and most of all by standing in his way at the door so that their forms touched and fired the spark of his passion, she would be set down as a brazen hussy by the strait-laced Sundown community. But for two reasons the thought gave her no distress: In the first place, no one ever would know; and in the second, it wasn't true. There might have been truth in it then, but there wasn't now. Since Donald's lips had touched hers the whole world had swung around. Now she knew that she wanted him, more tremendously than ever she had wanted anything, not for his money, but for himself.[168] If she had walked that road westward a scheming hussy she had come back a lady in love on the arm of her knight. And when she had paused in her stride and he had turned and at her invitation had taken her in his arms there was nothing of which she was ashamed. It had been the ecstatic moment of her life. She had known it again when they parted at the gate, Donald electing not to come into the house, and tremors of it were still running through her being as she slowly undressed and prepared for bed. At last this was love. She had not known it with Harvey Graves, who had faded into a faint impersonal impression somewhere on the outer orbit of her experience. This justified everything; made everything necessary, wise, sacred, adorable. In her dresser mirror she caught the reflection of her white body as it was partly disclosed by her unrobing, and it held her with a new fascination. She held out her arms to her image and, as she closed her eyes, felt the fire of his lips again on hers and the hot, sweet terror of his passion.

As she lay in bed she reviewed again the events of the evening, and one disturbing note began to clamor louder and louder in her brain. Donald had said nothing of marriage; indeed, nothing which could be interpreted as a word of love. Could it be that he was committed to Hester; that, indeed, there might be something irrevocable between them? Fear gripped her at the implications of that thought, and of the fear was born a terrific surge of longing and jealously. "She shall not have him," she told herself. "She must not have him. No matter what—I thought I was planning my life, but this is here." She tightened her hands above her heart; pressed it until they hurt. "My Don," she whispered. "My boy, my lover, my man!"

She awoke to find that a strange peace had succeeded the clamor of the night before.[169] Under the sunlight Hester faded just as Harvey Graves had faded in the darkness, and a radiance of delight hung about her mental picture of Donald. The fears of the night were dissipated and joy welled in her soul, and she sang as she dressed for her duties.[170]

As the efficient Katie placed breakfast before her with just the suggestion of a questioning glance Clara slipped her hands about the other's face and pressed her cheek to hers. "I hope I didn't worry you last night dear," she whispered. "I'm getting to be an awful owl."

"You're of age," the matter-of-fact Katie replied. "And there are no dangers in these parts excepts those one walks into."

"I was not in danger. I had the best of protection. I will tell you as soon as I can."

The birds were singing as she took the path down to the creek and the schoolhouse. She did not go by the bridge,[171] but crossed the deflated stream, picking her steps carefully on the stones, and the earliest children greeted her on the further bank. She drew them about her and entered the schoolhouse like a faithful hen mothering her brood. But before the opening hour she found occasion to slip out alone and look to the westward. Yes, sure enough; there was Donald's team against the black blackbground of his widening field. She could plainly see Donald's figure on the plow seat behind, and her bosom rose with unsimulated emotion as her eyes bridged the gap between them. She wondered whether he was looking at the schoolhouse and thinking of her, and whether he, too, had been thinking deep last night on the blankets her hands had smoothed for his body.

The long day and the longer evening wore by, and [172] just as she was giving up hope for the night, he came. Katie was ironing and Tom was reading in the kitchen when Clara, from her room above, heard the gate swing on its hinges. For an instant the blood receded from her head; then it returned with a rush, and she felt her heart beating as though it might be heard downstairs. But she went down casually, opened the door, and went out.

"Clara!"

"Don!"

For a long moment they hung upon each other. "Darling, I was waiting," she whispered. "I was sure you would come."

"Well, I'm here," he answered, trying to laugh, but the sound would not come lightly. "And you thought I would come?"

"I was sure you would come. Over and over I said to myself, 'He will come, he will come,' and I was right. Donald, I want you to come in to-night."

"Yes, I guess I had better come in."

"And"—her arms stole about him again and her lips were close to his ear—"I would like to be able to say, 'Katie, Tom—here is Donald. He and I are going to be married.' Oh, Donald, am I a dreadful woman that I should want to say that?"

For a moment caution pounded in his ear. Here was a parting of the ways; his foot was raised for an irrevocable step. All his destiny would be shaped by the decision of that moment. But her lips were against his ear, his cheek, his mouth.

"Sweet," he said, "I have never known, it doesn't seem possible—how much I love you."

101

Part Three

1

Mr. Donald Strand sat in the little room he called his office, making figures with a pencil on a sheet of paper. His[1] room opened off the front vestibule, affording a place where he could meet those visitors who came on business, or through curiosity, or on presumption of slight acquaintance, without disturbing his household. It sat as a sort of guardian at the gate of his family life, a filter to arrest those bodies on the current of his affairs which had no admitted claim to the privileges of the inner circle[2]. It was a sturdy[3], rectangular room with one window facing the east, with plastered walls adorned with calendars and red and blue ribbons captured at the Alder Creek and Brandon exhibitions, and a framed, enlarged photograph of a placid-looking bull bearing the inscription "Sundown Chieftain II". Above the roll-top desk sat the silver cup awarded Mr. Donald Strand[4] in the Better Farming Competition. Donald was fond of this room; it invested him with the dignity of business; it kept his triumphs continually before him; it was an intimation to all comers that he was a man of affairs.

Through the open window came the smell of ripening wheat borne on the warm air of a summer's night, and from time to time the stillness was interrupted by an automobile on the highroad a hundred yards away. Sometimes Donald would raise his eyes as a pair of headlights flung their long feather of brilliance[5] to north or south, and he would follow the darkness behind them until the red rear signal glimmered into the distance. Then he would return to his figuring. Many a time the result of this effort had given him pleasure, and he had folded his paper and put it away in one of the pigeonholes of his desk with a comfortable sense of well-being and success. But to-night there was a slight frown on his face; when he turned so that the electric light shadowed his features there was a sag to his cheeks[6] and the deepening lines held an unmistakable hint of advancing years.

The sum of his reckoning was as substantial as ever; indeed, more so[7], and he had been conservative in all his estimates. He had put in the land at thirty dollars an acre, when everyone agreed it was worth fifty; thirty times twelve hundred and eighty was thirty-eight thousand four hundred dollars. He had under-estimated his automobile, his farm machinery, his horses, his herd of pure-bred cattle headed by Sundown Chieftain II[8]. His bank account —$2,438.40—admitted no flexibility, and his farm mortgages were reckoned[9] at their face value, but he had included his few stock market investments at cost rather than at their present much-enhanced prices[10], and little items like his loans to Old Man Farquhar[11] and Walter Spence he had disregarded altogether. Still the total was[12] the substantial sum of $75,838.40, and he had allowed[13] nothing for his growing crop. He took off his glasses, wiped them, and re-examined his reckoning. Yes, there could be no mistake. He had passed the seventy-five-thousand-dollar mark. He smiled a little as he reflected how he once had thought of fifteen or twenty thousand dollars as wealth, and fifty thousand as an extreme flight of ambition. Now he was within measuring distance of double that sum, and he counted himself still a young man—only forty-nine in August, sound in wind and limb, never been sick a day, and still a long piece to go. It was a very creditable[14] accomplishment, and yet the contemplation of it failed to bring to him the satisfaction it seemed to warrant[15].

The germ of his unhappiness[16] lay in a letter on his desk, delivered that day in the mail box at his gate. He took it again from its envelope, scanned the first couple of pages at a glace, but read slowly as he came to the disturbing paragraph:

> Jim is doing wonderfully well. Of course he has a fine practice, but that is now only a minor part of his income. His professional work brings him into contact with many opportunities to turn an honest dollar. Only last week one transaction netted him over ten thousand, and of course he is making a

lot of money on the stock market. I know you have done well, too, Donald; you have done wonderfully, for a farmer, but I often think how big a success you would have been if you had gone into business. Men without half your ability are millionaires in the city. Why don't you come in and have a talk with Jim? He can put you in touch with anything that is going on, and I am sure nothing would please him more. Can't you spare a few days before harvest? Bring Clara, and Clarissa, too; I suppose she has holidays, if she has not already taken them[17]. The boys are welcome, of course[18], if they can come. We have a large house; room for everybody, and no inconvenience to me, as I keep plenty of help. Jim and I have made reservations for the Mediterranean cruise this winter, so you must come before harvest[19].

Do say we may expect you shortly. I know Jim would O.K. this invitation if he were not so busy with all his interests that I hardly get a word with him. But my time is my own and I am hungry[20] for a talk with you over all the things that might have been—and some of those that are. Ever affectionately, your cousin, Ellen.

He laid the letter down and sat back in thought. He could not believe that Ellen had meant to hurt him, she was merely enthusiastic over their own success and eager that he should share in it[21]. He had done wonderfully—"for a farmer". She could not know how that turned the steel in his ribs. For twenty years he had been demonstrating that a farmer is the equal of any man that walks — demonstrating it with the success that had gathered about him his two sections of land, that had built the finest house in Sundown district, had won the Better Farming Cup, had bred Sundown Chieftain II; that had enabled him to live at his own pace, taking orders from none, answering to none. And Ellen said he had done well "for a farmer". Well—seventy-five thousand wasn't so bad. She hadn't mentioned any sum that Jim was worth, but it was clear enough that anything Donald could be supposed to have made must be small by comparison. And just when he was congratulating himself upon turning the third quarter in his first hundred thousand she must come along and set up new standards of success which made his achievement seem trivial. Oh, well. Seventy-five thousand wasn't so bad, and everything clear. Perhaps Jim wasn't worth so much as he let her think. These city folk had a way of putting on a big front even if there wasn't much behind.

He folded up the paper with his reckonings and put it away in a pigeonhole with Ellen's letter beside it. Then, shoving his chair back a little, he opened a drawer and took out a box of cigars. Having selected one he held it to his nose, luxuriating a moment in its aroma;

then bit off the end and lighted it. "I guess a farmer can smoke a good cigar as well as a city man," he commented to himself. "I guess the city men wouldn't smoke many cigars of any kind if it were not for the farmers. I guess they wouldn't be making many reservations for the Mediterranean trip if some one didn't plow the land and grow the wheat." He was aware that bitterness was finding vent in his words, and bitterness is seldom fair. He always tried to be fair. As the smoke curled up, veiling the sturdy figure of Sundown Chieftain II in blue mist, the edge of his irritation was dulled and a measure of complacency was restored. After all, he was very comfortable. He had his farm—two full sections; there was Sundown Chieftain II; there was the cup awarded him in the Better Farming Competition; no one could gainsay that. He had Tom and Clarissa and Walter and, of course, Clara.

The thought of his family stirred a vague emptiness within him. No matter how well one did by his family he hardly could expect to score on every point. He admitted that his score, through no fault of his, had fallen short of perfect. The breach between himself and Clara had been widening year by year and continued to widen in spite of everything he could do. She had drawn Tom with her and they were like planets which had broken away from the central orb, circulating still about the parent body, but inevitably detached. He laid it all to his wife's unwillingness to rejoice in the life of the farm. The inferiority complex of the farmer, which he had seen manifested so often by parents who tried to educate their boys and girls for some more "respectable" calling, and whose sneers could not conceal their envy of the fortunate town-dwellers who were supposed to be parasites on the farmer's back, had, by some twist in his mental make-up, affected him in the very opposite way. He had gradually found his ambition taking the form of showing the townspeople that he could be as prosperous as they, that he could live in as good a house and drive as fine a car as the best of them, that he could give his family every luxury the lawyer or the banker or the doctor could command. He had proved his point—but he had not won Clara to it. Gradually, by a hundred evidences pieced together, he had come to realize that she had "caught" him, hooked him like a fish, playing a bait that no man could resist.

Then she tried to master him, to swing him away from the farm, from the milking and feeding and rough work which she detested, and when she found his will stronger than hers she had withdrawn into a hurt seclusion, walling him out of her life. Worse, she had taken Tom from him[22]. She had implanted in the boy her own repugnance to farm life, and Tom had broken away, preferring a white-collar job in the bank at Alder Creek.

Donald recalled the day of Tom's decision[23] as the deepest scar in his generally placid experience. Even now a dull pain hung[24] about his heart and his jaws slackened with the recollection. Tom had stated his case with enthusiasm but Donald had held him a moment without answer. Then: "So you want to leave the farm?" he said, and there was a tremble in his voice which the boy did not understand.

"Yes, Dad. It's a great chance. Not every boy can get into a bank, you know."

"I suppose not. And not every boy can succeed to a farm like this, Tom."[25]

The father looked at the son and the son returned his gaze. In that unspoken exchange Donald reached his decision. He could yield a point to gain a greater one, and his pride would not permit that it should be said there had been trouble in the Strand household. "What does your mother think of it?" he asked.

"She's all for it."

Donald had suspected that much. Tom had gone to his mother first, if indeed Clara did not initiate the whole plan. She had won this round, but Donald was too clever to let her know her victory. A slow smile softened his rugged features.

"Well, that's all right, Tom," he said. "I just wanted to be sure you knew your own mind. If it pleases you and your mother it is all right with me, but remember, I expect you to make good."[26]

Later Donald heard Tom talking with Clara and he guessed the gist of their conversation. He smiled grimly to himself. "She beat me," he said, "but she doesn't know it. And never will know it. That will leave it flavorless in her mouth."[27]

Of course, Ellen knew nothing of all this. When she had heard of Tom's position in the bank she had written him a note of congratulation and encouragement. Ellen had no children of her own; perhaps that was why she seemed to take a special interest in Donald's. Sometimes Donald was sorry for her on that account; sometimes he was not so sure. He began to suspect that Nature was a diabolical humorist, enticing men into marriage and parenthood and rewarding them with difficult women and rebellious children. Would Clarissa and Walter break away, too? Clarissa was a stenographer in Lawyer Smate's office in Alder Creek. Donald had not objected to that; it would do the girl good to have some business experience, and improve her chances of favorable marriage. Walter, his youngest, was still with him, and more and more his life circled around Walter. If only he could hold Walter! It seemed possible. The boy treated his mother with respect but his father with a certain healthy above-board masculine affection. To-night he had gone to Alder Creek to bring Clarissa home after her week's work, and Donald was waiting up for their return.

The mantel clock in the living-room chimed the quarter to twelve. The clock was a present from Ellen; it brought her back to his memory. Childless people were likely to set an undue value upon material success. Well, seventy-five thousand . . . and he had his home. Not a finer in the municipality. Right on the site of the old Strand farmhouse it stood, its many windows shouting success on the very spot where Uncle Jim had built his first log cabin. When Katie had died in childbirth Donald had taken over Tom's lease, for Tom had become restless and wanted to go further west; and when Uncle Jim had died, leaving the farm to Aunt Annie, he had persuaded her to deed it to him in return for a bond in which he bound himself to furnish her with room and board and a fixed allowance for the full period of her natural life. The terms of that bond he had observed scrupulously[28], even although Aunt Annie had developed a longevity greater than might have been expected. He had considered her convenience in the planning of his house; a room on the ground floor, immediately behind the office, with windows opening to the south and west, had been provided especially for her, and he saw that she lacked nothing. He had made her as happy as, he supposed, any old, widowed woman could be; indeed, he sometimes marvelled at her simplicity and her happiness[29]. Even now he could faintly hear the thin pipe of her voice as she sat in her room singing the hymns which yearly became more dear to her. Clara didn't like it, but Clara was a different type, and he had made it as easy as possible for both by giving Clara a room in the extreme opposite part of the house—upstairs in the northeast corner, just where her old room used to be, looking across the creek to the site of the schoolhouse, only the schoolhouse no longer was there, the spread of knowledge and mechanized agriculture[30] having reduced the child population of Sundown District to the point where it was cheaper to send them by bus to Alder Creek than maintain a separate school for their convenience.

Aunt Annie's thin treble penetrated the plastered wall[31], and Donald, half unconsciously, cocked his ear to listen:

"Are you washed . . . in the blood . . .
In the soul-cleansing blood of the Lamb?" . . .

The smoke from his cigar died to a tiny curling wisp as he followed the well-known words, stirred by a confliction of emotions he could not fathom[32].

2

Donald was aroused from his meditations by a blaze of light across his window, and, looking out, saw the wide-set eyes of an automobile glaring up the drive which led in from the highroad. He sighed gently as he sat back into his chair. Although Walter was a good driver it always was a relief to see him safely home[33]. He listened as the car lurched into the garage; the tires shrieked on the concrete floor from the sudden application of brakes, and Donald's lips twitched with annoyance. His ever-present problem was to know just how much discipline he could apply with safety to Walter and Clarissa[34]. He trembled to think how thin was the tie that bound them. A single unguarded word might break it.

The screen door slammed and Clarissa and Walter surged into the office. The girl, very fair, with hair of a deep russet red and lips colored to harmonize, allowed her cloak to drop from her shoulders and flung her bare arms about her father's neck. She smacked a kiss on his cheek.

"Now, now, no tell-tale stains," Donald pretended to remonstrate. "How are you and the law getting along?"

"It's a great graft, Dad. We've written four letters to Winnipeg about a mortgage on the Marble farm, and have had four letters back, and there's still something to argue about. Of course all these letters are charged to the party of the first part."

"Sounds interesting. How many letters do you suppose it would take to pay off the national debt?"

Clarissa shook her russet hair. "Search me," she said, "and what are you driving at?"

"Just this: that all wealth comes out of the earth, and all your letter writing doesn't add a nickel to it."

110

"Maybe not, but it shifts it into other pockets. Now Dad, I'm not going to argue with you. I may be a parasite—"

"She means she's a red-headed flea," said Walter. Then, sniffing the cigar: "Why the celebration?"

A glint of pride and banter flickered in Donald's half-closed eyes. "It might be over the return of the prodigal son—at five minutes to midnight," he suggested.

Walter was quite unabashed. "If I had been any later, I would have been early," he said. "But I have a good excuse. I was detained by the prodigal daughter."

"He was not. I was waiting hours—"

"Never mind." Donald signalled for peace with outstretched hands. But Walter was on the trail of a jest. "Do you know why there's no prodigal daughter mentioned in the Bible, Dad? Because the prodigal daughter didn't come back."

The boy waited for his father's laugh, usually so responsive to his humorous sallies. But Donald's face grew grave. "That's a cruel remark, Walter," he said. "I hope you may never know how cruel it is."

Walter was at once overwhelmed with contrition. "Gee, Dad, have I spilled something? I'm sorry."

"Well, let's eat," said Clarissa, breaking the tension. "I suppose Mother is in bed?"

"In her room, at any rate. Hours ago."

"Okay. I'll dig up something. I've got to put my old man in good humor." She was off to the kitchen, leaving Walter alone with his father.

"I see a touch on the horizon about the size of a ten-dollar bill—or maybe twenty," Walter prophesied. "Dad, as man to man, you let that girl wind you around her finger. She's earning good wages, and yet she's forever sticking you up for more. Not that I care, of course, but—"

"You shouldn't. When it comes to holding up the old man you're not exactly a novice yourself, Walter."

"But I work for it. I work on the farm. That's different."

"You are pleased to call it work. When I was your age —Yes, I know, as you so often remind me, times have changed, so I won't press the point. There's another matter on my mind at the moment. A mere trifle, of course; I believe I have brought it to your attention before. You went into that garage again to-night like Elisha went to Heaven—on high. Some day you'll go plumb through the end of it. And I suppose you broke another speed record coming from Alder Creek?"

Walter took out a cigarette and lit it before answering. "Eight minutes," he said. "Oh, yes, I know it used to take you sixty[35] with a team of wagon, but again I remind you that times have changed. Eight minutes figures out to an average speed of thirty miles an hour, which is just one degree removed from going backwards. Because it used to take you an hour you think we should still be living in the Stone Age."

"The tombstone age, you mean. They're putting up granite slabs every day to young fellows who thought their dads were too slow. But there is no use arguing with the uprising generation. Anything doing in Alder Creek?"

Walter gave him an unenthusiastic picture of their country town on a Saturday night. One broad street jammed with cars; sidewalks jammed with people who combined business with many social opportunities; zones of activity around the gasoline stations and garages.

"See Tom?"

"Sure. I understand the bank is still solvent."

"He didn't come home with you."

"No. I think he had to sit up with a girl. I'm glad I'm so heart-free, Dad."

"Stay that way if you can," his father advised him.

Their chat was cut short by Clarissa's clear shout from the kitchen. "Come on, folks; eats are ready." Donald swung to his feet and Walter slipped his arm around his father's waist, not so slender as it once had been but still strong and muscular. Together they strode across the living-room and into the kitchen.

Clarissa had raided the ice box and the booty was strewn in some disorder on the table. The girl seemed more domesticated here than in her father's office; she presented something of a picture with her short reddish hair brushed out over her ears and the nape of her neck, her sleeveless dress exposing her arms to the shoulder, its deep-cut V in front confessing a hint of the bosom it hardly concealed. As for a moment she stood holding a bottle in each hand she seemed to her father typical of that uprising generation to which he had referred.

"I didn't make tea, Dad," she apologized. "Can you slake your thirst with ginger ale? In this old-fashioned house there's nothing stronger."

"Suits me," said Donald, seating himself. He loved these domestic moments when his children took him into their circle.

"Believe me, Dad," Walter observed, as the girl filled her father's glass, "a lot of 'em ain't stopping at ginger ale. You should be very glad you have such old-fashioned children."

From a loaf of bread and a cold roast Mr. Strand constructed for himself a satisfying sandwich. "I *am* glad," he said, taking up the thought which Walter had dropped. "Not that you are old-fashioned, Heaven knows; a girl that dressed when I was a boy as Clare is dressing now would be considered—well, there would be only one conclusion. I don't hold with that at all, and I am glad you two are no more irresponsible than you are. Standards have changed. I remember at the dances if a girl showed her ankle we thought she was bold; now if she doesn,t show her knee you think she is deformed. Well, I'm not quarrelling with it. I suppose it's all in what you are accustomed to. But just as there were some who liked to show their ankles then, just to go a little further than where the line was drawn, so there are some now—"

"Easy, Dad," Walter interruped him. "As man to man, I think you are going to run into difficulties. What I gather is that you are too good a stockman to be indifferent to an attractive calf."

"And you don't really think me a wicked woman?" Clarissa slipped an arm[36] about his neck and deftly landed herself on his lap. "Even if I do expose a knee, or two—like that?" with an upward flip of her thin skirt. "Aren't they quite presentable? Did you even see better, in the course of your long and observant career?"[37]

Donald was conscious of just a suggestion of color crawling to his cheeks. He would have been ashamed for them to see it; he would have admitted that it confessed a mind baser than theirs. "You young folks beat me, altogether," he said. But he cupped his right hand about his daughter's knee, and his left arm drew her vibrant body close to this. With a love that was possessive as well as paternal he choked back an undefined jealousy that surged within him.

3

On his way to bed Donald turned off the downstairs lights[38], but he did not trouble to lock the front door, civilization in the Sundown district having not yet advanced to the stage which makes such precautions necessary. In the upper hall he met Clare in her pajamas *en route* from bath to bedroom.

"Good night, old bear," she addressed him. "For two pins I'd kiss you and throw in a hug."

"For two pins—go ahead," he challenged.

She flung her arms about his neck and pressed her lips to his cheek. And his arms wound about her and held her close.

"Not in love with anyone yet, Clare?"[39] he whispered.

"No one but you. Oh, I'm snooping around, but nothing definite. Tomorrow I'm going swimming after church."

"Swimming? On Sunday? After church?" Donald was like a man rocking on his heels. He never knew when he was going to be quite bowled over.

"Of course, you want your daughter to be athletic, don't you?"

"I want her to be wise," he said, gravely.

"Well, I'm wise."

"Clare, you're a young devil."

She answered him with a grimace. "I'm your child. Figure it out for yourself. And now that we understand each other, could you, out of your abundant wealth, spare your little girl say about twenty dollars?"

"Clare, what do you do with all your money—I mean, my money?"

"I do you justice, Dad. You are the wealthiest farmer in the district. Farming is a nobler pursuit than doctoring or lawing or selling,

115

consequently your daughter must be better dressed than the doctor's daughter, or the lawyer's daughter, or the merchant's daughter. And she is. I can turn more eyes on Main Street and hold them longer than the best of them. I make them envy you, Dad. Isn't it worth it?"

"Your argument is not on a very lofty plane, Clarissa. Besides, the doctor has no daughter."

"That is a mere technical objection. No doubt the doctor could have corrected it had he been so disposed. As for lofty planes—I simply cut out the bunk and get down to what we both mean. Do I get twenty?"

"Mention it to-morrow. Don't forget."

"I won't." She brought her eyes close to his and he felt the pull of their fascination. "You're a dear old devil," she said, half mocking. "I wish you and Mother could hit it better. Oh, don't kid yourself—I know. But I won't blab outside. Forgive me. I know it hurts." She shook her head as though to throw some unpleasant picture from her mind. "Now go to bed and dream about Sundown Chieftain the Second and don't call me early Father dear or to-morrow'll be the saddest day, etcetera." With a flourish she was off to her room.

4[40]

The upper storey of the Strand house accommodated five bedrooms. Clara had hers in the northeast corner. In the front centre was the spare room, kept always in order for the occasional guest, and in the southeast corner, over the office, was Donald's room. He had chosen it from no particular preference, but to let Clara have her old corner and any memories she could draw from it. Behind his room was Walter's—shared by him with Tom when both boys had been at home—and behind Clara's was Clarissa's. Aunt Annie, in deference to her old limbs, had her room downstairs, and Mrs. Fetch, the housekeeper, had for convenience a little place off the kitchen[41].

As Donald turned from his daughter's arms[42] his eyes swept a quick glance across the floor at Clara's door, but there was no gleam of light to indicate that she was still awake. He moved[43] a little wearily, not knowing whether or not he would have answered the gleam had it beckoned him. He acknowledged[44] Walter's cheery "Good night, Dad!" and went into his own room.

For a considerable while he lay awake, pondering, as he now often did, the whole mystery of life. The sense of failure which Ellen's letter had wrought in him, and which the buoyance of the children had lifted for an hour, settled again like a fog. He had been aware of other failures in his life, but the satisfaction of owning the best-kept farm in the municipality—he had the silver cup in his office—of winning the first prize with Sundown Chieftain II[45]; of having amassed a fortune of $75,838.40, not counting some small outstandings, was a sort of armor with which he had been able to surround himself whenever his sense of values was challenged. It was not that he envied Jimmie Wayne his success; it was that he measured his own success against Jimmie's, and by that measurement it began to look like failure. And

117

as the whole armor weakened certain spear thrusts of the past which he had hoped to forget or ignore shot their tremors of pain through his being with unsuspected force[46].

He had thought that Tom might come home for the week-end, but Tom was apparently more interested in some feminine acquaintance in Alder Creek[47]. His disappointment in Tom was the heavier because he had to bear it in secret, in secret even from Tom[48]. He had to dissemble toward Tom, to pretend an enthusiasm for his banking career which he did not feel. Behind this dissembling, and rendering it more tolerable, lay the hope that Tom, with a little broadening of experience, might tire of the profession he had chosen and turn again to the independent life of the farm. When Tom saw the manager of his bank opening letters from head office with a trembling hand in anticipation of the rebuke which they might contain, meanwhile affecting toward his customers an importance which he did not feel; or the merchants of Alder Creek smirking behind their counters afraid to give offence by an honest outspoken word lest they lose a dollar of trade, and accepting insults as though they were jokes, the product of a nimble and witty mind; or the lawyer caught between two fires when asked to press a suit against men who could swing business to him, or away; or old Doctor Harrison afraid to send a bill to the McDougalls lest they induce their young nephew, recently graduated in medicine, to begin his practice in Alder Creek—when Tom saw all these things clearly, surely the independence, honor, and authority of his father's calling would appeal to him with irresistible force. Donald must not admit he had lost his boy. The fight was still on; he would win him yet[49].

His mind turned to his wife in her room in the other corner of the house. They had been a disappointment to each other. He lived under a dull feeling of Clara's reproach, a feeling that was no longer acute, but which still disturbed him when he allowed his mind to run upon it. Clara had on various occasions set her will against his, and had found herself the weaker vessel. That was as it should be; there could be only one head to a household. On matters of policy his judgment must be supreme, but on many minor matters he would gladly have humored her if she had played up for humoring. She had known how to get him all right; there had been no coldness then, and how was he to foresee

118

that the arts by which she made herself attractive would in time become nauseous to her? The coinage of her desire had proven to be counterfeit; its brilliance had worn off leaving only dead lead beneath. He had given her a room to herself to escape the tantalization of her unresponsive presence, and she had accepted it, not as a reproof, but as an escape. The family pride which ran strong in both of them had concealed their virtual separation from their neighbors and had minimized it to[50] their children. When they went out together they were as respectable and courteous a couple as could be met in the whole Alder Creek District. But romance between them was dead. Probably Clara blamed him, laying it to his masterfulness and his masculinity, and was a million miles from guessing that he felt himself the aggrieved person, defrauded in the contract between them that was supposed to last for life. What did she think he was? A mummy, with blood dried to dust in his veins?

Perhaps it was a mistake that they had married at all, although he wondered if his experience was an uncommon one. Would it have turned out the same way with any one else? With Hester? Hester had married Jack Marble and they were doing well enough in their unimaginative, plodding way. Sometimes he met her at Alder Creek and they spoke casually, as though there was nothing to conceal. There had been an episode, but he preferred to forget about it if he could. It was dead. Hester was dead. Clara was dead. But Ellen remained alive. Ah, Ellen! Perhaps sometime he would tell Ellen. A man must have a woman to whom he can open his heart, and Ellen would understand, and forgive, and remain silent. If Clara knew, she would leave him, and all Alder Creek would say she did right. They did not know, and he never would tell, that Clara had left him years before. His checks on her had remained uncashed. There was no balance to his credit. Again he wondered if his lot was common or unusual. Perhaps men and women were made like that and it just could not be helped.

When he heard the clock downstairs strike two he got out of bed preparatory to making a new bid for sleep. Clarissa's door was open, and moonlight, now coming in from the west, fell across her sleeping form. For a minute he watched her, muffling his breath. Clarissa stirred within him something that was wholly different[51]. He wondered if she, too, would marry, and if some day the wedge of indifference or disagreement[52] would separate her from her mate. Perhaps. And then, perhaps not. This new generation, with its amazing frankness, its willingness to face facts, might perhaps escape the fog in which its more conventional elders were so hopelessly lost. He would almost dare, in spite of the shame which would envelope him, to throw about her feet the light of his own experience if only that would keep her on solid ground.

She stirred, and, not to wake her, she stole back to his room. He was happier from having looked on Clarissa; he had Clarissa and Walter. Must he, some day, lose them? God, no! God? What had He to do with it? Did He know? Did He care? Would He help? *Could* He help? Or was God merely the name given to the Primal Force which had set the world spinning under a code of laws inexorable in their operation? The orthodoxy of his childhood died hard, and at times he had glimpses of experience which revived his faith, but he wondered whether these were really experiences from an external source or just the running down or winding up of some unexplained mechanism in his own mind. He longed for some one with whom he could talk, and again his thought turned to Ellen. He would accept her invitation. The Alder Creek fair was over; Sundown Chieftain had won the first prize; harvest would not be pressing for another three weeks; there was no reason why he and Clara should not go to Winnipeg. When a man is worth $75,838.40 surely he may allow himself a holiday. Not bad, that—$75,838.40, in addition to some small accounts—no matter how much Jimmie Wayne had made. It would take a long while to count seventy-five thousand dollars, even in ten-dollar bills. He wondered how large a bundle it would make, how long it would take to count them, turning with his fingers, ten, ten, ten, ten—ten—

5

Donald was awake early. The habits of his farm life could not easily be broken even when the conditions which forged those habits had passed away. The sunlight was pouring over the fields open to view from his eastern window; it danced with the brilliance of diamond dust in a million reflections; it flooded with warmth his face and his hairy chest as he filled his lungs with the morning air. The smell of the ripening wheat smote him with a nostalgia for something never quite understood or quite attained, but at any rate it was good to be alive, to look over those long fields of ripening wheat, to see the glint of sunlight in the pools of Alder Creek and on the myriad dew-gems which hung on every leaf and blade. He drew on his underwear and pants, his socks and boots, postponing his shave and Sunday dressing to a later hour[53], and went out into the farmyard.

George and Ned, his two hired men, who slept in a bunk-house near the barn, were already about. George was bent over beside one of the cows, adjusting the milking attachment; his blue cotton shirt was drawn tight across the muscles of his back, and the sweat stains stood out upon it in tribute to his honest toil. As his employer's shadow fell across the door he turned and straightened himself, exposing a face fair and stubbly under its week's growth of whisker[54].

"Fine mornin', Mr. Strand," he observed. "It'll warm up as the day gets older, but that's the stuff to feed the crops. I was out around the fields last evenin', and the wheat is showin' some color. With good weather we'll be cuttin' in three weeks."

"I was thinking about that. Do you see it all coming in together, or is it going to give us time to handle it with the two binders?"

"Got a combine on your mind? They say they're doin' well in Saskatch'wan, but it don' seem to me quite human not to have no stookin' to do."

121

The machine was pulling at the udder of the cow; she stirred and Donald laid a soothing hand on her flank. "That don't seem quite human, either," he said, glancing at the milker, "but you two boys would hardly like to sit down to thirty cows before breakfast, eh? But I'm not saying I'm going to buy a combine—just yet. They'll be cheaper, and they'll be better. What I want is to be sure the two binders'll handle the crop. Better look 'em over, George; you've got a mechanical eye, and if there's any repairs needed get them done. I'm figuring on being away for a week or so,[55] and I want everything ready when I come back. Of course, Walter'll be in charge"—with a twinkle that was not lost on George—"but it is you I will hold responsible."

"Got you!" said the farm hand, returning the wink. "Goin' to give yourself a little holiday?"

Donald made his answer very casually. "Oh, just running down to Winnipeg, I think. Have some business. May look over a combine or two."

George nodded. "We'll run things all right, Ned an' me. And Walter," he added, as an after-thought.

"Sure you will. I'm not worrying." The talk ran on about farm matters[56].

It pleased Donald that his farm was the most highly mechanized of any in the district, that neighbors came to praise his equipment and seek his suggestions. He was proud of his barn, of his stock, of George and Ned, of the orderly methods by which they attacked the duties of the farm, of his own quiet but unquestioned authority. Banker, forsooth! The bank manager at Alder Creek worked for a fraction of his income and took orders, not always too courteously expressed, from a superior officer in a distant city, while one Donald Strand, who had elected to be a farmer, took orders from no one, not even the King himself!

He wandered down to the piggery and affectionately massaged the backs of his Tamworth hogs, as, with more enthusiasm than manners, they attacked their morning meal. He had a friendly regard for his pigs. They were born to be killed, of course, but they had a good life while it lasted, and were not too exacting in their demands. "Pigs pull a bigger load on the farm than all the tractors that were ever

122

built," he would say to his hired men[57], and leave them to ponder over his figure of speech. "The more squeal from the pig the less from the creditor," was another of his obscure remarks.

When he returned to the barnyard the work horses were being set loose for their day of rest and recreation. He shied a friendly hand at them and they responded with heavy capers which presently settled into a trot down the well-worn path to the pasture. Ned and George stopped beside him to share his admiration and the warm benediction of the morning sun. "I often think," he said to them[58], "that God must be fond of horses. That is why He made Sunday. Horses know how to use it—if you give them a chance. But humans! The up-rising genera-tion are tireder on Monday morning than they are on Saturday night."[59]

A turkey gobbler strutted by in prodigious pride, his huge tail feathers expanded, his wing tips touching the ground, his bulging neck as red as any woman's lips. At the apex of his pride he vomited a vol-ley of bulbous sound into the quiet morning air, provoking an immedi-ate discordant response from ganders and roosters who were of no mind to grant his turkeyship any position of superiority. The clatter, once started, grew in volume until even the mild-mannered ducks and drakes joined in the chorus. Donald whimsically observed the demon-stration. They were his, these creatures, so far removed from man in their appearance, so like him in their pride and self-assertiveness. He felt a possessive warmth[60] toward them. They were part of his life; they were like flowers in a garden, giving it variety and color.

"You'll be wantin' to see the Chieftain?" Ned suggested, knowing full well that the climax of the inspection was still to come. Mr. Strand feigned a moment's consideration, then agreed. "Yes, bring him out; let's see if his recent glory has gone to his head." When the ponderous Sundown Chieftain II was led forth[61] he viewed him as an artist might look upon his masterpiece. Ned led the bull by means of a fork handle snapped to the ring in his nose, and George walked along side, slap-ping his flanks and urging him to less leisurely movement. The Chief-tain's eyes were expressionless as the marbles the small boys play with in the spring; of what bovine intelligence, of what pride of place or malignance of nature lay behind they gave no glimpse. Donald ran his fingers over the well-kept sides and rested his hand on the pinnacle that capped the huge shoulders, swaying the Chieftain a little with the strength of his arm. This was achievement. He walked about the great creature, noting the points of his breeding, surfeiting himself with a happy lust of possession.

"All right, boys," he said at length, as one whose passion has spent itself. "Take him in."

6

Mrs. Fetch was busy in her kitchen when Donald entered. She was the wife of a neighboring settler whose interest in her had cooled and was suddenly supplanted by a flame from another source. The man had avoided mortgage proceedings and the wrath of the community by leaving his farm to his creditors and his wife to the sympathy of her neighbors. The indignant settlers would have tarred and feathered the wretch, but Donald paid only lip service to their indignation. So many wives, he reflected, will neither tend the fire nor let anyone else build it. So, while others voiced their outraged sense of morality in high words, Donald offered Mrs. Fetch a place in his household. It was an act that puzzled Clara, but it relieved her of much drudgery and moved her up a notch in the social scale. Not even Dr. Harrison's wife at Alder Creek, old and lame though she was (the latter affliction due, it was commonly said, to her husband's clumsiness in treating her broken ankle) had the luxury of a permanent housekeeper. And if she must have another woman in the house better the dead ashes of middle age than the combustible material of youth. That was what puzzled Clara about Donald.

Donald greeted Mrs. Fetch cheerily. "Morning, Sarah. Up and comin'?"

"Up, but not comin'," Mrs. Fetch returned from the sink where she was de-seeding grapefruit. "Goin'. Always goin', Mr. Strand."

Donald was accustomed to this retort. Mrs. Fetch enjoyed stressing the hardness of her lot.

"Oh, come," he said, "it's not as bad as that. Look at me. I was up hours before you, and hours last night after you went to bed. And I'm not complaining."

"An' neither would I, if I was the richest farmer in the county.

125

An' what were you doin'? Last night, smokin' your cigar; I could smell it all through the house th'smorning; like a doggery, your office was. An' th'smornin? Fondlin' that overgrown steer!" Mrs. Fetch, although quite unawed by her employer, felt a decent reluctance to describing the Chieftain by his proper classification. "If I'd your money I'd lie in bed."

"A woman would," Donald answered, bluntly. Then, revealing the sequence of his thought: "Is Mrs. Strand up yet?"

"I heard water runnin', an' it won't be Walter or Clarissa, unless she yanked 'em out o' bed. No," barring his approach, "you can't wash here. I'm usin' the sink."

So ordered, Donald started for the bathroom. On the stairs he met Clara.

"Sleep well, Clara?" he asked, willing to be agreeable. "You're all dressed up."

"Not more than usual for Sunday morning," she said, as though there had been criticism in his comment. "I don't usually prowl around in my underwear. I suppose we're going to church?"

"I suppose so."

"Then you better try and get some action out of that family of yours. It's always a mad rush at the last moment."

Donald had it on his tongue to mention that he did not take entire credit for the children, but he closed his lips and went on up the stairs. What was the use in arguing? he asked himself. Women were supposed to be pleased when you mentioned their dress but Clara had treated it as a criticism. Oh, well.

He paused at Clarissa's door, knocked, and, when there was no answer, opened it. A curling heap on the bed suggested the outline of the girl's body; the morning sun disclosed the disorder of her room which the moonlight had chivalrously concealed. To reach her side without stepping on them he had to stoop and lift her scanty and discarded clothes. But her little round head lay like a red flower on her pillow; she was beautiful even in her sleep. He let his fingers toy with her hair until she stirred, opened her eyes, saw him, and yawned.

"Oh, gee, Dad, I suppose it's all hours. You shouldn't keep me up so late. If I didn't have to go swimming I think I'd cut out church."

"You don't have to go swimming on my account," he answered. His fingers stole down over her cheek, her shoulder, her arm, coming to rest in her soft palm. Clumsily he sat down beside her while the bed springs squeaked their protest against the unaccustomed weight. "You know, Clare, when I was a boy sometimes we went swimming on Sunday, up in the big pond in the pasture, but we had to sneak out of[62] it and we always knew it was very sinful. And when the papers brought news of Sunday swimmers being drowned we thought it was very sad but that was what must be expected."

"And you thought they went straight to Hell, didn't you, Dad? Well, I don't. I think a girl drowned on Sunday has just as good a chance before St. Peter as if she arrived Saturday afternoon. Of course, she must[63] present herself in a bathing suit that does her justice. You should see the new one I'm going to break in to-day. It's a knock-out. Yellow and black, with the sides knocked out and the back left off. I hope to do it justice."

"I suppose you carry it in your compact. I sometimes wonder just how far you modern girls would go if the law—"

"Now don't be vulgar, Dad. It's all in what you're accustomed to, and I bet we think less about—what you're thinking about—than you do. And perhaps you're just a little jealous and a little sorry you're not a boy again—"

"Jealous, perhaps," Donald's face hardened; his jaw muscles stood up beneath the weathered skin. "Damned jealous of you, Clare. Never forget that. But as for the other—being a boy again—no; I wouldn't want to have it all to do over. I'd do it differently, but perhaps no better."

With a remarkably strong grip on her father's arm the girl swung herself into a sitting posture. Her free hand found his face and affectionately massaged the bristled cheek. "There, Dad; you shouldn,t[64] worry," she soothed him. "I suppose I'm one of your big mistakes, but I'll come out all right—you see if I don,t. Now drag Walter up; he can have his bath while you shave, and I can't. There'll be the usual rush at the last moment." With one of her quick, dexterous movements she planted a foot against her father's hip and shot him off the bed.

Walter was still asleep. The boy had a trick of pulling the covers over his head and leaving his feet exposed; Donald looked down at the hairy shanks and marvelled at the mystery of life. Only yesterday, it seemed, they had been little baby legs, clothed in skin like satin; now they were as big and unprepossessing as his own. He drew his fingers across the sole of a sleeping foot, producing an instant upward contortion; then, wrapping his arms about the entangled figure, he lifted the mass bodily and dropped it on the floor. "You're up, Walter," he announced. "Get a wiggle on. We'll be late for church."

Half an hour later the three went downstairs together. They found Clara seated by a window in the sunny dining-room, gazing out across the fields. Slowly, as one who has grown patient through long adversity, she turned toward them, cutting for an instant a profile against the outer light which still would have tingled Donald's veins had there been any answering flicker in her cold reserve.

"Good morning, Mother," the boy and girl said, dutifully, together, and Walter added, disarming criticism, "We're late again, aren't we?"

With slow grace Clara moved to the waiting table. "I always expect that," she said. "Your father rises early enough on Sunday, goodness knows, but he's always late for breakfast."

"That's because he spends so much time holding hands with Sundown Chieftain the Second," Walter suggested. "When I fall in love it won't be with hoofs and horns."

"Shut up, Walter," his sister chided him. "That's vulgar."

"Nor with lipstick and powder," Walter continued. "I prefer a dog."

Through carmine lips Clare thrust a red tongue at him and they took their seats at the table. Donald sank to his chair, a momentary stone in his stomach. The children were capable of wounding him in so many unconscious ways. Walter's remark about making love to the Chieftain; burlesque, of course, but with just a tiny thread of truth running through it, a thread which sometimes seemed to wind about his chest and make his breathing difficult. If only Clara could feel it, too. It might in time draw them together again. As he glanced across the table he thought how beautiful and inaccessible she was, how unaware

128

of the little thread of truth that ran through Walter's thoughtless witticism.

At that moment Aunt Annie came out of her room. She moved across the polished floor with careful steps; she was bent and thin and gave the impression of frailty, but there was still great vitality in her old veins. She had cultivated sweetness in her declining years in an effort to be an agreeable member of Donald's household, and without knowing that her very amiability was a constant source of irritation to Clara, who found it hard to return her measure for measure.

"Dear, dear," she apologized, as she saw them all seated at the table, "I hope I haven't kep' you waitin'. It's such a fine mornin'—I suppose we were all goin' to church?"

"The others were late, too," Clara answered as the old lady let herself down into her accustomed chair. "We always have a rush on Sunday morning. Donald—the blessing, please."[65]

From long force of habit, or in obedience to a custom he was loath to discontinue, Donald bowed his head and mumbled a hurried and somewhat confidential blessing into his grapefruit. If he was conscious of addressing the Primal Force he gave no evidence of being deeply impressed; indeed, he treated the ceremony as an amiable courtesy on his part rather than as a one-way message to the Heart of the Universe.

"We're away," said Walter, as his father's Amen ended in a whispered gasp. For some minutes the business of eating occupied all their attention, but a momentary pause before the poached eggs gave Donald an opportunity to introduce a subject which was on his mind, and which might as well be dealt with at once.

"I had a letter from Ellen yesterday; that is your Aunt Ellen, in Winnipeg," he added quite unnecessarily, directing the remark to Walter and Clarissa. He was aware that Clara entertained an unspoken resentment toward Ellen, possibly due to some intuitive jealousy, and he was glad of the cover the children gave him in introducing the subject. "She wants your mother and me to pay her a visit. Do you think you could run the farm for a week or two, Walter, with a little assistance from George and Ned?"

"That'll be all right," the boy answered promptly, "but if you're

129

going to take the car you'll need me to drive it. I wouldn't feel easy about you going alone in the city traffic."

Donald smiled on his son. "I appreciate your concern," he said, "but on the other hand I would not be satisfied to leave the farm without an experienced man in charge[66]. As for driving the car—I'm only forty-nine, Walter; I suppose that seems very old to you, but with some suggestions from you before we leave I will probably manage."

"Smoke that," Clarissa suggested to her brother. "Dad has his moments of understanding."

"Why don't they visit us?" Clara asked. "It's no farther one way than the other, and it's[67] years since they have been here."

"It is also years[68] since we have been there," Donald answered. The comings and goings between the Waynes and the Strands had not been overdone. Perhaps Ellen, too, had her intuitions. "Jim and Ellen are taking a trip to the Mediterranean this fall," he went on, "and I suppose he has his practice to attend to until he leaves. As for us farmers, we have a slack time before harvest, and I think it would be a pleasant change. Just as you like, of course. I thought you might want to do some shopping; the stores in Alder Creek don't give much choice."[69]

Clara had reached her decision. If she had any dislike for Ellen she was too proud to show it, and she had no intention of giving Donald good excuse for a week or two in the city alone.

"Yes, I'll go," she said. "Have you fixed a day?"

Peace surged back into Donald's soul. That was one hurdle easily taken. He had expected Clara would go but not so agreeably.

"No, I haven't fixed a day," he said. "By midweek, if you can be ready. I'll need to be home again when the harvest comes in, and it's ripening fast."

7

They made a good turnout in the new car, bought that season as an intimation that, when it came to quality, the Strands took nobody's dust. Donald himself drove to-day, with Aunt Annie, small and old and happy, at his side, and Clara, Walter and Clarissa in behind. Thrilled by the purring response of the eighty horses under his toe he took the highroad at an easy pace[70]. The wheat fields, yellow half-way up the stalk, slid by like a ribbon of green and gold; the smell of ripening wheat beat in through the open windows. The road now followed the checkerboard square of the prairie survey; Donald never travelled it without thinking of the old days when, disregarding section lines, it wound around the sloughs and along the hillsides like a huge rope carelessly flung across the prairie in the general direction of Alder Creek. Often he had walked that old trail; every step of it knew the imprint of his foot. Now it was submerged under crops of wheat and barley, its identity destroyed before the resistless march of settlement and cultivation[71].

The old Calder homestead floated by on the right. The elder Calders had passed to their reward, leaving as their only monuments a quarter section snatched from the wilderness and the indelible impressions planted by its president in the young hearts of the members of the Band of Hope. Never again would Mrs. Calder's voice be heard in uncertain soprano at the meetings in Sundown School; according to good orthodox belief it had been retuned and was now lilting praises with the celestial choir. Donald wondered. Winnie Calder had married and was somewhere in Alberta; Ralph was somewhere in France[72].

Donald slowed up to take a corner not yet rounded off for the convenience of motorists. Ahead, now, lay the Crisp farm. In reminiscence he saw the old man's parchment-like face and white hair; his

131

wife, with her white hair, too, but an inviting, ruddy color under the skin. Their pride in their children—how they had sought to conceal it, but how the old man's foot would tap when the youthful trio throbbed out their conception of "The Campbells are Comin'" on mouth organ, Jew's harp, and concertina. Katie lay in the narrow chambers of Alder Creek cemetery; Gordie's bones were marked with a cross in Flanders; Charlie had gone farther west. Gordie had been one of the comrades of his youth, most peaceable and well-disposed of all the boys at Sundown School; Donald tried to focus the impossible picture of Gordie thrusting a bayonet into a German belly and getting one in his own. It would not focus; it drew away like a little revolving disc into the distance, then, growing suddenly, rushed down upon him in a malignant fog—

"Dad!" Walter's sharp voice brought him back to consciousness. Walter's hand had shot past his shoulder to the wheel. "What's the matter, Dad? Gone to sleep?"

Donald pulled himself together. "Nothing; just swung out for something—some loose gravel on the road." But Walter,s lips were at his ear. "Don't kid me, Dad. Are you all right?"

"Sure, I'm all right." Walter sat back, satisfied with the assurance, and Donald congratulated himself that the women had not recognized that instant of danger. Something in Walter's voice and action stirred him deeply. Never before had his younger son—or Tom either—used that tone of authority or that note of concern. His heart warmed to Walter. He was something to fall back on; someone ready to take the wheel if his hands should fail. It was a comforting thought.

A car whipped by them, throwing gravel against the fenders and cutting in dangerously close in front. Donald caught a glimpse of young Fred Hardy[73], from the old Sinclair farm, showing off in his father's new machine[74]. "Crazy young fool!" he muttered, but smothered his complaint, remembering his own very recent lapse. Certainly the life of to-day was full of hazards. A new Earth had come in the last twenty years. "And," he added, whimsically, to himself, "the old Heaven has passed away."

He slowed up as he came to a point where a slight depression broke the even surface of a field of wheat. "See, Auntie; that is where

132

the old trail ran down to the ford on Gopher Creek. You remember the sidling hill? And there was a gravel bottom, and the suckers used to scoot at the splash of the horses' feet."

The old woman's eyes were bright with memories. "Indeed I do. Many's the time your Uncle Jim upset his load o' wood on that same sidlin' hill, an' me sittin' up late o' night, with the children in bed, wonderin' whether he was lost, or hurt, or froze. It's a changed world, Donal', wi' your telephones an' roads an' bridges an' automobiles. Changed, yes."

"But not improved?"

"I wouldn' say that. But I don' think people are as happy now as we use' to be. Maybe it's just because I'm old, but folks don' seem to laugh like they use' to."

"Perhaps there is not so much to laugh at," Clarissa observed[75].

8

Many cars had assembled at the United Church at Alder Creek when Donald drew up among them. He helped Aunt Annie and Clara to the sidewalk and sent Walter with the car to find parking space.

Clarissa touched his arm. "So long, Dad. I'll have to skip to get in with the choir, and I'm not going home with you. Going swimming, an' everythin'."

Donald looked at her soberly. She was very lovely in her light summer dress and her rich, ruddy hair, and in spite of their relationship possessive jealousy stirred within him[76].

:"Oh," she said, suddenly, "I almost forgot—you wanted me to ask you for twenty dollars."

"That isn't just how I recall it, but here's your money. Don't spend it all in one place. And watch your step."

"Trust me," she said, and her frank eyes reassured him.

The morning congregation was thronging into church. Everyone knew Mr. and Mrs. Strand; everyone spoke in passing; some stopped to shake hands. Smate, the lawyer, unable to reach them, smiled his broadest assurance that all was well; Goad, the bank manager, had a good word about the crops; Lang, general merchant, remembered to congratulate the owner of Sundown Chieftain the Second, winner of first prize at Alder Creek fair; Lester, publisher of the local paper, had a nod for a good subscriber. Donald was in his element; he returned their greetings heartily, and was not afraid to crack a joke even on Sunday on the church steps. The women were more effusive and less sincere than the men; but Clara, though she saw through them like glass, played her part with just the right touch of dignity, reserve, and condescension. Though she could not shape her life to her liking she felt that she might as well have the sweet with the bitter, and the homage of these women was sweet even while she knew that Mrs. Smate was under orders to be cordial because the lawyer was grooming himself for the party nomination, and that Mrs. Lang shared her husband's respect for a good customer. Clara had her smile and her soft word for each of them. Even that wizened little bachelor, Harry Long, who, despite innumerable rejections, still believed himself to have a way with the women, purred audibly when she spoke to him by name and took it as a good omen for the renewal of the fire insurance policy which he carried on the Strand buildings.

Clara, resting her hand on her husband's arm, and preceded by Aunt Annie, moved into the church, presenting a picture of domestic harmony and worldly success which baffled and exasperated many of the contemporary couples. They found their way unaided to their pew and Clara bowed her head a moment in an attitude intended to indicate prayer. It was a practice followed by most women and a few men, but Donald never had been able to bring himself to it. He noted mentally that Walter had not joined them; probably he had found Tom and as like as not the two had gone for a drive in the family car. Well, youth would be youth, and it was hard to know just how much to insist upon. He let his glance run along the choir until it came to rest on Clarissa, prettiest and best dressed, according to his judgment, of all that very presentable group. He saw her lids flicker in response to his and settled back in his seat, content to let the service take its course.

It ran true to form. As the minister entered the pulpit the congregation arose and the choir struck up a short morning hymn. Then a few words of prayer, a longer hymn, a reading from the Psalms, and the taking of the collection. Donald could remember when collections used to be taken after the sermon, in his uncle's stiff hat, and often he smiled at the thought that the result of that practice must have proved unsatisfactory, and the pay-in-advance system had been introduced. But he placed his envelope with a dollar bill on the plate; no one could say that Donald Strand didn't pay his way. Then came a short dedicatory prayer while the six young men who had gathered the collection felt the backs of their necks redden under the gaze of the congregation. Donald was never sympathetic to that prayer; it was too artful a means of impressing upon the congregation that they were giving to the Lord, meaning, in this instance, the minister's stipend, the janitor's wages, and the mortgage on the building. He supposed it helped to squeeze money out of reluctant givers, but it didn't fool him. Then followed an anthem by the choir in which he[77] caught at times the soaring of his daughter's voice and voted the performance a success; quite a step from those old days at Sundown School when Mrs. Calder and Andy Wayne differed by an octave and a half as to the starting-point of Old Hundred. There was more reading, during which Donald's thought involuntarily wandered to the relationship between $75,838.40 and the reputed wealth of one James Wayne with whom he had smoked whip-stalk cigars under the willows beside Alder Creek, and from whom he had learned that gol darn was almost as effective as damn and did not involve any danger of eternal punishment. He wondered if Jimmie had really made more money than he, or was he just putting up a bold front to Ellen? The congregation, rising to sing, jerked him back to consciousness of his surroundings and he joined in the hymn lustily. The words had become meaningless to him, or worse, but that they were the vehicle for an exercise that had in it something of spiritual uplift could not be denied.

The sounds of the hymn died away, the congregation resumed its seats with much creaking of joints and timber, and the minister launched into his long prayer, obviously designed, at least in part, for the edification, direction and discipline of his congregation. Donald could have quoted in advance many of the expressions in which the prayer abounded. He would have liked sometime to ask Mr. Munro to translate some of his figures of speech into literal English, but he knew he never would; that would open the way to a discussion of religion, and Donald, though he wondered and wondered, had an insistent modesty about exposing the smallest corner of his soul. Besides, it wasn't done. One might challenge a politician, a lecturer, or even a school teacher, but one could not, without offence, challenge his minister[78].

During the sermon he ran up a mental estimate of the number of his acres of wheat multiplied by the probable yield per acre multiplied by the probable price per bushel. From that must be subtracted the cost of threshing, the cost of twine, the additional labor necessary during harvest. Even then it came to a comfortable total. Of course there were still the hazards of hail, grasshoppers, and hot winds and rust. The farmer's life was beset by hazards; he had to fight the elements to get his crop and the craftiness of his fellow men to keep them from taking an undue share of the proceeds. To be a successful farmer called for a combination of intelligence, judgment, industry and business ability not demanded in any other pursuit. It wasn't enough to raise a crop; you had to learn to say no or those smiling sycophants would take it away from you. Uncle Jim had emphasized that, and Donald never had forgotten. What if[79] some people, behind his back, called him hard? That was because he wasn't soft. This combine affair. He must look into the matter. Perhaps they were all right, but he would have to be shown. Never be the first—nor the last. He had thought the combine idea out for himself, long ago, but hardly expected ever to see it in use. Well—the world was moving along. It was a far cry from the day when Andy Wayne hauled his bright new seeder up in front of Uncle Jim's log house, unconsciously ushering in the era of big farming and bursting the bounds of the quarter section[80]. No tractors then, no motor cars, no electric lights in farm homes, no gasoline engines, no radios.

He glanced to his side. Clara was as passive as stone, as beautiful as a cameo. For all the gulf that separated them a little tide of worship-fulness surged within him. So close and placid they sat; not the wisest in that congregation could know what worlds divided them. He wondered if the other vignettes of life around him were as misleading as his own. At any rate he was glad Clara had made no open break; it was better so; immeasurably better at least for Walter and Clarissa. If Clara were to die to-morrow everyone would say she had been an ideal wife. He himself would say so, and perhaps, during the emotional strain of separation and readjustment, would believe it. But Clara had not played the game. Of course, no one would ever know. She would not tell, because she herself did not know—she blamed it on him. He would not tell because his pride forbade him. But she had won him by fire and the fire had gone out. Whose fault? Well . . . he could love her yet if she would let him. If she would reach over and press his hand right now he would return the pressure. But nothing, he knew,

137

was further from her mind. She was respectable and moral and cold and dead. If only she would come to life! If only, some way, he could bring her to life! But not by bribery, not by concession. . . .

The sermon came to a close. Donald caught a few words of exhortation which, detached from their context, suggested to him vaguely a roof without a house—a protection, a shade, without support. He bowed his head dutifully for the benediction, then filed out behind his wife.

9[81]

The afternoon fulfilled the morning's promise of heat. A rising wind whipped clouds of dust from the highways and the bare summerfallows; the air was thick with it, the sky went grey; the sun was an indistinct luminous mist. Mrs. Fetch closed the windows to keep the dust out; even in the house the atmosphere was close and hot. Donald removed his coat and his tie, and, a little later, his shirt; he took off his boots and stretched himself on the couch in his office. Clara was in the living-room reading a magazine, but Clara objected to his going about the house without a shirt, so he lay in his office, reflecting that even yet he was wearing more clothes than a couple of women. Aunt Annie had gone to her room; she tried to snatch a sleep in the afternoon, or perhaps she was writing her weekly letters to Ellen and her son Tom, and Walter had gone off somewhere with the car before the storm became so thick.[82]

The hot, close air brought little beads of sweat to Donald's forehead, but they were born, too, of some tangle of emotions going on within. He had disappointed Clara; Clara had disappointed him. Clara was not strong enough to master him, and too strong to yield. She maintained a perpetual armed truce; invisible outside the household, vaguely suspected by the children, known in all its iron rigidity only to Donald himself. "The heart knoweth its own bitterness." Sometimes old sayings like that would come to Donald, and he would grope about in his memory for their origin. When he was a little boy he had heard a chapter of the Bible read every night. He never had set up that practice in his own household; life seemed to get speeded up, and it was impossible to do so. Besides, it had all been so true to him then, but now he did not know what he believed. He believed something; he believed there was a purpose from somewhere running through everything, but when he tried to disentangle its threads as they wove in and out about his life they became hopelessly confused. He was no longer sure there was another life to follow this. Perhaps; perhaps not.[83] The old fear was gone, but the old hope had gone with it. Never would the dry bones spring through the turf at the blast of a trumpet, clothe themselves with flesh, and crowd about the Throne. And yet—and yet—there must be something. Otherwise everything was chaos, and life a riddle to remain forever unsolved.

There was Aunt Annie, for instance. Her beliefs had been modified, but her faith had not been broken. She looked forward to reunion with Uncle Jim with as much assurance as Donald anticipated his meeting with Ellen and Jimmie Wayne in Winnipeg next Wednesday. As for Clara, he never had fathomed her beliefs. He had an idea that she just went on and on.

He heard Clara's footstep on the floor, and a wild momentary surge rushed through him. If she would come to him, even now! And she was coming! He traced the sound of her footsteps across the floor; he saw her trim figure framed in his doorway. If she would come, if she would kneel down beside him, if she would let his arms steal about her, her hair fall about his face!

But she stood in the doorway. "Sleeping, Donald?" she asked, gently enough.

"No." His voice was husky. "Just thinking."

"What day do you want to go to Winnipeg?"

"Wednesday, if it suits you."

"It will do. I need some things, but I suppose I can get them there. Ellen will not expect too much of one travelling by motor.[84]

"Did you take notice of Lizzie at church?" she asked, after a pause. "Really, she is getting worse. Her figure is terrible."

"It is pretty bad. But some people, who *have* figures, don't make the most of them."

She was silent for a moment. "I don't understand you," she said.

He lay still, hearing the beating of his heart, not knowing whether to answer her. "You never did, Clara," he said at length.

"Nor you me. You have not considered me. You have had your own way. In everything."

"In everything!" he repeated, bitterly.

Because of the darkness of the room, for the blinds were drawn to keep out the heat, he could not see her face clearly. He wondered how much she read into his ironical assent. But when she spoke the moment had passed by.

"Be careful you don't catch a cold, lying there without your shirt," she said, and returned to her magazine.

10

Toward evening the wind went down, the sky cleared, the sun flooded the fields with long red[85] light. Mrs. Fetch bustled about, opening windows and wiping the dust from sills and furniture. Donald sauntered through the barn, saw the evening milking well on its way, and, feeling an urge for movement, turned down the old trail which led through the pasture field in the direction of what once had been the Farquhar farm. The trail[86] pierced the windbreak of Manitoba maples which sheltered the house from the west; the storm had broken down leaves and twigs; they rustled against his feet as he walked. Then his course[87] swung down to the creek. It was dry now at the ford,[88] and the mud had hardened and caked into rough corrugations bearing the imprint of hooves of horses and cattle. The smell of stagnant water and the low murmur of a wild duck still mothering her half-grown brood came from around a bend. In the bed of the creek Donald was quite out of sight from the surrounding levels; he thought of the times he and Jimmie Wayne had smoked their whipstalk cigars under its sheltering willows, luxuriating in a sense of wickedness that compensated for the lack of nicotine. No doubt Jimmie was smoking a better cigar now. Well, he smoked a ten-cent brand himself. He felt in the pocket of his shirt, for he was without coat or vest, and regretted that he had not brought one to lighten his way. Nearly forty years ago, that was, and how little they then foresaw all that would happen in between! The reflection saddened him for a reason he did not understand; there was a nostalgic yearning[89] for the little boy he once had been and never again could be.[90]

Donald clambered up the opposite bank, and in a few minutes the trail brought him to the road allowance along the northern side of his farm. From this position he could see his wheat fields stretching away to the southward, the intervening gap of the creek lost in their gentle undulations. The field had been seeded north-and-south, and the stalks stood in firm, grenadier-like ranks, row on row, their heads hanging with the weight of the firming cereal within, their leaves whispering continually in the slight motion of the evening breeze. Donald strode a few paces into the field; drawing the heads upwards in his hands they reached almost to his armpits.[91] He rubbed a few heads in his palms;[92] the chaff was still tenacious; the kernels were large and opal-green. Fortunately the wind had done little harm. Two weeks later, when the grain[93] would be ripe, it would be a more serious matter.

The sun, more than usually red, was setting in the north-west against a honey-colored abyss of sky; overhead a few fragments of cloud caught and held its orange and yellow rays in an entanglement of copper and gold. Donald's eyes narrowed as he faced the horizontal light, but in a few moments the great orb had disappeared, the honey-colored abyss threw out a veil of mauve and purple, and in the far east in the iron-gray[94] curtains of the night began to fall, fold on fold, across the plain. The prairie sunset had always had a fascination for Donald, from which he argued that his soul was still alive, knowing in how many of his neighbors it was long since dead. He took off his hat and wiped the sweat from his forehead, for the coolness of the night had not yet settled down, and resumed his walk.

To the right lay the section on which he had herded cows that first summer, where Billie and Hester Harp had come to join him, and he and Hester had begun to be aware. Its sloughs had dried up with the cultivation of the surrounding area, and wheat and barley waved where once the curlews ran along the muddy flats. The whole face of the country had changed, but not more, nor as much, as the faces of those who had known it in its virginity. Hester was Mrs. Jack Marble now, bearing her husband six children and a secret that she could not share. Sometimes he met her in Alder Creek and they stopped and spoke a minute about the weather and the crops, as though they had nothing mightier on their minds. After all, what did it matter? Just a musty memory for both of them to carry, if they could not forget. So far as he was concerned Hester might as well be dead—might as well never have lived. But if Clara knew she never would forgive.

Thought of Clara tightened his heart a little. It was out here she had sought him that day, pretending to be in quest of strawberries, but really in quest of him. It was in the old Farquhar house, now torn down to make way for unbroken fields of wheat, that she had entagled him in the web of her domesticity. It was on this very trail, at this very raise in the road, that she had turned to him that night as no one ever had done before. He had thought then it was her surrender; he knew now it was his. Oh, well, it might have been worse. Deep as his disappointment in Clara had been, there wasn't a woman in the neighborhood to-day for whom he would trade her. She had appearance, she had poise, she had pride; at least she did him justice in those respects. And she had saved him from the featureless satiety of Hester Harp; but for Clara he might have married Hester. God!

He swung homeward, walking faster than he had come. It was cooler now; there were little zones of cool air through which he passed, plunging into zones of warmth, then cool again. A few stars had come out. The creek, when he reached it, lay in heavy shadows; he found his way across its sun-baked bottom by memory[95] rather than by sight. The cows had been turned into the pasture; the sound of their deep, satisfied breathing reached him from every side. Here and there through the gloom he could discern a huge recumbent figure on the grass. Suddenly he stumbled on one in his path, almost falling over her; she arose lazily and without alarm, humping her back and stretching herself prodigiously. He ran a friendly hand along her spine and pushed around her.

11[96]

The windows of Winnipeg were reflecting[97] the red blaze of a low-hung August sun when Donald drew his car up before the substantial place[98] of James and Ellen Wayne. The deep-verandahed house sat well back from the street in the quiet dignity of a home which can afford spacious lawns and ample breathing room in a high-priced residential district. In threading his way through the city traffic Donald had fallen back unconsciously on the doctrine of predestination, but he heaved a subdued[99] sigh, not intended for Clara's ears, when he saw the stout word WAYNE cut in the artificial granite of the curb.

"Well, here we are, Mother," he proclaimed cheerily. "All stiff and sore?"

"Neither—but somewhat relieved," Clara answered, with a sigh distinctly unsuppressed.[100] "There's a drive-in somewhere, and you're on the wrong side of the street."

Donald surveyed the situation. "So I am. Always get directions wrong in Winnipeg. Thought I was on the other side. Well—guess I can make a Y turn and that'll put me right."

"You made a number of turns that weren't so wise," Clara remarked, allowing herself the luxury of a far-fetched pun. "Only reason we're not arrested is you frightened all the policemen off the street.[101] You certainly mowed a swath through the traffic."

As Donald went searching for an appropriate rejoinder, one that would justify his driving without ruffling too deeply Clara's uncertain humor, he caught[102] sight of Ellen coming down the walk to greet them. "Why, here's Ellen! he exclaimed.

"Yes, I saw her," Clara answered.

"Well, here you are!" Ellen's hands were extended, one to Clara, one to Donald. "Tired? It's dusty driving. Don't bother with a thing;

145

Holmes will put the car away and look after your baggage. My, I believe you are both looking well?"

"You carry it well yourself, Ellen," Donald ventured, careful not to be over enthusiastic in Clara's presence.

It was the same old Ellen; a little rounder of face, a little fuller of throat, a little plumper with the years, but still the bright eye, the cheerful, half-bantering voice, the smooth olive complexion. Her head was bare and her bobbed hair seemed to deny the flight of time, but on closer examination there were threads of grey among the brown, and little thin wrinkles gathered to a centre at the eyes. Donald held her hand a moment and the touch of her fingers carried him back thirty years, but his words were casual as they sauntered up the walk together.

Ellen showed them into a spacious hall where they caught a glimpse of deeper rooms with sunlight filtering in through richly-curtained windows. "Now how do you sleep?" she said, turning to them again. "I can give you a large room or two smaller ones with bath between." It was a question which ran to the core of their married life, but she asked it without embarrassment. Donald hesitated, feeling a little prickle of color under the skin in spite of himself, and looked at Clara. Obviously the question awaited her answer.

"We have our own rooms at home," she said. "If it isn't too much trouble—"

"Not a bit." Ellen gave no hint of the significance of Clara's request. "I will show you up now, so you can wash and refresh yourselves a little, and the maid will put your things in order later. Sorry Jim isn't here at the moment; he plays golf Wednesday afternoons when the weather is fit, and I don't discourage him, for he's putting on weight dreadfully. You're holding your own, Donald." She ran an affectionate arm about his substantial waist. "But you're hard. Jim's soft. I think we shall have to go back to the farm—when we've made enough money."

"How much is enough?" Donald asked, wondering what she would say.

"Does anybody know?" she parried. "Of course, you have used the farm to make money, but Jim couldn't do that. You are that much

146

cleverer than he—yes, I really think so. It's harder to make money farming than in business or in the law. Oh"—turning to Clara—"I forgot to ask about the family. We knew, of course, that Tom and Clarissa have their positions, but we thought Walter might come. Is Mother as well as usual? I would have asked her particularly, but I thought the trip might be too hard."[103]

"They're all fine," Donald said, coming to his wife's assistance. "Walter's running the farm—with the aid of two good hired men, of course. Walter doesn't shed as much sweat as I did at his age. Remember my shirts and underwear? You washed them often enough."

"Donald!" his wife protested. "Is that very delicate?"

"Not a bit. None of us was delicate in those days. And it was the making of us. We'll see whether the new generation will carry through as far."

"Unfortunately, I won't." It was Ellen speaking. "I haven't any new generation."

Donald's eyes sought hers, but she seemed to be looking into far distances. Then, recovering herself: "But come to your rooms.[104] Jim should be home any minute."

She showed them into their adjoining rooms. Donald looked about his spacious chamber. She had spoken of it as a "smaller" room, but it was larger than his at home and much more luxuriantly furnished. Through an open window he caught a glimpse of green lawns and gardens and ribbons of placid water beyond the trunks of trees. He took off his coat, collar, and tie, and sank into a chair which received him with deep and comfortable complaisance. The bathroom door was slightly ajar; from his position he could see that the floor and walls were tiled, and the sunlight danced on polished fittings. "Often wish I'd tiled my bathroom," he observed to himself, conscious of a little twinge of envy. The finest house in the Alder Creek district looked rather cheap and bare compared with this. Jim had succeeded. But then, as Ellen said, it took more ability to succeed on the farm. Or was she just trying to make it easy for him?

Half an hour later, at Ellen's summons, they went downstairs. Jim met them in the hall. "Well, well," he said heartily, taking each by the hand. "It's like old times to see you again. Sorry I wasn't here

147

when you arrived—golfing, you know. You've heard about the man who said his wife was going to divorce him if he didn't give up golf? He was awfully cut up about it; said he didn't know how he would get along without a wife. Couldn't very well help it to-day, though; mixing a little business with the nineteen holes. Tell you about it later, Donald."

Ellen was right; Jim was putting on weight. Donald remembered that as a boy Jimmie had been thin to skinniness. Now he filled his well-cut clothes rather more than comfortably, and his jaws curved heavily into his neck,[105] but his eyes still carried a glint of their strange old audacious curiosity of life.

Ellen led them through the large, thick-rugged living-room into the dining quarters. It was sundown now and the blinds were drawn to prevent the unpleasant mixture of natural and artificial light; in the centre of a large, oak-paneled room was a massive round table, set for four. Light from electric candles sparkled on silver and crystal.[106] There was no food in sight.

"How about a little cocktail, folks?" Jim asked, when they were seated. "You need a pick-up after your long drive."

"I didn't serve any to-night," Ellen hastened to explain. "Donald and Clara are teetotallers. Or were?"

"Are," Donald assured her.

"It's all right, of course," said Jim, amiably. "Just thought maybe times had changed. I used to be that way, too. Remember in the old Band of Hope how we used to recite 'Wine is a mocker, strong drink is raging?' Well, I suppose it's a good way to start off-keeps one from going to extremes. We thought then that every person who took a drink was a drunkard. I've found out since that nearly everyone who cuts any figure in the business or professional world can put a few under his belt without inconvenience."

"Not everybody, Jim," Ellen corrected, anxious for her guests.

"I didn't say everybody. There are exceptions. But they *are* exceptions. Liquor is a great mixer. Of course, on the farm you don't have to meet that problem. I suppose that's why farm communities always vote dry and cities vote wet."

"Perhaps there is another reason," Donald suggested, sturdily. "In

148

the farm communities everybody knows everybody else, and they see what liquor does to those who give way to it. In the cities I suppose those who give way too much just gradually disappear[107] and others take their place, but in the country we still have the old sots as neighbors to remind us of what they might have been."

Jim shot a quick glance at his guest. "Sorry, Donald. I didn't know you felt so strongly about it. Forgive me for bringing it up."

A little embarrassed over his display of vigor, Donald fumbled his cutlery.[108] "Oh, that's all right," he said. "But I have two boys coming up, and, you know, it makes you think. I suppose," he conceded, "we are quite old-fashioned. The times are travelling too fast for us."

Ellen switched the conversation onto safer ground and the meal passed as pleasantly as possible with both Donald and Clara a little afraid of a tactical misdemeanor among so many pieces of silverware and so many comings and goings of a quiet and efficient maid. It differed as much from the slap-stick service of Mrs. Fetch as an automobile differs from a buckboard. The farmer and his wife were swallowing with their meal the unhappy conviction that Alder Creek was not Winnipeg.

"Well, you smoke, anyway?" said Jim, when they were about to leave the table. "Come down into my smokehouse; I'll give you something better than a cane whipstalk. Remember the old days, under the willows, with our bare feet sunk in the damp soil and us puffing and choking and being regular devils?" Jim threw an arm about his guest, feeling for the old comradeship. Turning to Clara, half whimsically: "Perhaps you'd like a cigarette, Clara? Ellen will find you some. Oh, she's not inveterate, but she knows how."

Donald came to what he believed to be his wife's assistance. "Of course Clara doesn't smoke," he said.

"*Didn't* smoke," Clara corrected him. "Yes, I'll have one. When in Rome, you know—"

"Thata girl," said Jim, with enthusiasm. "Good sport, Clara," he added into Donald's ear as they moved along the hall. Donald, looking back, saw his wife pulling on a cigarette, and a thrill ran through him that he could not explain.[109]

12

Jimmie Wayne led Donald to his billiard room in the basement of the house. It was floored with brown tile and the walls were tinted in colors restful to the eye. Huge masculine chairs offered[110] comfort before an open fireplace which, because of the season, was not in use. Jimmie produced cigars and for awhile the two old friends sat in a silence interrupted at long intervals by brief observations, while their personalities groped for the old contacts and the old confidence. Environment and habit had set up an insulating wall between them. They were still friends, but something had gone which could not be replaced. It was hard to find a meeting ground on which they were both at ease.

"Tell me about your farm," Jim suggested, groping, as was his guest. "I hear you are setting the pace for the whole Sundown district. You were always a good farmer, Don, and I'm glad to see things coming your way."

Donald's tongue was loosened. This was something he could talk about. Half an hour later he was surprised to find that he had disclosed more to Jimmie than he ever had done to anyone else—even to his banker, or to Clara. Jimmie showed his interest and was generous with his commendation. Donald had done well; he had a right to be proud of his achievements.

"You haven't done so badly yourself, Jim—judging by this house, and these cigars. That's the smoothest smoke I've had since the last election."

"You like them?" Jimmie was pleased[111] with his guest's approval. "Smoke 'em up; that's what they're for."

Donald helped himself again, and Jimmie extended a lighter. The blue wreaths hung about their heads; the beams of the ceiling, the deep tints of the walls, the angular form of the billiard table,[112] were softened and mellowed by the sedative smoke.

"Yes," said Jimmie, picking up his friend's thought. "It's a long jump from the willows beside Alder Creek and two barefoot boys feeling very manly and wicked."

"What do you pay for a cigar like that, if you don't mind?" Donald asked, feeling his way back to commercial subjects. He had no intention that the confidences should be all on one side.

"I get them wholesale—friend of mine—eight dollars a box. A little extravagant, perhaps, but a box does me a week, and after all it's not much more than a good bottle of Scotch. Which reminds me I must have a drink." He touched a spring in a table beside him and it opened up, displaying a bright array of glasses and bottles. "Sure you don't care of any? Well, you'll have a glass of ginger ale, anyway." He filled a tumbler with the bubbling fluid and poured a stiff draught of whiskey for himself.

"Now you want me to tell you how I've been getting on," he began, as they sat sipping together. "I've done well, Donald; so well that it almost frightens me to think of it. You've told me you've made seventy-five thousand on the farm, and it's a great credit to you. Nothing that I've done detracts from that. But when I make up my statement for the bank I add another naught."

Donald almost choked over a swallow of ginger ale. "You don't mean seven hundred and fifty thousand—three quarters of a million dollars!"

"Just that. Easily. If the market holds—and it's getting stronger every day—I'll turn the even million before New Year."[113]

Jimmie's instinct for the dramatic indicated a pause, and he sat sipping his whiskey while the weight of his deliverance sank into his friend from the farm. It was a happy reflection that both of them had done well. It was an even more happy reflection that he had done the better of the two.

"There is nothing more dangerous than offering financial advice," Jimmie resumed, "and you know your own business, but it does seem to me that Fate has thrust a golden spoon into the mouth of this generation, and all we have to do is swallow. Have you kept out of the market altogether?"

"Oh, not altogether," Donald claimed, with a little feeling of weakness about the belt. He would have denied strenuously that he was guilty of envy; he wished Jimmie nothing but the best of luck, but why should this man with his easy life and his golf and his drinking and all that make ten times as much as he? "I usually buy wheat in the fall; make some money on it, too; and I've some sound stock, but not a great deal. Guess I've been too busy digging my money out of the land to watch the market."

"Quite so.[114] And it is absolutely necessary that someone should dig the money out of the land, but it isn't necessary that it should be you. I'm not suggesting that you leave the farm; I believe the happiest life in the world is on the land, and I'm looking forward to having a place of my own. Summer on the farm and the winters on the Mediterranean or in Bermuda—that makes a very happy combination. But it takes money. I'm busy making the money now, with something like that in view. And while my judgment is not infallible, I haven't made many bad guesses. If I can be of any service to you I will be glad, for old times' sake."

"That's very decent," Donald murmured, cautious not to commit himself.

"Oh, not a bit. I'm sure if I went to you for guidance in the buying of some purebred stock you'd give it in a minute. By the way, I saw where you had cleaned up at Alder Creek fair.[115] Bully for you, and that's not intended for a pun. So if I can help you to pick out a little gilt-edged stock on the market I'll be only too glad. We'll take a trip down to the brokers in the morning and place a little flier, just as a try-out."

Jimmie, with his water-tight mind, dismissed the subject and turned the conversation to other matters.

"This thing of drinking," he suggested. "Of course, I'm old strong for temperance, but I'm disposed to think that in those old Band of Hope days we were a little intemperate—the other way 'round.[116] I often wonder if what we were taught as truth was not largely superstition. God was very close in those days, and made a note in a book every time we said damn. On the other hand, if we did anything commendable, such as going to church or learning our Sunday School verses, a note was made on the credit side of our account, but if any-one was unfortunate enough to die while the balance was against him and without having obtained forgiveness he was sent to Hell to be burned for ever and ever." Jimmie shrugged his shoulders with a ges-ture indicating something like despair. "That's the kind of civilization we were bred into, Donald; is it any wonder every kind of orthodoxy is having a hard ride?"

Donald did not know how to answer. He never had discussed such matters with anyone; he had wondered and wondered, but he had not talked. There always had seemed something indelicate in talking about God and religion; something like going out naked into the street. And yet he had a great yearning to check other people's doubts against his own. For a long while he had refused to admit that he doubted, fearing that such an admittance would jeopardize his future life, but of recent years doubt had grown over him as a cataract grows over the eye.

"A man must believe something," he ventured. "The world didn't come about by accident."

"Oh, I believe in God," Jimmie returned his thought instantly. "Only He isn't the same God. He has moved out from behind the nearest cloud and has His headquarters a few billion light-years dis-tant, somewhere in the centre of the universe, but He exists every-where, like the ether, or the attraction of gravity. I would say He *satu-rates* everything, if you know what I mean, so completely that every hair of your head comes into the reckoning. I am not trying to quote Scripture, but that's what I think. And I don't think He cares whether you say damn or tut-tut, or whether I drink Scotch or ginger ale. But if I drink too much I'll break down my health and pay for my excess, and if I use foul language I'll soon have a mind that smells. You see, we're surrounded by law; law everywhere. And the punishment is not vindictive; it is simply automatic. My quarrel with our teachers is that they made the punishment vindictive, and I think they were wild on their law. Take divorce, for example. You remember how we used to regard a divorced person as some kind of blight upon the society which he or she contaminated? Now divorce has become respectable."

Donald raised a hand. He had not known any divorced person in-timately, but he had a good old belief that the whole thing was evil.

153

Jimmie greeted the objection with a tolerant smile. "You don't agree? Well, I'm a lawyer, and perhaps my prejudices have been more modified than yours. Suppose for a moment we look at this marriage business sensibly,[117] instead of sentimentally. Marriage is one of the few contracts which are supposed to be binding 'until death do us part'. It is therefore a contract which should be entered into only after the most serious and unbiased consideration. Now why do young people marry? You know, and I know. Nature, the subtle jade, is planning for the reproduction of the species. She doesn't give a whoop about the two individuals concerned, and as she is leading them into a position which they would not accept if in possession of all their senses, she has a way of investing them with emotions which temporarily upset their judgment. Under the influences of these emotions the two young things rush into a contract which binds them for life. Well —what can you expect?"

The argument was disturbing Donald more deeply than he would have dared to admit. He was trying to frame a comment when Jimmie resumed:

"How many do you suppose are happy, Don? Of course you are, and of course I am; everybody but a quitter pretends to be. But how many really are? How many do you suppose find a means of evading their contracts? How many more would like to, but don't dare? I am a lawyer; I get occasional glimpses of life in the raw, and I tell you there are some things worse than divorce." He paused, then continued: "Would it surprise you to know—" He broke off again. "Oh, I'm in favor of monogamy. But marriage, like the Sabbath, was made for man."[118]

Jimmie arose from his chair, a little heavily, and walked about the large, luxurious room. "I shouldn't harangue you like this," he said. "It's no way to treat a guest. But it isn't every night one meets an old friend and has a chance to really open up. I don't want you to think that Ellen and I are not hitting it off. I suppose I get along with her wonderfully—for a second choice."

"What do you mean—'second choice'?"

"Don't pretend to be dumb, Donald. You're not. Let's go upstairs. The women will think we have deserted them."

A branch of the stairs led through a porch to a wide verandah. Jimmie took that way. "A breath of outside air will do us good," he suggested. The night was warm and still; stars,[119] which would have shone with intense brilliance over Sundown Farm, were dimmed by the lights along the street. The distant roar of traffic fell on Donald's ear; Jimmie did not notice it. They filled their lungs, and, without speaking, went into the house.

Ellen was reading by a chair-lamp in the living-room. Donald thought how young and beautiful she still looked under its pink light. The years had used her easily—as they had Clara. Hearing their footsteps[120] she laid aside her magazine, a smile parted her lips, and she moved to meet them, gracefully as a girl, across the deep rug.

"Clara was tired and has gone to her room," she said. "Would you like something to eat, Donald? It's no trouble."

"No, thanks," he answered; then, dropping into the vernacular: "Guess I'll be hitting the hay, too. When do you city people have breakfast? Six-thirty is our time, on summer schedule."

"We burn the candle at the other end, Donald. You can have breakfast just whenever you like, or not at all, if you'd rather rest. Tell you what I'll do; I'll have your breakfast and Clara's sent up, say about nine-thirty?"

Donald's throat gave a little gurgle. There was something infinitely ridiculous about the idea of having breakfast in bed at nine-thirty. Before he could protest he was guided to his door. "Good night, old man," Jimmie called from the head of the stairs. "If I'm gone in the morning Holmes will drive you down when you're ready, and we'll look into a broker's office and put a tag on some of the easy money that's floating around."

"Good night, Donald," Ellen said gently, and there was a caress in her words which followed him into his room.

Donald dropped into a chair and began the removal of his shoes,[121] but the process came to a pause as he tried to piece together again the conversation of the evening. Just what had Jimmie been driving at? There was the challenge to the old faith; the tolerance of divorce; the talk of being a second choice, and the shaft, "Don't pretend to be dumb,[122] Donald; you're not." Just what was Jimmie driving at?

Donald did not yet dare put into concrete form thoughts which flashed by and eluded him. His mind, stimulated by Jimmie's conversation, was whirling like a fog, a fog through which he could see nothing clearly. A phrase from the old war days came back to him; "low visibility". That seemed to describe his present condition. But he wondered again if Jimmie had just been generalizing, or if his arguments had a purpose deeper than a mere exchange of observations. Out of the confusion his thought presently centred upon Clara; Clara, who was tired and had gone to bed and was probably sound asleep in the next room. Jimmie had spoken in a complimentary way of Clara. Nothing wrong about that. But there had been something underneath. It occurred to Donald that Clara would enjoy being Jimmie's wife. She would fit into these surroundings. She never had quite fitted into Sundown Farm. And Ellen? He could not misunderstand the way in which Ellen had said good night.

He[123] arose from his chair, and, without any conscious purpose, moved across the floor to the door which connected with Clara's room. He tried the lock gently; it turned, and the door swung partly open. Clara's lamp was out, but a finger of light from somewhere outside drew a parallelogram on the wall. He stood still a moment, listening for her breathing, but not hearing it above the sudden pounding of his heart. If she was awake she gave no sign, and after a moment's irresolution he softly closed the door and returned to his own bed. Glancing down, for the first time he noticed that it had been prepared for occupation. The counterpane had been removed; the white sheets lay open in an inviting gore; the pillows were in place. His mind swam in a mist of memories.[124] It was such a little thing, and yet it might mean everything. Everything. Everything he had missed by one mistake. Or was it a mistake? Ellen had no children; the fear and wisdom that had guided them, as they thought, aright, might have been for no cause. At any rate that cause was now removed. Was Jimmie suggesting a—a rearrangement? Marriage was made for man, he had said. Standing stupidly beside the bed Donald pressed a big finger into the yielding sheet.[125]

13

Notwithstanding the promise of breakfast in bed Donald was awake before six with no prospect of further sleep. He raised a blind and let the morning light flood into his room. Moving as quietly as he could, he washed, shaved, and dressed, and sat down to wait for signs of life below. He was in a cheerful mood; the fog of the night before had cleared, or, rather, had blown away.[126]

At the first sign of domestic activity he went down stairs. Finding neither Jimmie nor Ellen about he spent a while surveying the well-kept lawn and then took a turn down the quiet street. It was the most delightful hour of the day; strange that city people should prefer to spend it in bed! Later he found Jimmie on the verandah,[127] and the two breakfasted together, sharing the morning *Free Press*. Neither Clara nor Ellen appeared, but Jimmie seemed to take that for granted and plowed through his paper and his meal[128] together, with occasional comment on the news of the day. He[129] looked well-dressed and very fit; the previous night's liquor apparently had left no hang-over; he impressed Donald as a man who knew his job and was abundantly capable of handling it. He made no reference to the matters they had discussed, a fact which made them seem more than ever like a dream in Donald's mind.

They drove down town together, Jimmie detouring through the parks and arriving, for once, later at his office. But the machinery was already in operation; Donald was impressed by the efficient and expensive furnishings, and the well-dressed clerks and stenographers at work at their desks and typewriters.

"Quite a crew you carry here," he mentioned to Jimmie, when they had reached his private office. "You must have some wage bill!"

"Quite a bill," Jimmie agreed, producing a box of cigars for his guest, "but what we pay them is only a fraction of what they are making. That is one of the problems in an office like this, or in any office; it's hard to keep staff at any price. They are all in the market, and when a stenographer makes say a couple of hundred dollars in a couple of days on her favorite stock it dampens her enthusiasm for pounding the keys for twenty-five a week.[130] But I must take you in and have you shake hands with Sutherland. Then we'll go out and unravel the market."

Mr. Sutherland was older than his partner, and balanced Jimmie's round and somewhat florid face with his own pale and lengthy features. He greeted Donald with interest and plunged at once into an intelligent discussion of crops, rust, hot winds, and 'hoppers. "You know, Mr. Strand," he said, his long forefinger picking Donald out as though he were a witness in the box, "the world has entered into a new era. We are approaching the time when the old scourge of poverty is going to be removed from our civilization. But the source of all wealth is still the land, and while one may have an eye on the market he should have the other on the farm, not to speak of the forests, the mines, and our wonderful water powers. From these sources wealth is accumulating at an unprecedented and ever-accelerating pace. We are entering a new era, Mr. Strand. But we will do well to still give honor to the homely virtues of industry and enterprise."

Donald ventured an observation. "We are increasing the wealth," he said, "but it doesn't seem to be very equally distributed. Hard work may be a virtue, but does it pay as well as—well, as being on the right side of the market?

Mr. Sutherland's long features broadened perceptibly. "I see you are a man who thinks," he complimented Donald. "And I won't argue that the distribution of wealth under our system is absolutely just. I doubt if it can be quite just under any system. But I do say that hard work is better rewarded to-day than ever before in history. You know," he brought his long hands together above his desk, "there is a common delusion that there is just so much money, and if I have a dollar, you haven't it. That's an absolute delusion. If millionaires were abolished to-morrow the poor would not be richer; they'd be poorer. Wealth is a matter of confidence. When confidence goes up, wealth increases, and everyone is better off; if confidence were to decrease wealth would decrease, and everyone would be worse off. Fortunately our confidence is on a sound foundation; we have a great country magnificently endowed, a sturdy people, a liberal system of government. No man can foresee the future that lies before us."

Jimmie interrupted. "I'm taking Donald out to capitalize that future a little, Andrew,"[131] he said. "He's going to give confidence another little boost."

"Quite right," Mr. Sutherland agreed. "Good luck, Mr. Strand." He took Donald's hand in his. "If Jimmie can't steer you right, no one can. He's the luckiest man on the market I ever saw. I shouldn't call it luck; it's intuition; sometimes I think it's genius. Good luck!"

Donald was fascinated by the crowds in the brokers' offices. Not only men but women and girls thronged about the boards, the hysteria of sudden wealth in their eyes and voices. Of course he had heard of all this before; even Alder Creek had its little band of speculators, watching the market pages, running up bills for long-distance telephone calls to Winnipeg. He even had made a few careful investments himself,[132] but this was the first time he had seen the actual machinery in motion. Jimmie explained the processes, helped him to understand the abbreviations on the boards, followed with him the charts showing the curves of popular stocks.

"Now, of course, you're of age," Jimmie said after a while, "and I'm not going to urge you. But there are a lot of people getting rich who haven't a tenth part of your intelligence, Donald."

But no urging from Jimmie was necessary. The mob enthusiasm was already engulfing Donald. "Suppose they would take my check?" he asked. "I don't carry an account in Winnipeg, and I brought only enough cash for expenses."

"Of course they will, but I can do better than that. I suggest a couple of hundred shares of—"[133] He indicated a division on the board with a long column of figures below it. "It's active, and it's going up. Opened this morning at four-ninety; last sale at five-fifteen. You can have the purchase charged to my account and if you sell before you go home you can clear it up; otherwise you can send me a check later. Okay?"

Donald nodded, and Jimmie caught the eye of a clerk. "Two hundred for Mr. Donald Strand, of Alder Creek, Manitoba, but put it on my account for the present."

"Very good. Thank you, Mr. Wayne." The clerk made a notation and Jimmie initialed it. They waited a few minutes longer, then went out into the street.

Donald had been making a mental calculation. Two hundred at five-fifteen; why that was over a thousand dollars! By a nod of his chin he had plunged into a debt of a thousand dollars. His insides went suddenly hollow. Suppose the thing went bad; suppose he were to be stuck for a thousand dollars! But he was ashamed[134] to mention his fears to Jimmie. "Just the same, the cows have to be milked," he observed, obliquely.

"Of course they have," Jimmie agreed. "But so has the market, and it yields a lot[135] more cream to the gallon."

From the Wayne lawn Donald was half-way down to the street to meet the boy with the evening *Tribune*.[136] For the first time in his life he plunged straight to the market page. It took him a moment to find the quotation; the long list of figures swam up and down and around about him. But at last—there it was! Five-sixty! That was an advance of forty-five cents—forty-five times two hundred—ninety dollars! He had made ninety dollars that day. More than he paid both Ned and George for a month's labor. And this had been going on for ever so long—for years, perhaps. Certainly the stock market yielded more cream to the gallon.

He began to think his trip to Winnipeg might prove to be a turning-point in his life.

14

The days that followed were filled with interest and action. Ellen took Clara to the stones and to teas and bridges, and gave a tea in her honor;[137] Jimmie made Donald feel at home in his office, introduced him to men prominent in the business and professional life of the city—men whose names he often had seen in the Winnipeg papers; showed him through the Grain Exchange and the Parliament Buildings, where he called even Ministers by their first names, and cajoled him out for an unsuccessful but exhilarating afternoon on the links. Donald, who had played baseball in his boyhood,[138] had no idea that a golf ball could be so elusive and so exasperating; but the open air and the hot sun were familiar to his face; there was something primordial about them, something linked with Sundown Farm and the smell of wheat.[139] When he watched the boards in the brokers, offices, jostled by the milling crowds, it was hard to believe that all this was within one day's drive of his ripening fields, his full-uddered cows, Ned and George sweating in the sun, Mrs. Fetch cheerfully complaining in the kitchen, the intermittent thump of the gasoline engine, and the slow evening with its amber light and its long shadows and its deep silences. Surely these things were a thousand miles away! But out on the golf links they became real and possible again; he had his feet on the earth and the blood coursed steadily through his veins.

It was Sunday night before he had an opportunity to talk with Ellen. It seemed to come about quite accidentally, although he knew she had contrived it. Clara had gone to visit friends in part of the city; Jimmie was to call for her at ten, and Ellen thought she was tired and would just wait on the verandah. "Then I'll stay and keep Ellen company," Donald suggested to Jimmie, making a joke of it. "If I risk my wife with you in the car you should risk yours with me on the verandah."

"I would take the risk if it were twice as great," said Jimmie, somewhat enigmatically.

The depths of the verandah were cool and quiet, with little fingers of light pointing[140] through lattice-work from a street lamp on the corner. Ellen brushed by Donald, leading him to a seat. "We have half an hour, perhaps an hour," she said. By manner as much as by her words he knew the value she set on time. This was their opportunity; make the best of it.

"Happy, Donald?" she asked, cutting right to the core of things.

"Why, yes," he answered. "Yes, of course."

"Why do you say 'of course'? Do you mean that happiness is the natural order of things?"

"Isn't it? You are happy, aren't you?"

She sat in a rocker, and as she swayed slowly with her chair a square[141] of light cut across her face, tracing its white, smooth path along her cheek. But a moment later she was veiled in semi-gloom, and he could not catch the answer in her eyes.

"If you were anybody but you, Donald, I would say yes, of course, just as you did. But you are you. Do you remember when I used to take your lunch to the field and we would sit together in the shade of a stook[142]—can you recapture that feeling, Donald, or has it slipped from you as utterly as it has from me? Oh, people think I am happy. I have a fine home, money to spend, a successful, generous husband—why shouldn't I be happy?"

"Well, why shouldn't you?" he asked, as she seemed to pause for the answer.[143]

She was silent, as though weighing within herself whether she should answer. Finally: "Two reasons, Donald. The first is—no children. Could you be happy without children?"

"When you've no children you don't have to worry about what is to become of them; you don't have the heartaches when they choose their way instead of yours."

She leaned forward and her hand touched his. "You don't mean that, Donald. You don't even think you mean it. Life isn't all having your own way; life is creating, bearing, bringing forth. Who wants an unfruitful tree?"

162

He had a question on his tongue, but he changed it. "What about all those unmarried women in the shops and offices?" he asked. "They seem to be happy."

"But they're not, really. Some of them won't admit it, even to themselves, but they're not. Society is running to all kinds of excesses in trying to forget that it's unhappy. But I want to talk about us, not everybody in general. We gave each other up for the sake of the children we thought would come. In your case the sacrifice, if it was a sacrifice, was justified. But what have I?"

The words rather stunned him. Here was a woman who had everything, and she was saying, What have I?

"Your home, your husband, money to spend," he ventured.

"Don't mock me, Donald."

"Forgive me. I didn't mean—"

"I know. But things are not what they seem. With me, as with you. Of course, we put the best face we can on it. We are too proud to admit defeat. And it *is* defeat, isn't it? We have been close to life; we have grasped at it—and missed. And life has gone streaming by. Do you not often feel that there is something beyond you, just outside your grasp, which you have never reached? And as we grow older we begin to believe that we never shall reach it. We begin to feel that there was a door—or should have been a door —somewhere in the past that would have led us into life, but we failed to find it. And isn't that defeat?"

Donald was uneasy under an attack which so directly and so sincerely challenged his success. Since young manhood he always had thought of himself as a success, and in recent years that belief had been abundantly confirmed. He was the wealthiest farmer in the Alder Creek district. Only since Ellen's letter had a disturbing doubt crept into his mind that he had been using a wrong measuring-stick, and the standards he had found in the city—in Jimmie's success—had deepened that stream of doubt which was eating away at the foundations of all he had thought solid. And here was Jimmie's wife confessing failure for herself, implying failure to him.

"Anyway, Jimmie has been successful," he suggested.

"You think so? He does, too. But some day I expect a tremendous awakening for him. You know this thing," she waved her hand as though to indicate all about her, "this thing he calls success can't go on forever. I don't know why; I can't argue; but it just can't. I suppose it's a woman's intuition. There will be a slip some day; a point at which the circle breaks. I hope he will be able to take the blow when it comes, but he has found what he thinks is success so easily and so continuously I wonder if he will have any anchorage against defeat."

"You. You are good anchorage against any man's defeat," he said, earnestly.

She laid her hand on his. "Thank you. I hope it may be true. I suppose the happy people are those who have never dared to face the truth. Has it ever occurred to you that we are all dupes in a little game played by old Mother Nature, whose only concern is the continuance of the race? We have built around that concern all kinds of superstitions and prohibitions, but what does she care so long as the children come? But when they don't— You will live on in your children, Donald. But I will be through."

The finality of sadness in her last words touched him deeply, even while he recognized threads of Jimmie's argument and wondered if they had discussed the matter together.

"Through?" he said. "Altogether? Do you suppose there is nothing after?"

She was silent for a while; then she answered hesitatingly, questioningly, as though venturing into strange fields and not sure of her way:

"I don't know. Perhaps. Does the butterfly know it was once a worm? And if it doesn't know, what difference does it make? Perhaps we had an existence before we came into this world, but we don't know it; we have no memory that reaches back that far. Perhaps we have an existence after we go out, but if we have no continuing consciousness what difference does it make?"

"But suppose there is a continuing consciousness?" he suggested.

"Ah, that means everything. If only we could[144] be sure! So much that seems wrong might then prove to be right, and so much that seems right we might then know to be wrong." She arose and stood beside his chair; she leaned over and rested her cheek against his. "Oh, Donald, I would claim you then," she whispered, and a moisture touched his face with her breath. "I would claim you now, but I am afraid. Dear, you have always been mine. You were right, but what you feared does not matter now."

Her lips met his, and he was amazed that the ashes in his veins leapt into fire. But even as the flame enveloped them[145] a car stopped before the house and they heard the voices of Jim and Clara. They were laughing and in high spirits. It wasn't like Clara to laugh like that. They were coming up the walk, arm in arm.

"Mustn't let them know," Ellen whispered, as she drew away. "Must never let them know. I have coaxed him into the Mediterranean trip, hoping to break up—something I can't tell you about. Hello, you folks!" she called aloud. "Had a good time?"

"Never better," Jimmie answered, and led Clara into the house. Later he had an opportunity to whisper to his wife: "Clara took a chance on a cocktail and it fussed her up a bit. Do her good. Wake her up."

Donald went into the country to see a combine. Crops in the Red River Valley ripened earlier than those on the higher land at Alder Creek, and he had an opportunity to see the machine at work. But in spite of all the persuasiveness of the salesman who accompanied him, he did not buy.[146]

"Perhaps next year," Donald suggested, and that was as far as he would go. There was just the possibility the combine would not work under all conditions, and he was too shrewd to let his Alder Creek neighbors, by any chance, have the laugh on him. Besides, he had begun to think he might use the money to better advantage. His stock that morning was selling at six-ten.

15[147]

Both Donald and Clara found so much to interest them in the city that they stayed[148] longer than they had intended, but a note from Walter saying the harvest was ripening forced them to reluctant action.[149] Before leaving, Donald paid a final visit[150] to Jimmie in his office.

"Thought I'd drop in and sort of square things up," he said. "Guess we'll have to hit the trail to-morrow."

"What things?" Jimmie asked,[151] a puzzled expression stealing over his broad face.

"About the stock. The shares you bought for me."

"Oh, that. I thought you were going to offer to pay for your board, or some such deadly insult. Here, square this up first," and he extended his box of cigars.

"Now about your shares. To-day's quotation is six-fifty. You bought at—what was it?—five-fifteen. That's a dollar thirty-five a share—two hundred shares—two hundred and seventy dollars. Of course there will be a small charge for brokerage and interest, but you should net at least two hundred and fifty dollars. Not so bad for a holiday?"

Donald's smile answered him. "I should say it's not too bad. I am indebted to you, Jim."

"Not at all. But now what do you want to do? You can sell your shares, pocket your profits, and go home. Or you can leave them and speculate on a further rise. Or you can convert your equity into margin for some other stock."

Donald hesitated a moment. "I don't particularly need the money," he said, "but I'm green at this game, and you're a busy man—"

"Don't say another word. If I can help you I'm only too glad, and there will be no legal fees, either. They will be written off against an

166

old friendship account I have. I suggest that you sell these shares and re-invest the proceeds. If you would like to put in a little more capital of course it would count up quicker. How are you fixed?"

"I have a couple of thousand in the bank at Alder Creek," Donald answered, hesitatingly. He always had regarded his own affairs as extremely confidential; it was an effort to him to reveal this much, even to Jimmie Wayne. In their talk that first night he had dealt in generalities. "And there will be some expense in taking off the crop before I turn it into cash," he continued. "Of course, I could get more at the bank. My credit is good at Alder Creek."

"I am sure of that.[152] But you give me an idea. Why disturb your bank account at all? I can arrange a loan for you here.[153] Be glad to do so. Will endorse your note, if necessary."

Donald was embarrassed. There seemed no limit to his old friend's willingness to help. "I've never asked a man to back my note in my life, Jim," he said, "and I'm not going to start now."

"You haven't asked me. I'm asking you. It's not as though I were taking any chance. I know you are as well worth, say, five thousand dollars as you are fifty cents. If you are squeamish about it you can leave the stock account in my name, and I will pay the bank out of the proceeds whenever it may be desirable to do so."

Donald demurred about a sum so large as five thousand dollars but Jimmie assured him that is what banks are for, and five thousand would count up twice as fast as twenty-five hundred. "In fact," he added, "if I were you[154] I'd make it ten, but perhaps it's just as well to start in a small way and let you find your feet."

There was an interview with a banker, and Donald was surprised how readily a trifling loan of five thousand dollars could be arranged—when Jimmie Wayne offered to sign the three months' note. Then there was a study of the stock lists, a selection of investments, and the orders were placed.

"I can't tell you how much I owe you, Jimmie," Donald said, when the business was completed. "I don't know who else would take such a chance on me." His eyes were moist with emotion.

"Chance nothing! There's no chance about it. The market is going up every day, and neither you nor I will ever have to put up a dollar of that money. That's the way fortunes are made, Donald; using someone else's capital. And while you are comfortably off already you are now on the way to bigger things. In more ways than one."

There was a stress on the last words that arrested Donald's attention. "'In more ways than one?' What do you mean?"

Jimmie piloted him along the street and back to his office before he volunteered an answer. Not until they were alone together did he speak:

"Ever think you'd like to represent your constituency in Parliament?" he asked.

Donald's new cigar wobbled with his surprise. "Who—me? Never thought of such a thing."

"Then think of it now."

Donald's astonishment[155] found relief in laughter. "Quit kidding me, Jim. I know my limitations."

But Jimmie was very much in earnest. "That's just where you're wrong, Donald. You *don't* know your limitations. You think you do, but you don't. You are drawing altogether too small a circle around your ambitions. And I'm calling you as our candidate in the next federal elections."

"But I've had no experience," Donald protested. "Oh, the municipal council, you know, but no real public life. I'd be all at sea."

"You're all the better without experience. You have no past to explain. And you have just about everything that goes with a winning candidate. You have grown up with the country; you are a successful farmer; you have sufficient education to get by with the English language, and—I don,t mean to flatter you—you have a sturdy, he-man appearance which won't do you any harm, especially with the women voters. Remember about half the votes are cast by women. Now women just get fed up on political arguments, but there are certain fundamental instincts which can always be trusted."

"You are not[156] trying to tell me I'm a ladies' man?" Donald interrupted, his masculine vanity tickled by the suggestion.[157] "It's the first time that's ever been laid against me."

"Well, it may not be the last. I said you put too small a circle around your ambitions. But to get back to business: Of course I haven't the whole say-so, but I have some, and I have friends who have more. If I press your name it has a chance of being accepted. True, you would still have to be elected, but the first step, the really big step, is to get the nomination. About the only way we can carry the field next time is to have an honest-to-God farmer as our standard-bearer, and you look like it. I think you can almost take it as settled."

Donald sat for some moments in silence. Visions of his suddenly enlarged circle were whirling through his head. After the first shock of the unexpected there really did seem no reason why he should not make a good candidate. His mind even leapt the distance to Ottawa, not far from his childhood home. There would be some satisfaction in going back as Member of Parliament. That was another expression of Success. He supposed he would be pretty green at first, but some one would guide him through. There must be some way of doing those things.

"You see," Jimmie resumed, "that is one of the reasons I wanted you to get into the market while the getting is good. Some easy money will come in handy in the fight, and afterwards. Oh"—to Donald's rising eyebrows—"everything on the square, of course. There are plenty of legitimate ways to spend money.[158] Perfectly legitimate. And if you give your life in public service, why shouldn't you have something in return? I'm taking it that I have your consent. He closed Donald's hand in his own chubby fist, and for a moment the two men held each other in a grip of recaptured friendship and confidence.

16

Sundown farm seemed strangely changed after the visit to Winnipeg. Donald could not analyze the change, but he knew that something subtle and mischievous had happened. For one thing, he always had[159] taken great pride in his house, the largest and finest farm home in the whole Alder Creek district. Now it offended him. There it sat in its box-like, angular rigidity, stubborn and unreceptive. It was a stupid house. Its square,[160] hard rooms affronted him. He had a feeling that something was missing, something gone, and yet he knew it never had been there. Something was gone, too, from within himself; he had a lonely, empty feeling as he sat in his office trying to restore his pride, fingering the ribbons won by Sundown Chieftain II, holding in his hands the silver cup awarded by the Better Farming Competition. It's gold-lined bowl was no emptier than he. Even the Chieftain, with his well-kept hide shining in the sunlight, failed to restore that old sense of achievement which had been his greatest[161] delight. He would walk in his fields, depressed by the premature ripening of his crops and the havoc wrought by grasshoppers, and blame his mood on these two causes. Then he would go back to his office and re-calculate his assets, making allowance for the disappointing harvest. The sum was substantially the same; the sum which had given him so much satisfaction until that fateful letter of Ellen's had resulted in the recasting of his whole sense of values.

Thought of Ellen—and she was forever in his thoughts—worked within him a strange compound of happiness and disappointment. He could not explain[162] the emptiness of his heart, but he knew that Ellen would fill it. He could not visualize the architectural changes that would soften his house, but he knew that Ellen would soften it. He did not know where he had lost the old rapture he once had felt in the possession of his broad fields, but he knew that with Ellen's help he could re-discover it. And yet Ellen he could not command. In spite of all Jimmie's modern theories, that way lay destruction.

It was fortunate that the rush of harvest swept him into its vortex. He put Walter on the tractor, hitched the two binders behind, and engaged extra men for the stooking. While he no longer planned to do personally[163] any large amount of physical labor, he was busy early and late superintending operations and maintaining a constant stream of supplies. He felt that had it been a good crop his old enthusiasm would have come back; even as it was he re-captured it to some extent. As Walter's tractor went surging by, perforating the air with its staccato punctures, and the sheaves bounced on the carriers, and the drive-chains sang in the heat, and the smell of warm oil and wheat-dust mingled in his nostrils, he again felt himself to be a man of destiny. Like a memory out of some half-forgotten dream came the suggestion[164] that he was to be a Member of Parliament and that wealth beyond any earlier imaginings might yet be his. Then he would tramp through his stubbled fields, his lungs full again. What though everything so far had been failure—comparatively; he would show them yet! He was barely fifty; he was strong and sound in wind and limb, and he had got a new vision of Success. He would show them yet. A new way had opened before him and in it he would walk boldly.

That new way divided his heart. Even in the heat of harvest he would come in from the fields in mid-afternoon when he saw the mail-man go by, and plunge to the market page in the morning paper. Then he would sit in his office[165] and figure his profits. Jimmie had been a good guide; his stocks were well selected; the market still was going up. He hardly could believe the result of his reckonings. Even with the crop a comparative failure this was going to be the most profitable year he ever had known. He would study his rows of figures until in some way they seemed to transcribe a happiness into his soul; then he would take out his box of ten-cent cigars and smoke one with luxurious deliberation. "Not eight dollars a box," he would say to himself. "Not eight dollars—yet. But some day. Some day."

Donald told Clara no more about his investments than seemed[166] necessary. It was not his practice to discuss his financial affairs with

171

her in any detail. He had long ago learned that if he went to Clara in the glow of some new financial success it was but the signal for a demand for fresh expenditures upon the house or upon her person. She had the gift of cooling his enthusiasm under the douche of some new extravagance. Clara believed that money was made to be spent, as food was made to be eaten, being extinguished in the process; Donald believed that it was made to be planted, to grow, and to multiply. Their theories were irreconcilable, so he satisfied his conscience by providing her with what he considered a liberal amount, and kept his business to himself.[167]

Jimmie Wayne made weekly reports, all in concise and business-like[168] form, showing the progress of Donald's investments, usually with a congratulatory line or two at the bottom. "Old man," he wrote on one occasion, "you'll break into the hundred-thousand class before you know it." Another time: "About that other matter, everything is moving smoothly to the desired end. I have discussed it with two or three who have a good deal to say, and they are with us. We'll spring a publicity drive for you at the right moment, and I think it's as good as settled." Jimmie also made generous, and, as it seemed to Donald, extravagant use of the long-distance telephone. Often he was called from the fields to hear a report on some new market development or to give his assent to some switch in investment. To all suggestions Donald had one answer: "Use your judgment, Jimmie. You know more about this game than I do."

The signal announcing a telephone call was a flag flown from the house. In answering such a signal one day Donald, instead of going in by the back door as was his custom, for some trivial reason went around the front. His course led him by the open window of his office, through which he was surprised to hear Clara's voice in conversation. He paused, thinking one of the neighbors might have called, but there was a quality in his wife's tones[169] which stirred something reminiscent, reaching far into the past. "Of course I do. . . . Don't be silly. . . . No, I haven't mentioned it. I'm afraid Jimmie. He wouldn't understand. . . ."

Donald thumped in over the verandah. Clara met him in the hall, a picture of composure, although there was a heightened color in her cheeks. "Winnipeg is calling you," she said.

"Who wouldn't understand what?" he demanded, facing her abruptly.

Her hesitation was for only a split second. "Oh, you heard? I was chatting with Jimmie. I thought while the line was being held I might as well use it. He wondered if I could persuade you to join them on the Mediterranean trip." Her composure was almost overdone.

"And you thought I wouldn't understand that?"

"I meant that you would hardly agree to spend that much money on a trip. Of course, if you think you would—"

For a moment he held her with his eye, but she returned his gaze, smiling and unafraid. "No, I wouldn't," he said, and walked to his telephone.

Jimmie had heard of an impending split in a popular stock and recommended it for investment. Nothing was said about the Mediterranean.

17

Donald turned the incident over in his mind as he walked to his work, the forest of stubble crumpling under his farm boots at every step. It wasn't so much what Clara had said as the voice in which she said it. He had no objection to her chatting with Jimmie; certainly he had no objection to that. But there was something more, and her studied composure could not throw him off the track. Jimmie had said to him not a word about the trip to the Mediterranean; had not even mentioned that he had been talking with Clara. Donald wondered why he himself had let the opportunity pass; why he had not said, "Clara tells me you have been talking with her about your trip and that you would like us to go with you." If Clara had manufactured the story that would have taken him by surprise, and even a quick-witted lawyer might have been guilty of the momentary hesitation that would have convicted her. But he had let the moment pass and it hardly could be recalled now.

He sat down in the shade of a stook and tried to think clearly. What did it all mean? There must be one of only two explanations; either Clara's conversation with Jimmie was innocent chatter or it was something which he could not bring himself to face. He recalled now how they had seemed to seek each other's company on more than one occasion during the recent visit in the city; he had not noticed it at the time, being absorbed in the opportunity of having Ellen to himself. A twitch ran through his being at the implications of that thought.[170]

He wished he could talk with Ellen. Ellen was so sensible and so wise, she would know what to say. But[171] here was something he couldn't tell, even to Ellen; perhaps least of all to Ellen. It concerned his wife and her husband. Here was something touching his honor. If there was a wound it was too deep and vital to be revealed. Yet Ellen's presence would soothe and steady him. He recalled the touch of her hand, the cool fire that flowed from her lips—

He sprang up from his shelter, confused and baffled. The sun was swinging well to the west; the shadows of the stooks were stretching[172] eastward across the stubble. From a distant part of the field came the coughing of the tractor;[173] the clatter of the binders was cushioned in the deep hedge of wheat that almost hid them from view. Well—here was work to his hand. Life was too complex to be understood. Emotions one had neither sought nor desired sometimes caught one in the current and swept him out to sea. But not always out to sea. If one were sensible he stayed near the shore. . . .

He tramped across the field to where fresh-cut sheaves were lying in the stubble and began setting them up in stooks. The stride and swing came easily to him and as he worked he quickened his pace, planting the butts with an almost vicious thrust, dropping the surrounding sheaves into position with machine-like rapidity; striding on to the next. The sun sank beyond the rim of the world like a golden coin into a slot; the air turned quickly cooler; grey night stole up from the east, but overhead the sky was mauve and to the westward all was lemon-colored. Sustained labor brought a measure of peace to his soul, and peace made possible the shaping of a policy in his mind. He would wait—he would wait. Perhaps it all would dissolve like a mist. If not, when the time came to act, he would act. But not now. He would wait. He would pretend it never had been. But he would watch; he would see; they should not take him unawares.[174]

The sound of footsteps in the stubble recalled him to time and place.[175] He looked up to see Walter approaching through the twilight.

"Well, Dad, have you bust your balance-wheel?" Walter's voice was cheerful and assured, the voice of man to man.[176] "Or just showing us young bloods there's life in the old horse yet? Showing us how they used to do it, when you and the world were young?"

"Yes, for a dollar a day," Donald answered, straightening his back and pressing his hands against his kidneys. "Now I pay four for men that quit at six."

"And you make more money than when you paid a dollar," Walter answered.

"Not out of this year's crop, I won't." Then, feeling that some kind of explanation was needed: "Just got the notion to try my hand again, and I guess I didn't know when to stop."

"You never did, Dad," Walter told him. "Come on. Mother's wondering what's got into you."

Walter took his father by the arm and together they picked their way through the stooks, vague and silent in the closing night. Donald felt the tight grip of his son's arm; it was strong and reassuring. He had Walter. Whatever came, he had Walter. And, whatever came, Walter must never know.

18

Clara's concern in sending Walter to bring him from the field was something of a development; and when Donald came in to his late supper she served it with her own hands,[177] relieving Mrs. Fetch of that duty, to the good woman's mingled surprise and annoyance.

"You shouldn't work so hard, Donald," she said. "You're not as young as you used to be."

It was strange to hear Clara chiding him for overwork. He could not recall when she had objected to his working unless she required his time for some other purpose. "Oh, it won't hurt me," he answered. "Have to show these young fellows once in awhile what a real day's work looks like."

Clara made one or two attempts to lead him into conversation, but Donald was too tired or too moody for easy speech. He finished his meal in silence and soon after went to bed.[178]

Donald's policy of watching yielded nothing. If Clara had been indiscreet she either was indiscreet no longer or more cunning in her indiscretions. Donald saw nothing, heard nothing, amiss. Indeed, Clara seemed to soften somewhat toward him.[179]

September blended into October with no more shock than the tearing of a leaf from the calendar, but the days were shorter, the mornings carried a nip of frost, the fields took on a sere and empty appearance. Through the morning air would come the bark of a tractor driving a thresher miles away. It recalled to Donald his boyhood when through the October mornings had come the crescendo whine of the horse-power. Those were the days when threshing-time meant the feeding and lodging of many men and teams, and slavish work for the women of the household. Now Clara hardly knew when the thresher was on the farm, and Mrs. Fetch grumbled early and late about the two extra men engaged for harvest. Later the steam engine had crowded the horsepower out of the scene and had supplanted the whine of gears with a shrill whistle and the patter of its exhaust. And now the steam engine also had gone, except for isolated cases where good management or good fortune had saved it from the scrap-heap, and gasoline power had come into undisputed control, even to the hauling of the wheat in gasoline trucks to the elevators where gasoline engines hoisted it into bins or waiting freight-cars.

Donald reflected that in his own lifetime all these changes had come about, and he counted himself still a young man—at least, not old.[180]

Day by day his stocks were moving up. He was almost afraid to reckon his profits. Sometimes he felt like telephoning Jimmie to sell out, clean everything up, make sure of these fabulous figures which looked so impossible on paper. He had hinted that once or twice, and Jimmie had laughed and asked if he was losing his nerve. "Why, we haven't started yet," Jimmie would say.[181]

Meanwhile a new tenderness, or a revival of the old tenderness, seemed to have taken possession of Clara.

19[182]

It was perhaps well for Donald that the reawakening of his wife's love loomed large in his life at this period, for the long succession of favorable reports from Jimmie Wayne suffered an interruption. Monday's mail brought a statement which showed no net improvement over the previous week. Donald studied it carefully in his office, making figures on the back of a calendar pad. True, there was still a handsome profit, although[183] some of the stocks actually were down from the previous report. This was something which never before had happened[184]. But Jimmie's accompanying letter was reassuring. "There has been some weakness in the market," he wrote, "but don't let that disturb you. Some of the nervous ones have been letting go, the profit-takers have been cashing in[185], and the short interests in New York have jumped in with[186] a series of bear raids. It's only temporary; it can't be more than that; everything is fundamentally sound; the country never was so prosperous; I expect by next week to have good news for you again."

Donald tried to respond to the optimistic note in Jimmie's letter. He assured himself that all was well, but underneath the assurance lay a disturbing doubt. Jimmie had said the country never was so prosperous, but Donald reflected that the price of wheat had dropped eight cents since September[187]. His native caution urged him to sell, but he found it hard to act against Jimmie's advice, which might easily deepen into ridicule. Still, it was his name that was on the note at the bank, and surely he could express an opinion. He called Jimmie on the telephone.

"How's the market?" he asked, when they had exchanged greetings. There was an uncontrollable tremor in his voice, and his heart was thumping. He hoped Jimmie could not hear it.

"It's steadying down", came the answer. "Not much change to-day; I guess the scare-cats have all scurried to cover. It beats the devil[188] how little confidence some people have in their own country. Here we're sitting on the top of the world, and just because some bogey-man in New York says 'Boo' shares are flung on the market like they were infected with smallpox. I only wish I had the money to jump in now and take on a real load, but I've been running pretty close to the wind[189] and my hands are tied for the moment."

Donald hesitated, and the wire hummed emptily. How could he say "Sell" in the face of such an indictment? How could he classify with the scare-cats? And how set up his judgment against Jimmie's? Yet it was *his* risk.

"I was wondering if it might be a good idea to unload a little, just to be on the safe side," he ventured. "Of course, I trust your judgment, but if we were to sell a bit we could strengthen the margins all 'round."

It was Jimmie's turn to hold the wire empty for a moment. "If you say sell I'll sell," he said at length, "but I'm not afraid—not a bit. I'm in hourly touch with the best brokers in the city, and they assure me it's only a temporary waver. Why, they're looking for International Nickel to go to a hundred, and you'd sell to-day at forty-nine and a half! I can't see it, Don, but you're the doctor. By the way, that other business is lining up all right. I've got you sold to the Powers that Be, and I think you're going to find yourself in politics—and Parliament —before you know it. Of course, you're not the only one who's mak-ing easy money these days. Farmers all over the country are into the market up to the neck, and some of them won't have to be prodded to put their best foot forward. If you don't want it there are plenty to take your place, but I'm banking on you, and I want you to make a bigger pot of money than any of them, for, after all, money means success. What do you say?"

The picture, so artfully suggested that it did not seem to be art at all, floated before Donald's vision as he leaned against the telephone on his office wall. Through the window he caught a glimpse of Ned and George plowing in the stubble—his act of faith against the coming year. And success was very dear to him. People would say, "That's

Donald Strand; you know, the new Member from Alder Creek." Bank Manager Goad would say to Tom, "Talk about farming! Look at your father's balance. You guessed wrong that time, my boy." At the church they would make way for him[190] and he would know by their covetous glances —

"Well, what do you say?" Jimmie broke in. Tell you what I'll do. If the market slips to-morrow I'll sell ten percent of your holdings. Ten percent every day it slips, and buy ten every day it goes up. Is it a bargain?"

"It's a bargain," said Donald.

Tuesday[191] Jimmie called him. "Market's stronger to-day," he reported, friendly triumph in his voice. "I was sure a little fright couldn't hold it back. According to our agreement I should have bought for you to-day, but the margin is so thin I thought it better to strengthen it a little. Okay?"

"Okay," Donald answered him. A weight seemed to be lifted off his chest. He came upon Clara in the living-room and drew her face to his a moment as they passed. This new love, more wonderful than the old! And he had not told her how rapidly he was becoming rich, or that Jimmie expected to get the nomination for him at the next election. After all, these were secondary things, but valuable to pour into the lap of the wife who loved him. What experience, what contemplation, what conclusion, he wondered, had so suddenly reversed her attitude toward him? It would be idle to pursue that question. Enough to drink the glass that was placed to his lips.

20

Donald was reading his farm paper in his little office Wednesday afternoon, when his number was rung on the telephone. "Winnipeg calling you, Mr. Strand," said the Alder Creek operator. "Just a moment, please."

"All right, Bessie," Donald answered, in cheerful mood. "Take your time."

"I'll get you through in a minute," the girl answered. "Tremendous pressure on the lines to-day. Something doing in the market. But I guess[192] you're all right, Mr. Strand. You're too clever to be caught."

It was the friendly remark of a neighbor's daughter whom he had known since childhood, but something in it chilled Donald's blood and set the hair twitching at the base of his skull.

The next moment Jimmie Wayne's voice burst through. "Hello, Donald? That you, Donald Strand?"

Donald's hand was shaking with the receiver. "Yes, Jim. What's the trouble?"

Jimmie's voice was steadier. "Don't mean to alarm you, Don. Market's had another sinking spell. Bad enough. We'll need every dollar of securities we can rustle. Must protect our holdings. Day or two—it'll be all right again. Everybody says it'll be all right again. I'm throwing everything I've got into it. what time is it?—two thirty. I've been trying to get you for two hours. Wires jammed. You've just time to get to Alder Creek before the bank closes. Get all your securities and drive in here to-night. Let Walter come—he can drive. Everything. Come straight to the office. I'll be here, no matter how late. It's life and death, Don; we've got to protect our account in the morning or be sold out. Can't talk longer now—everybody calling—rushing—see you later."

There was a click at the other end of the line, and Donald found himself hanging weakly to the empty receiver. For a moment he stood as one dazed, his knees threatening to fail under the dead weight of his body. But it was only for a moment. The situation called for action —immediate action.

"What's wrong, Donald?" Clara exclaimed, as he came into the living-room. His face was grey; the lines about his mouth had deepened; he placed his hand upon the back of a chair. Clara sprang to his side. "What's wrong, Donald?" she repeated. "Is anybody hurt?"

"Not badly," he answered, trying to reassure her. "Jimmie's in a jam. I'll have to go to Winnipeg at once."

"Oh!" Clara's eyes had grown big and round; fear lept in their deep recesses. "He's not hurt? He's not badly hurt?" she pleaded.

"Not physically—financially." Hardness had crept into his voice. He resented her too great[193] concern. "I must leave at once—must get to the bank before they close. Where's Walter?"

"Somewhere about. Let me go with you. Donald, I must go with you!"

"No. Not this time. You couldn't help. Get Walter, and throw some things together. He'll have to go, to drive."

For a moment their eyes met, and she bowed to the stronger will. Mrs. Fetch was sent scurrying for Walter, while Clara hurried upstairs to throw night clothes and shaving things into a grip.

"What's the matter, Donald?" Aunt Annie asked, hurrying out from her room with a step surprisingly easy for her years. "What's the matter?"[194]

In a few words he told her[195].

"You need money? I have a little in the bank. I have been saving the rent from the cottage; never spent a cent of it, Donald, to provide for my last sickness, and burial." She hurried to her room and in a moment returned with a bank book. "There's six hundred dollars," she said, thrusting the book into his hands. "Will you need a check?"

For a moment he held the little red book. It blurred and swam before his eyes[196]. "No, Auntie," he said. "I couldn't take that."

"It isn't much, but it will help," she urged. But he pressed the book into her palm. "Keep it. You may need it," he said.

Walter appeared from somewhere. "What's up, Dad?" he asked, concern in his eyes.

"Market trouble. We've got to get to Alder Creek before the bank closes, and to Winnipeg to-night. I want you to drive. Pull the car out—your mother is getting your things."

As they swung down the driveway to the road Donald looked at his watch. "You've got eight minutes," he said.

"Easy," Walter answered, taking the turn onto the highway on two wheels.

The hard gravelled road, rutted with October traffic, wound under them like a fast-flying belt. A car going the same way loomed ahead. The distance between them shortened momentarily.

"It's Fred Hardy—and his Dad," Walter said, as they drew nearer. "Fred boasts that no car ever passes him on the highway."

"One will to-day, Walter. Step on it."

It was the order the boy wanted. His father's restrictions had made him eat Fred Hardy's dust on many a bitter occasion. The Strand car lept forward and with a roar of horn and exhaust[197] surged by its rival, showering it with gravel as it passed.

"Tom would let you in, anyway," Walter remarked, without lessening his speed.

"I know. But my securities are in the vault, and if it should be locked—I don't know whether they have a time lock, or not. But we'll make it easily." The elevators of Alder Creek were rising rapidly before them.

"Good driving, Walter," Donald commended, as they drew up among the cars parked in front of the bank. "Just four minutes."

"I could shave that if I had to," the boy[198] answered, flushed with his speed and his father's praise. "Go on in, Dad, and I'll fill up with oil and gas."

Donald found an unusual number of customers for a midweek afternoon in the corridor of the bank. They were neighbors and business men who greeted him respectfully[199], but all too intent upon their affairs for conversation. He edged his way to Tom. The boy was pale, as from overwork, and his hand trembled on his ledger.

"I want to get my papers, Tom," he said, as quietly as he could.

"Walter and I are driving in to Winnipeg with them to-night."

Tom beckoned him through a gate in the counter. "Are you caught, too?" he asked, as he found the package of papers sealed and labelled with his father's name. "I didn't know you were in—deep. Look at all these people. Drawing their last dollar. But I didn't know you were in? Your checks have not been going through here?"

"Jimmie Wayne was handling it for me in Winnipeg," Donald answered. "I'll have to help him out for a few days, but he says he's sure it will be all right."

A look of relief came over Tom's face. "I hope he knows," he said. "It's pathetic—I mean, all this." His glance indicated the anxious line before the wickets. "They're covering up as far as they can, but some of them can't cover. I hope you're all right, Dad."

Donald took a second look at his firstborn. The gulf that had separated them was closing.

"Want to draw your cash, Dad?"

"I guess so. Make a check and I'll sign it."

Tom went to prepare the check, and Mr. Goad paused at Donald's side. "Lucky you are not in this, Mr. Strand," he said. "You're too wise to be caught."

Donald checked an impulse to correct him. After all, it was none of Goad's affairs.

"I suppose bank regulations are all that kept *me* out," Goad continued. "There's always something to be thankful for. What goes up must come down, but a lot of people wouldn't believe it."

Tom returned with the check, and Donald signed it on the counter. "Seventeen hundred and forty-eight dollars and forty cents," he read. "That cleans me out?"

"I drew it for the amount of your balance as shown in the ledger. Perhaps you won't need it, and you can re-deposit it when you come back."

"I hope so," Donald said. "This makes it hard on you boys in the bank, Tom. You look all in."

Tom shook his head, as though to throw off the signs of weariness. "It isn't the work," he said. "It's—it's—the whole damnable business!"

185

Donald caught his hand in his and for a moment held it tight. This was no time to talk about the farm and mistakes that couldn't be helped.

"Safe trip, Dad," said Tom. "And back. Maybe things won't be[200] so bad. Perhaps the market will pick up to-morrow."

"I hope so," Donald answered, fervently.

21

Darkness had long fallen[201] when they rolled through the wide and brightly-lighted[202] streets of Winnipeg. Donald guided his driver to the tall office building which housed the firm of Wayne and Sutherland. Lights were still burning in many windows; people were coming and going through the revolving doors.

"I suppose you can park here," Donald suggested. "Better come and wait for me. No saying how long I may be."

In a few moments they found themselves in the outer offices of Wayne & Sutherland. The warmth of the building was comforting after their cold drive[203]. Through glass partitions they could see clerks at work over their desks.

"Mr. Wayne is very busy," said the young man who came to wait on them. "He cannot see anyone before morning."

"He can see me," Donald answered, mastering a desire to sweep this trifling obstacle out of the way. "Tell him it's Donald Strand, from Alder Creek."

The clerk departed and was back in a moment, his attitude of obstruction suddenly changed to one of almost eager welcome. "Come this way, Mr. Strand. Mr. Wayne will see you at once."

"You bet he will," Donald answered. "Come along, Walter; you may as well be in on this."

They found Jimmie in that private office where Donald and he had sat together one morning about two months before. He was alone. Masses of papers were piled on his desk. His round face seemed to have shrunk; shadows lay across his eyes. He did not rise, but beckoned Donald to a chair beside his desk. Then, noticing Walter: "Ah Walter. A heavy drive for you. Take off your things and rest while I talk with your father."

He turned his eyes toward Donald, and, without speaking further, reached into his desk and produced a bottle and glasses.

"I know you don't take it, usually," he said, "but a drink will do you no harm after your drive. You may need a bracer."

Donald hesitated. "Well, just a spoonful."

The liquor sent fire rioting in his unaccustomed veins, but his head remained steady[204].

"Well?" said Donald.

"The pincers have closed on us," Jimmie answered. He locked his fingers and drew his palms together, unconsciously illustrating his figure of speech. "But not us only. We're not alone. They're burning midnight current all over the city."

"That won't help us any, as far as I can see," said Donald. On his long and silent trip resentment had gradually welled within him against the man who had led him into this situation, and he mixed no honey with his words. "Where do we get off at?"

Jimmie eyed him from across his desk. "You can't take a licking, Donald, eh?"

"I've never had to. No man has ever licked me at my own game. Can you say as much?"

Jimmie's voice went through the motions of laughter. Then suddenly his thick fist came down on the table. "Yes, by God, I've never been licked, and I'm not licked yet. Glad to see you've got fight in you, Donald, even if you do turn your guns on me for the moment. I might hold the line myself, but your reinforcement makes it a cinch. Now I guess you don't need any lengthy explanation. Your stocks and mine are all carried in the brokers' accounts in my name. That was how we started, and, for convenience in handling, it was never changed. In my own accounts they have been kept scrupulously separate, as you know from my weekly statements. But so far as the brokers are concerned, they can't be segregated now. We have to stand or fall together. The slip in the market has narrowed, and in some cases, obliterated our margin. We have to deposit cash or securities tomorrow morning[205] to protect that margin, or our stocks will be sold. A good many, I am afraid, will not be able to protect their accounts, which means that there will be a lot of distress selling, and the market will go lower under that pressure. Which will call for more margin. But as soon as the distress is relieved the market will bulge[206] up again. We're like two men pushing a cart up a hill. We're almost at the top. If we let go now the whole thing will go crashing to the bottom, but if we can put just a little more weight behind it we'll be up and on Easy Street, which, as you know, lies at the top of the hill. I've got these securities gathered together." He indicated a bundle of papers at his hand. "Everything from my life insurance to the deed of my house. That's what I'm putting in. Now what is your contribution? Use your own judgment, Donald. I got you into this, and it's not for me to say. If you want to stay out, stay out. If I go down you'll lose your five thousand, but you'll soon get over that. If I survive, you'll get whatever your share may be. Now shall we sink or swim together, or do you prefer to strike for the shore?"

Donald took a large sealed package from his coat pocket. He broke the seal and counted out a number of Dominion and provincial bonds, some good industrials, some fully-paid common and preferred stocks. When he came to the deed of his farm he held it for a moment suspended in his fingers, then laid it to one side.

"That doesn't go?" There was a rasp of challenge in Jimmie's voice.

"That doesn't go," Donald answered, firmly.

"I'm putting in my house."

"That's different. Your stocks paid for your house. My farm paid for my stocks. That's putting it broadly. But the farm has never let me down, and I'm not going to let it down now. It will be no pawn in this gamblers' game."

Jimmie's eyes softened a little. "Very well," he said.

"And the life insurance doesn't go, either," Donald continued. "It's not very much, but I bought it to protect my family, and it doesn't go."

"Very well," Jimmie agreed, without argument. He knew human nature well enough to recognize a stone wall without butting his head against it. "This stuff you have is gilt-edged, worth almost dollar for dollar. Along with mine it will carry us over the top. And don't kiss it good-bye. You may think you're casting your bread on the waters, but it'll come back—it'll come back, buttered."

189

"I hope so," Donald said. He was breathing easier now, and was even prepared to see some light through the gloom. There was no doubt, at any rate, about his partner's sincerity, and something of his old liking for Jimmie began to revive within him.

"Sorry I was a bit blunt, Jim," he said. "I haven't got the polish of you city fellows."

"Polish? If you were polished, Donald, you'd be polished granite."

"You think I'm as hard as that?"

"I wasn't thinking of hardness. I was thinking of solidity. A good thing to tie to. Never mind, old man; we'll make the grade, and some day we'll talk about this night, and laugh as we talk. Take another nip, just to steady you?"

"No thanks, Jimmie. It would have the opposite effect."

"Well, excuse me." He poured himself a stiff drink and downed it at a draught. "I know I take too much," he apologized, "but in a pinch like this it sees me through. Leave it alone, Walter. Your Dad rides through without it, but I can't—not now.

"You know, Donald," he continued after a moment. "I never thought it would come to this. Sinking spells, of course, I expected them; but this is more than a sinking spell. This is a submersion, and a lot of people will never come up. Members of my staff; clerks, stenographers—cleaned out." He wiped one palm graphically across the other. "They've been around my desk all day, pleading, weeping, threatening, cursing. Clients, too—asking what to do. What do you do when an earthquake shakes your buildings to the ground, or a tidal wave engulfs them? I'm supposed to know. Well, I don't know. Still,[207] I'm sure everything is basically sound, and those who can weather the storm will find themselves sitting on the top of the world."

But Donald's thoughts had swung from the market crisis to another peril which lay like a cloud across the horizon of his life. He had meant, with the same direct bluntness which characterized his business dealing, to learn from Jimmie the truth about Clara. If there was anything between them he meant to know it. But that purpose had slipped his mind when he asked Walter to come in with him, and the subject could not be discussed in his presence.

Thoughts of Clara brought Ellen into his consciousness. "Does Ellen know?" he asked.

"No. That is, of course she knows about the break in the market, but she doesn't know how hard I'm hit. I haven't been home since morning; I let her think I'm looking after the business of clients in distress. You and Walter will spend the night with us. We may as well go now."[208]

Jimmie placed Donald's securities with his own and locked them in his dispatch bag[209]. "We'll take these home with us," he said. "Save coming back here first thing in the morning."

Ellen met them in the living-room. A fire was glowing in the grate; luxury lay about her, but Donald thought she had grown Whiter since he saw her in August.

She extended both hands. "Glad to see you, Donald, but sorry for these business disturbances. I hope you are not much hit."

"A mere scratch," Donald assured her. "And a little blood-letting will do me good. Think I was running a bit of pressure, anyway."

The grip of her fingers tightened. "I'm glad it is not serious with you," she said. "And Walter! Why, a young man, now. How the years do go! I hope you're as good as you look, Walter."

"Oh, that would be expecting too much of me, Aunt Ellen," Walter answered, with a laugh that disarmed his words of all conceit. "I know you're not really my aunt, but I always think of you that way. You don't mind, do you?"

"Mind?" She caught the boy's cheeks between her hands and pressed a kiss against his face. "That's how much I mind!"

"Now I suppose you are all starving?" Ellen said, briskly. "I've a salad and some cold chicken, and cheese and biscuits and coffee. Tell me about Clara and Tom." She led Donald into the dining-room.

Donald and Walter were given twin beds in a large room. As Donald undressed a problem in behavior took shape in his mind. It was many a year since he had shared a room with Walter; he remembered him as a tow-headed chap, saying his prayers before he vaulted into bed. Whether Walter had continued that practice in recent years he had not troubled to inquire. His own habits had become desultory. Whether prayer really sought out a source of power which reponded to and reacted upon the seeker, or whether it was simply a mental process producing its own results, were questions to which he had found no satisfactory answer. The invention of the radio had tended to make belief in prayer reasonable. If man, by a mechanical device, could thrust his voice around the world, what were the possibilities of the infinite mechanism of the spirit? And yet he was unconvinced. The Receiving Set never answered back. Some claimed to have heard it, but not he. Perhaps it was themselves they heard. Or perhaps he had not tuned in properly; perhaps he was on the wrong wave-length. These were things to be thought out some day, but here was an immediate problem. Should he let Walter think he still believed, or that he did not believe? He slipped to his knees beside the bed, amazed at the courage required for this simple symbolism. What he said he did not know; his words were a blur. But when he arose he saw Walter kneeling at the other bed, and there was a glow in his heart which came from somewhere.

When they were in their beds and the lights were out Walter spoke to him quietly. "I was going to ask you something, Dad."

Donald's heart hurried in its beat. Was Walter going to raise this question of prayer? Why not? And if so, what should he answer? "Yes?" he said, waiting.

"I noticed you didn't put the check in with the securities. You know, you mentioned to me on the road that you'd drawn all you had in the bank, and would probably be broke until you got something from the Pool."

So it was only that. "No, I didn't put it in," he said.

"I wondered if you had forgotten, but I didn't like to mention it."

"No. I had not forgotten."

There was silence for a moment, and when Walter spoke again there was a note in his voice that skewered into something quivering in Donald's vitals. "You held out on him," he said.

"I held that much out on him. I changed my mind about putting it in."

"Aunt Annie didn't hold out on you."

"No, but Aunt Annie knew who she was dealing with."

"And don't you know Mr. Wayne? Didn't you go to school together?"

"I'm not sure that I do know him, Walter. I wish to God I did."

There was a long pause during which, through the darkness[210], each heard the other's breathing. "Sorry, Dad," Walter whispered, at length.

"Okay," Donald answered, borrowing an idiom from the boy's language.

22

Ellen presided at the breakfast table. Donald sat at her right and noted the dexterity of her lovely fingers as she ministered to his wants. Ellen was fifty now, but the satin lustre had not all worn from her olive cheeks, and her lips were as fresh and mobile as a girl's. Across the table from her sat her husband, much restored by his night's rest; his good humor this morning was spontaneous rather than forced. Walter, talkative at home, was silent under the pressure of strange surroundings, feeling his way carefully through the breakfast courses with sly glances for guidance to Ellen and Jimmie.

Jimmie had already been through the market pages of the *Free Press*. "It's not as bad as I thought," he commented, cheerfully. "A slump, but not a crash. The old machine will be rolling along in a day or two as though nothing had happened."

"Some people will know it happened," Ellen said. "Mrs. Blaine called me last night, in tears. She said her husband was wiped out. It could hardly be that bad, could it, Jim? Why, the Blaines—you know—one of our wealthiest families—She wondered how we had stood it. I told her of course we lost something, but nothing serious. That was right, wasn't it?"

"Quite right. I'm sorry for Blaine, though, if he was caught."

Ellen was not so sure of her undivided sympathy. "Of course I'm sorry," she said, "but they should have seen it coming. If you could play safe, why couldn't they? Anyway, you always have your profession, and you, Donald, have your farm. You know, Jim, I often wish we had a piece of land. There's something so safe about land."

"That's your ancestry speaking up," Jimmie told her. "We who were born on the land never get our roots quite clear of it."

"It's more than ancestry," she argued. "It's something deeper.

194

We came from the earth, and to the earth we return."

"Perhaps, but I'm in no hurry about making the return trip. It's so hard to be sure about the destination. You remember, Donald, how sure we used to be? Now we wonder."

"That is because we are materialists," Ellen asserted. "But there *is* something more. Don't you think so, Donald?"

Thus directly appealed to, Donald found it necessary to make a difficult confession of faith. "Yes, I think so," he said.

"You *think* so," Jimmie took him up. "When we were boys we *knew* it. If one generation has passed from knowing to thinking, what will the next generation do? What do you think, Walter?"

"I don't know," the boy answered, a little embarrassed at the trend of the discussion. "I often wonder."

"You see, even the boys now wonder. When we were boys we *knew*. What we do know is that we have this life to make the most of. We make good here and now or not at all."

"And making good may depend on a turn of the stock market?" Ellen challenged.

"Exactly. And Donald and I are going down this morning to make good. I think Walter would have more coffee, Ellen."

Ellen saw them to the door. "You'll be back for lunch," she pressed.

"I am not sure," Donald answered. "If we get through with our business I think we'll start for home. The days are short, you know." He was thinking of an interview with Jimmie which might make further hospitality under his roof difficult or impossible. "But Walter can stay and pick me up at the office later."

"Why not let Walter drive us down?" Jimmie suggested. "Holmes can bring my car when I want it[211]. Let Walter come with us. It will give him a chance to see how the wheels go round."

There could be no plausible objection, so Walter accompanied them. For an hour or two they were busy with their brokers, and had the satisfaction of leaving their accounts protected against any moderate disturbance of the market. On Jimmie's assurance that it was all in order Donald signed certain papers, necessary for the negotiation of his securities, while Walter followed the transaction with keen attention.

"You should let this boy come to the city, Donald," Jimmie said, when they were on the street together. "He has a head for business. I would be glad to find him a place."

Donald mumbled thanks, but a new fear had shot through him. Would Jimmie take Walter? If there should be a break between them, would Jimmie—and Clara—take Walter? Tom was already gone; Clarissa would some day marry; Walter—That price was too big to pay.

"How would you like to come and work for me?" Jimmie continued, addressing the boy directly. "Of course, I wouldn't start you on a director's salary, but you'd be drawing one within ten years or I don't know human nature, and I do. Not in the law. In business. I'd put you in business."

"That's a very fine offer," Walter managed, "but I think Dad is figuring on keeping me on the farm."

Donald's heart warmed again. The boy was sound, and loyal. "Yes," he said. "Must have one farmer in the family."

"Well, think it over," Jimmie suggested. "In the meantime, Let's get back to the office."[212]

But Donald was not to be baulked forever. "Take a look at the city," he managed to whisper to Walter. "There's a reason."

"Okay," the boy answered.

When again[213] they were in Jimmie's office Donald did not know where to begin. His host produced a box of good cigars, and as Donald fingered one Jimmie[214] pressed a handful into his pocket. "Smoke 'em on the way home," he said. "Smoke—if you won't drink—to our future and greater prosperity. We're over the hill, Donald, and I'm grateful for the way you stood by me. Ellen said we were materialists, but there is something more to it. We measure our success in material things for lack of another yardstick, but it's not the *things* that are success—it's the winning of them. There's a spiritual value in it somewhere. There's the maintenance of one's home, the support of one's wife, seeing that she has comforts—luxuries, if you like—the same for one's family, if he has a family; you beat me there, Donald; I'd give all I've got for a son like Walter. Fine boy; you should be proud of him."

"I am," Donald said. Where to begin? Where to begin? How could he lay against this man, with all his evidences of friendship, a charge of base behavior? How subject his own family honor to the insinuations such a charge must imply? It was just possible, from the distance of Sundown Farm, to attribute treachery to Jimmie; it was impossible to think such things in the glow of his presence, under the pull of his personality. And suppose the whole thing were false, a suspicion built upon incidents easily explained, he would have shamed himself forever and ever.

A clerk tapped on the door and entered with early quotations from the market. Jimmie seized the paper avidly; his quick glance took in the columns of figures. "Not so bad—not so bad," he said, thrusting the sheet before his guest. "A slip, but not a crash. I'm betting it will be stronger by to-morrow. Oh—we'll weather it yet." He threw an arm about Donald's shoulders, he sank in a chair by his side, his body trembled against him.

"Why, Jim—are you not well?" Jimmie had buried his face in his hands; from time to time his body shook spasmodically. "Do you want help? Do you want a doctor?" Donald asked, deeply disturbed.

"I'll be all right in a minute." Long silence followed, but at length[215] Jimmie lifted his head, shaking it as though to clear a mist from his eyes. "Sorry, Donald," he said. "A little reaction. Think I'll have a drink."

The talk turned to trivialities as the hand on the electric desk clock swept the seconds away. As it made its relentless rounds the knowledge came to Donald that the weight which lay so heavily upon his heart must be carried by him, and by him alone. What was this mystery of life that he should seek to unravel it? How much were he, and Jimmie, and Clara, and Ellen, the product of forces acting upon them, and beyond their control? Jimmie's moment of collapse, his trembling body against his friend, had made accusation impossible.

23

On the way homeward Donald turned the situation over in his mind, examining it from every angle, probing it for some piece of solid substance. As the car, with Walter at the wheel, rolled rapidly over the hard highway, the brown fields of October slipping by on either side, thin regiments of leafless trees standing at stark attention against a steel-blue sky line and herds of cattle feeding under lonely, mushroomed straw piles, Donald found himself evolving a new sense of values. For the first time in his life he probably would have to write down his assets at the end of the year; only when the waters had cleared would he be able to know how much had been saved from the wreckage. The prospect of the party nomination which, in their engrossment over other matters, Jimmie had not so much as mentioned, seemed something distant and unreal. His relationship with Clara was obscured in fog. All his old anchorage seemed to be gone. Only Walter at his side, holding the car at a steady fifty, driving with the skill and assurance of a locomotive engineer, seemed altogether dependable.

And yet Donald was not so unhappy as he would have expected to be in such circumstances. Whatever might be the behavior or the fate of others, he had been born into a new conviction with respect to himself. If things were slipping, things were not so important, after all. Perhaps it all would come right; perhaps the market would revive and he would find himself richer than before; perhaps the doubt about Clara would be cleared away; but in any event he would follow his own course. That course took form in his mind as an attitude in which he would be superior to his surroundings. He would be captain of his soul. He would be self-contained and self-assured, and, whatever happened, he would bear no malice. Whether or not he should be able to find happiness he would at least hold himself above anger or despair.

"Like me to spell you off, Walter?" he suggested.

"Not worthwhile stopping, Dad," the boy answered[216], his steady eyes on the long straight road ahead.

The sun slipped down to earth, filling the western sky with a haze like burnt smoke; its light blazed straight into the windshield, and Walter slackened his pace. The[217] huge gold disc dropped into a slot beyond the world, and the cloud of burnt smoke thinned along the horizon, its fringes lost in darkness to north and south, but at its upper edge[218] glowed a lemon-colored clearness in which was posted one bright sentinel star. It was the death of another day, illumined by one clear candle of hope. So, thought Donald, life may be, but can one be sure of the candle at its close? To-night he felt surer than for many years.

With the death of the day the air dropped quickly colder. Donald drew a robe from the back of the car, wrapped it about his legs, and laid a corner over Walter's knees. The lights were on now; they pierced the straight stillness like a thin electric wedge[219], and the miles rolled by unceasingly. At length they found themselves upon familiar highway; they were in Alder Creek; its buildings looked strangely low and squat against the picture[220] of the city still carried in their mental retina, its shop windows dark and unkempt, its main street wide and empty in contrast to the Saturday night throngs to which they were accustomed. Through the little town they slipped[221] without stopping, and a few minutes later were in the yard of Sundown Farm.

George met them at the garage. "Glad to see you back, Boss; good trip?"

"No trouble at all." Donald had stamped out of the car and was straightening his cramped limbs. The farmyard lay in darkness save for the blaze of the headlights trapped in the garage and one thin square of brilliance from a kitchen window. He felt that something was slipping[222]. The mood of resignation which he had experienced in the car—would he lose it[223] under the impact of familiar things?

He noticed where oil had been spilled on the garage floor, and mentioned it.

"Sorry," George said. "I was getting oil for the gasoline engine and the can slipped."

"Oil costs money, George," he reminded him.

Clara met them in the kitchen. "How's everything?" she asked.

"Jimmie's as well as could be expected for a man who has just come through a financial crash," he answered.

"Oh! And I suppose Ellen is well, too?" There was no mistaking her meaning. That was a great way to start.

"They are both well," he said, more gently. "There has been a bad shake-up in the market, but there's no saying how things will turn out, and we're all hoping for the best."

"I thought you would have telephoned me," she said. There was reproach in her voice.

"I should have. Very busy with other things." He was annoyed with himself that he should have overlooked something so obvious[224].

"I called up when I couldn't stand it any longer, but you had started for home."

So she had been talking to Jimmie again.

"I suppose you ain't had your supper?" Mrs. Fetch inquired.

"Not yet."

"I knew they wouldn't have their supper," the housekeeper[225] confided to the kitchen stove. "You'd think there wasn't a hot dog stand 'tween here an' Winnipeg."

"How's the old world, Mother?" Walter asked. He slipped an arm about her waist and planted a kiss behind her ear. "Miss us?"

"Of course I missed you. Now get away, you big tease!" Clara beat him off, but there was a flush of pleasure on her cheeks.

"Now why couldn't I do that?" Donald thought. But he couldn't. Something separated them. Something held him back.

Aunt Annie appeared, and Donald kissed her cheek without thinking.

Afterwards Clara reminded him of it. "You had a kiss for your aunt, but none for me," she said.

"Well, I have one for you now, if you want it," he answered, eager to make amends.

"Oh, I'm not suffering. How did you get along? Have we lost much in the crash?"

"Maybe yes, maybe no. It depends how the market moves from now on."

"Anything new about the nomination?"[226]

His eyes widened. "What nomination?"

"Oh, you thought I didn't know. I suppose you thought I wouldn't be interested?"

"You have talked of this with Jimmie?" There was accusation in his voice.

"Why not?"

He brought himself under control, groping for the sense of power and security he had felt on the road. "No reason, of course. I suppose you talk of lots of things with Jimmie?"

She had an answer. "Not more than you talk of with Ellen, I'll warrant." Then, less aggressively: "Donald, why do we go beating about the bush? Are you afraid to face the facts?"

He had not expected her to force the issue, and he sparred for time. "What are the facts?" he asked.

"You should know[227]. You're in love with Ellen. You always have been in love with Ellen."

He was about to deny it, but he knew a lie would stick in his throat. "That's hardly fair," he said. "Ellen is my cousin. We grew up together. We were like brother and sister. We were children together."[228]

"Well, you're not now. Did you think I didn't know? That I haven't known all these years? And in Winnipeg you were so absorbed with her that when I started a flirtation with Jimmie to distract your attention you couldn't see it."

"So you were flirting with Jimmie?" He was amazed at the ease of her confession.

"Why not? If one can't have love one must have—something."

"Love? But you didn't want love. You have never encouraged love. You have kept me at arm's length. Until lately—"

"Thank Jimmie for that."

"Jimmie?"

"Of course. Oh, Donald, do you know so little? I found flirtation pleasant, like a healing rain after a long drought. Does it surprise you that I came to life again?"

So that was it. As she stood smiling coldly he had a sudden impulse to slap her beautiful face[229]. He conquered it with an effort.

"Well, what do you suggest that I should do about it?" he asked. "You see, I am trying to face the facts."

"Suggest? Why should I suggest? Don't you know? But you haven't the courage."

"Just what do you mean?" It seemed almost laughable that she should charge him with lack of courage.

"If Jimmie thought as much of me as you do of Ellen he would know what to do."

"Perhaps he does."

"No, he doesn't. That is why things are as they are."

"Oh, I see." The fog was lifting.

"Your second sight comes slowly, Donald."

"But it's clear when it comes. You would run away with Jimmie, only he has more sense."

She laughed. "Oh, dear no, nothing so crude as that. It is not necessary to tell the world—at least, not at present. Any scandal would spoil your chance of election. Jimmie realizes that, and for some reason he has his heart set on making you a Member of Parliament. It appeals to me, too. I think I could do the position justice."

"If I am not good enough for you now I never will be."

"Perhaps not, but I might be reconciled to my fate—if you were a Member."

"I haven't done so badly for you," he defended himself. "I have the best farm in the municipality. I have had a measure of success—"

"Success! Your kind of success! Bulls and cows and hogs and wheat! But what about my kind of success?"

Her vehemence won from him a gesture of sympathy. She had spirit, and he loved spirit.

"What *is* your kind of success?" he asked gently enough.

"Oh, let me see?" Her eyes lit up with one of their rare glows of enthusiasm. "A fine house, in the city. A house like Jimmie's—only better. Beautiful clothes—much better than any you have given me. Invitations. People coming and going. A feeling that one is someone in the world. Have you noticed that no one ever comes to see us here?"

"Why, Clara! Surely we are popular?[230] Everyone who knows us treats us with respect."

"Not respect. Envy. They fawn on you, but as for friendship—bah! You are too cold, Donald."

She was calling him cold! "As for coldness, you are a concentrated[231] iceberg," he retorted.

"But I can be melted, if you know how. The trouble is you don't, and you have never tried to learn. You have wooed your beautiful Chieftain more than you have me. Oh, don't you see the futility of it all? Ellen would suit you, Jimmie would suit me. Why should we continue being four fools because we made a mistake thirty years ago? We are not young now, Donald. Why not seize what happiness we can?"[232]

They were standing under the light in the living-room. Aunt Annie and Walter had gone to bed; Mrs. Fetch was in her room at the back of the house; Aunt Annie's door was closed. They faced each other in a combat of wills.

"Sit down," Donald suggested, and when they were seated: "Now, if I follow you aright, what you have in mind is divorce?"

"No! Divorce, like running away,[233] would ruin your chance of election, thanks to a public which thinks it is moral when it is only bigoted. I want you to be elected. I want to gloat over your victory. I want all your position will give me. I want that much compensation for the drab years I have lived with you. But there might be—an understanding. Oh, I am willing to give as much as I take."
loose folds of its flesh lapped over the edge of his collar[234]. The crash was worse than he had expected. A sudden fatigue sank though his body. So this was what she had to offer for all the success he had brought her.

"I see," he said, at length. "I see."

He remained again a long time silent, and at last she got up and stood beside his chair.

"It isn't pleasant, Donald; it isn't pleasant for either of us. But we may as well face the truth. Love comes—and goes. Sometimes it goes. Yours and Ellen's seem to live on. I envy you that, Donald. As for me—we shall see. I have decided to go to Winnipeg—oh, just for a visit, a week or two. You need have no fear that your name or reputation will be involved in anything I do. Perhaps when I come back I will see the course more clearly."

"Clara," he said, speaking so low in his throat his voice was almost gutteral[235]. "If you go you need not come back."

She drew away from his chair. The muscles of her hands[235] were tightened with anger.

"So that is your ultimatum," she answered. "I have tried to meet you on a fair basis. I have tried to spare you public reproach. But all my life you have ruled me. You will rule me no longer. I am going."

24

For the next few days Donald went about as one under the influence of an opiate. He suffered dully, but not sharply, enjoying that respite provided by nature for one who receives a blow too great to be borne in full consciousness. He did not blame Clara as much as he would have thought. His disappointment in her had been a development of years; now that the climax was reached he found in it almost a measure[236] of relief. He even felt a sort of inverted respect for her resolution and her indifference to consequences. She spent much time in her room, apparently putting her things in order, but when they met about the house they spoke as usual. The other members of the family must not know that anything had happened to reflect upon the name of Strand. That might have to come, but not yet.

Donald, left more than ever to himself, wandered about his fields in the golden-brown days, and sought his little office with the fall of early darkness. He made innumerable calculations with pencil and paper but found no happiness in the result. If the market survived he might still come out on the right side; if it subsided further, even the securities he had poured in would[237] be lost. And there was still the five-thousand-dollar note at the bank. How was that to be paid unless he could realize on his stocks? He might have to mortgage the farm—this farm which had been out of debt for twenty years. Jimmie Wayne had gone on the note with him; it would be humiliation unbounded if Jimmie had to pay it. Yet if there were some way that he could get rid of the farm, some way to bury his assets that remained, Jimmie might have to pay the note, and it would serve him right. He toyed with the idea but abandoned it. It was his debt and he would pay. No one should ever say a Strand had failed to pay his debts. Aside from that nothing mattered much. He was astonished how little anything mattered.

For the first time in his life he found himself floating with the stream instead of fighting it, and the sensation was rather restful. He supposed it had some relationship to what people called faith; leaving everything to God and not worrying about it. His sense of the existence and presence of God had grown during his recent experiences. To ignore Him in prosperity and turn to Him in distress filled Donald with a certain feeling[238] of shame, but there was comfort in it, too, and strength from hidden springs he had not known existed. As he sat with Aunt Annie through the old hymn hour on Sunday night and heard again "There is a fountain filled with blood", although he could not accept the words[239] he was aware that underneath stirred a Power which opened the way to some kind of salvation. Salvation perhaps from self, from over-concern about self, from desire for success expressed in gratification[240] of self. Only when a man was unconcerned about self could he be really free. Never in his life had he been free; always he had been chained to his ambition. He had the sense of humor to smile inwardly at the thought that the thwarting of his ambition might be the thing to set him free.

Clara had named[241] Tuesday as the day she would go to the city, and Donald had surprised her and himself by offering to let Walter take her in the car. If there must be a break between them he proposed that, as much as possible, it should be decent and without rancor or ill will. "You will be more comfortable travelling by car," he said.

She looked at him quizzically, as though she suspected a catch in his generosity. "Thank you, but I have planned to go by train," she answered.

"But can't your plans be changed? You are welcome to the car."

"All my life I have been changing plans for you. I am going by train."

Donald withdrew to the privacy of his office, to think, to try to see the situation clearly. He heard Clara moving about in the livingroom, going up and down stairs, completing preparations for her journey, and he wondered in a sort of impersonal manner if ever he should hear her footsteps in his house again. Not that it would make much difference. In all his experience only Clara—and Tom, instigated by Clara—had opposed his will. It seemed strange that the two disturbing elements in his life should have been in his own family. With Clara's[242] influence removed better relations with Tom might be possible. Under the management of Mrs. Fetch the comforts of his household were assured. Yes, Clara was by no means indispensible. If she thought he would weaken under the threat of her absence she would be disillusioned; the prospect brought him rather a sense of relief. If it were not for what people would say when they knew; for the implication that he had made a failure of his domestic life; that[243], knowing only part of the truth, they probably would place the blame on him, he could have viewed the possibilities of the situation without much concern[244].

The fact that Clara preferred Jimmie did not trouble him deeply. He assured himself that he was too big for jealousy. She probably would find that she had misinterpreted what Jimmie intended only for a rather jovial friendship, and the discovery would bring her all the punishment she needed.

In the meantime he would go on as though nothing had happened. In a day or two he would call Jimmie on the telephone to discuss business matters, and casually he would mention Clara's visit. That would give Jimmie an opportunity to clear the air, if it needed clearing. Or maybe he would write to Ellen. That was a good idea; perhaps he would write to Ellen. She would know what to say; she always could be depended on in an emergency. With a picture of Ellen in his mind he began to toy with the idea which Clara had suggested. She had said she was willing to give as much as she took. Ellen, he knew would be his ideal mate. But that meant breaking the thongs of convention and of a certain moral restraint which seemed to be woven into his fibre. He might break them secretly—somewhere in the dim shadows at the outeredge of his consciousness he became aware of the dead presence of Hester Harp—but openly? That was impossible.

He had not bothered to turn the switch, but lay on his couch in a darkness relieved only by a wedge of light falling through the partly-open door. He had left the door open; there was just the possibility that at the last moment Clara would come to him, but as she proceeded with her unhurried preparations that possibility grew more and more remote. Suddenly he heard the outer door of the kitchen open and close, and strange stirrings and movements gave news of something afoot.

"Where's Dad?" said a voice which he did not recognize.

"In his office, savin' light," answered the observant Mrs. Fetch. "What's a-matter[245], Tom?"

But Tom did not answer. A moment later he was standing in the office door. "You there, Dad?" The strain of haste and anxiety were in his words.

Donald pulled himself to a sitting position. "I'm here," he said. "Anything wrong?"

"I want to see you alone, Dad."

"We are alone here." A presentiment of evil was twitching at the base of Donald's skull, but he kept his voice steady. "Close the door and turn on the light."

Tom did so, and dropped into the big chair before the desk. Donald's eyes blinked in the sudden brilliance. He was unable for a moment to get a clear picture of his son, but when his pupils were adjusted he saw that Tom's face was drawn and distressed, and weariness and something like fear were in his eyes.

"What's the matter, Tom?" he asked, gently. His affection for his first born, never quite dead, was rekindled by his evident distress.

It was a moment before Tom could command words. His hands worked nervously, clasping and unclasping, and his lips moved, but no sound came. He moistened them with his tongue, and suddenly words came like a flood breaking through a barrier.

"I'm in a jam, Dad. I hate to come to you, after all that has been, but no one else can help. You will help, won't you, Dad? You see, I didn't steal the money; I'm not a thief; I borrowed it, and I borrowed it on good security, but of course I had to fix it in the books[246] as I couldn't show it in my own name. A month ago I could have cleaned up with ten thousand dollars, but the market was still going up, and I thought I'd just hang on to the end of the year. The crash last week gave me a scare, but no one wants to sell right at the bottom, so I held on, and then to-day—"

"What about to-day?" Donald interrupted. The circle of his fear had suddenly widened.

"Haven't you heard?" Tom looked at his father as one who has wandered off a trail and must go back to correct his course. "I thought you would have heard. The bottom went out. And I'm sold out. Utterly. Had a wire about an hour ago. I may cover up for a while, but they'll get me, and it means jail if I can't pay, and disgrace and a lost job even if I do. My only hope is to replace the money before it's missed. Oh, Dad, I'm so sorry—"

But Donald did not seem to hear. "The bottom went out," he repeated, almost stupidly. "The bottom went out. And I went with it. Strange that Jimmie didn't 'phone me. Isn't it strange he didn't 'phone me?" Donald's face was toward Tom but his words seemed addressed beyond him, beyond the wall, into outer space.

Drawn by their common distress Tom moved over to the couch. He sat down by his father's side; he slipped his arm about his father's shoulder. "You cleaned out, too?" he said. There was fear[247] as well as sympathy in his voice. "I didn't know you were in so deep. Does it mean—you can't help me?"

"Perhaps I shouldn't say 'cleaned out'," Donald answered. "There is still the farm, and the stock, and all that. But it looks as though the securites were gone." He paused, breathing deeply, filling his lungs as though the air were too thin. "Oh, well, what is one more blow on top of another? How much do you need?"

Tom avoided the direct question as though he could not bring himself to name the figure. "I'm not a criminal, Dad," he said. "I always meant to pay it back, and I'll pay you, if it takes all my life. If only I'd sold at the right time—"

"I wonder how many people are saying to-night, 'If only I had sold at the right time'?"

"Yes, I know, Dad, but it does seem such a rotten break. No one need ever have known, and I'd have been away to a start, and no doubt would have become a successful financier and a pillar of society and all that sort of thing. I am no different from those that were lucky, but I suppose all success is pretty much a matter of luck, don't you think, Dad?"

"Perhaps," Donald answered, unaware that he was renouncing his most cherished belief[248]. "How much will it take? Out with it! We'll meet it like Strands."

"About three thousand dollars."

Tom relaxed his grip on his father's shoulders and sat up straight, his body rigid, as though braced against the blow he half expected. Donald did not speak for a moment. Then, very quietly:[249]

"That's a lot of money, Tom. I don't know where I am to get it. Perhaps you had better ask your mother for it. It was she who encouraged you to leave the farm in the first place. No doubt she will be glad to help you."

The boy's rigidity was gone, but his spirit flared up under the lash. "That's right, Dad; tramp on me when I'm down. You know there's no use in my going to Mother. She would help me if she could, but she hasn't a dollar except what you give her."

"Quite true. And, apparently, neither have you. The farm wasn't good enough for you, Tom, for a career, but now you expect it to keep you out of jail. But I suppose you are just running true to the form of the new generation. You can't be told, of course; but when you get in a jam you come to your father—"

"Why not? And where else? But I won't embarrass you further, Dad. It was my one chance. I realize[250] that you have been hard hit, too, and there is no reason why I should add to your burden. But I'm not going to jail without a fight. See that!" He drew from his pocket a thick bundle of bank notes. "That should be in the safe to-night, but it isn't. I can steal a car and to-morrow morning I'll be in South Dakota. The next morning I'll be in Texas, the next in Mexico. Of course they may catch me; they probably will, but I'll give them a run for their money. Sorry it has to be that way, but you leave me no choice."

He replaced the notes in his pocket, and stood up. His shoulders were back, his head erect[251], his eyes defiant. Donald felt himself stirred with pride that even Tom would fight when cornered. His strategy in placing his father in an untenable position was too clever to be entirely condemned.

"Sit down, Tom," he said. "I'll come through. You have boasted that you are not a thief, and I believe you; but you will be if you take that money that's in your pocket. It must go back before it's missed. I don't know just where I'm going to get three thousand dollars—"

210

"You have over seventeen hundred in your account. You can easily raise the balance on your note. You are in good standing at the bank. I'll pay the interest out of my salary, and the principal when I can. And I won't forget."

"All right. There is just one condition. Go and tell your mother. Tell her the whole story. She should know."

"Thanks, Dad, I will." He extended his hand and Donald drew it to his chest in a moment of atonement and reconciliation.

Their moment was broken by the ringing of the telephone.

"Winnipeg calling Mr. Strand."

"Mr. Strand speaking." Aside to Tom: "Here comes the bad news."

There was a moment of empty humming. Than a voice:

"Mr. Strand?"

"Yes."

"This is Andrew Sutherland, of Wayne and Sutherland, speaking. I have bad news for you, Mr. Strand."

Donald released a mirthless laugh into the receiver. "I have heard it already," he said, "but I thought Jimmie would have called me."

"It is about Jimmie I have to speak. This must seem very abrupt over the wire, but you may as well know the truth at once. Jimmie is dead."

For a moment Donald stood dazed by the calamitous information. Then: "Not dead! Not Jimmie Wayne! Not dead! It can't be possible!"

"I am terribly sorry to say it *is* possible. He left the office about the usual time this afternoon. Of course you know the market had broken badly, and he was greatly disturbed, but I had no idea he would do anything so rash and terrible, or I should have gone with him. When he didn't turn up for dinner they started a search. Holmes found him in the garage. The doors were closed and the engine was still running."

"Oh!" Donald's answer was less a word than a moan. "Poor Jim. Does Ellen know—of course she knows?"

"She is taking it as bravely as she can. She asked me to call you at once. You will come?"

"Of course[252]. Within an hour. No—I can't. I have business here that must be done in the morning. When the bank opens. I'll leave immediately after."

For a minute or two Donald stood hanging to the telephone as though for physical support. Jimmie dead! The implications were more than could be comprehended in so brief a time. With unseeing eyes he gazed into the hard wall. Before them marched the pageant of events. Jimmie, a barefoot boy, under the willows at Alder Creek. Jimmie, a college youth, somewhat skeptical about prayer. Jimmie, a man of affairs, planning on making a million dollars. Jimmie, a power behind the political scenes, pulling the strings that were to land a nomination. Jimmie, the occasion of Calra's infatuation.

Tom pressed by his side. "Jimmie Wayne is dead?" he asked, gently.

Donald nodded. "Suicide," he managed to say. "Where is your mother?"

"Upstairs, I think."

"I must go to her," said Donald, wearily.

25

Letter from Andrew Sutherland:

Dear Mr. Strand: I have not forgotten my promise to write you as soon as I could about poor Jimmie's affairs, but it has taken some time to get them into even a semblance of order. Although there are still many details to be worked out before an exact statement can be made it is apparent that after his debts are paid, little, if anything, will be left. It is hard on Ellen, but she is adjusting herself to new conditions like the brick she is.

Your own affairs are in somewhat more hopeful condition; a detailed statement will be sent you as soon as it can be compiled. Although Jimmie carried all accounts in his own name he kept a book of his own in which your investments were carefully segregated and faithfully recorded. I think we shall have no difficulty in establishing that this was a trust account, and that the securities you deposited are applicable only against the purchases made for you[253]. There will be a balance, but probably not enough to cover your note at the bank. I think it likely that in addition to whatever may be realized out of your securities—and there will be a battle with the brokers about that, as they will try to establish that you were really a partner with Jimmie in his speculations and therefore responsible for his debts—you will need to put up between one and two thousand dollars[254] to meet your note. I hope that this will not greatly embarrass you. You may be assured of my best services in protecting your interests.

The blow which we have all suffered in Jimmie's death is staggering. I look at his empty desk, and the whole world seems empty, too. He was the soul of energy[255], of cheerfulness, of goodwill, but these very qualities made him an optimist, and his ambition and optimism sadly outweighed his prudence. I blame myself greatly that I was not more insistent in my efforts to convince him that the market structure, for the last two years and more, has been fundamentally unsound. I should have seen, too, that at the pace he was driving, something was sure to break. The papers have been decent enough to treat it as an accident, but everybody knows.

I shall write again as soon as I can give more detailed information. Faithfully, **Andrew Sutherland**.

Letter from Ellen Wayne:

Donald, dear: The days and nights—particularly the nights, are endless, but still they come and go. It is two weeks since we laid him away. It might be a century. The world has turne d[256] inside out since then; the very faces I

213

meet on the street have a strange expression. A dozen times a day I think: Surely this is a dream. He will be home to dinner. I can't make myself understand that I shall never, never hear his voice again; never see his smile light up as I greet him at the door.

I shouldn't burden you with this. A million times I have promised myself that I will be brave. But if I don't talk to you, to whom shall I talk? You are my oldest and truest friend. Often I thought I loved you instead of him, and sometimes I wondered—dare I say?—if that love would one day be realized. But now such thoughts seem shamefully tawdry and unworthy. There are experiences which cause us to make a new evaluation of life, and I have passed through one of them. Nothing is as it was before; nothing ever can be.

Andrew has been wonderful. Jimmie always called him Andrew, and the name trips off my pen before I know it. He is doing the best he can with my affairs, but he cannot hide or change the fact that I am next thing to penniless. The house and the life insurance were pledged. I have a few stocks which Jimmie gave me, fully paid up. They will realize something. Then there is my jewelry, gifts from Jimmie, precious to me, but with no place in the new life to which I shall set myself.

I shall leave Winnipeg. If I stayed, they would put me out of my house, and the bitterness of that might overwhelm me. I have many friends here, but I can no longer live as they live. One by one they would begin to forget, and I would remember. And I think—don't you?—that as we grow older the memories of our childhood's environment become more and more insistent. The quiet and peace of sunny mornings on the prairie are what I need to restore my soul. We knew them together as boy and girl. We shall never recapture that, but I must reach for it, reach with outstretched arms and the prairie wind blowing about my cheeks.

So I want to come back to Alder Creek. Not to the farm, of course; that is impossible. But Mother still owns the Brown cottage. Here is my plan: Let Mother come back to me, and we will live in the cottage. I am not unmindful of your great kindness to her all these years, but I need her now. It may not be for long, but it will bridge this chasm that lies before me. Clara has been good to her, but Clara is not of her blood, and you will be happier by yourselves. Say you approve of it. I think I shall have enough to live on, if I am frugal. I want to dig in the earth again, and keep my own hens, and listen to the mothers brooding over their chicks. Oh, Donald, how I envy you your boys and girl! You cannot know how empty the vessel of life may be.

We wanted children, but they never came. Perhaps that is why he grew to be[257] so absorbed in business. It was a game to him, and he played it all too strenuously. But he did not have your background. The Waynes never were as solid as the Strands. You would never have done as he did. I am not blaming him, but item by item[258] the things that steady one slipped away from him, and when he needed them they were not there. Not that I am fearful for what may lie beyond, but neither am I sure. As I listened to the preacher's words they brought a comfort to my heart, but they might have been the tolling of a bell. If we *really* believed what we profess, everything would be so different, wouldn't it? But we only hope.

214

Give my love to Clara. I hope she is quite well[259] again. I was sorry she did not feel able to come with you, but she wrote me a sympathetic note, which I deeply appreciate. Your presence was a tower of strength to me on that terrible day, as always it has been. Perhaps that is why I want to come back where I will be near you, but not too near—for your sake, and mine, and Clara's. It all seems so futile. The things that mattered so much don't matter any more.

I shall write to Mother in a day or two, and I hope you will support the suggestion I shall make. I must get hold of something solid. Ever yours, E.W.

Donald stood for a long while in his little office, Ellen's open letter in his hand. It had been a laborious composition; there were erasures and interlinings, and it ended with an abruptness that suggested exhaustion. She had been so careful, so restrained. What thoughts, he wondered, had clamored in her mind, only to be suppressed under her careful phrases? He folded the letter slowly and placed it in a pigeon-hole in his desk. All that he saw clearly was the picture of a woman with her arms outstretched toward the sun and the prairie breezes playing in her hair.

Another letter from Andrew Sutherland:

Dear Mr. Strand: In my previous letter I made no reference to the nomination for Parliament which Jimmie was trying to secure for you. He was the political end of the firm, and that is a field in which I have no great influence. I have talked with some who may speak with authority, and I find that you are well regarded, but of course Jimmie's death greatly changes the situation. There are other aspirants whose claims will be aggressively and influentially pressed. You might let me know how you feel about it.

Excerpt from Donald's answer:

As for the nomination, I am afraid I have lost interest in it. It was always Jimmie's idea rather than mine. I have too many doubts. I doubt if I could get it; I doubt if I would make a good member if I were elected. I suppose one essential of a good member is that he must not doubt[260]. Besides, I have had one experience in getting into things I do not understand, and the result has not been altogether happy. So suppose we just forget it. My hands are going to be full enough with my farm and my obligations.

26

Ellen Wayne arrived at Alder Creek on a bleak day in December. Donald and Walter met her with the car; Clara had been invited to come, but pleaded that[261] she was taking cold. Ellen was the centre of observation for the loafers at the station as she walked with Donald along the platform[262] while Walter went forward to claim her baggage. Many of them knew her; some remembered that once upon a time it had been said that Ellen would surely marry her cousin, Donald Strand, and speculations, neither delicate nor strictly confidential, were again afoot among them. Ellen, acutely self-conscious under their half-veiled glances, affected the commonplace; she smiled at those she recognized, and paused to shake hands and chat a moment with one or two who, cloaking their curiosity with a special show of friendship, pressed forward for that purpose. But Alder Creek, which had remained poor, could not forgive Jimmie Wayne for becoming rich, and Ellen must bear at least a share of the blame. Her husband's tragic death had done something to restore her to good standing, but the best she could hope for the moment was acceptance on probation.

She[263] was keen enough to sense the situation and clever enough to show no sign. On the short drive to Sundown Farm she chatted quietly and casually with Donald and Walter; the more serious matters on her mind could wait for later discussion. Clara received her with a show of hospitality, and Aunt Annie with trembling lips and[264] a courage that would not let go.

Clara showed her to the spare room. "We shall try to make you comfortable, Ellen, until you are ready to move into your own home," she said. Then, abruptly: "Do you miss him terribly?"

"Terribly, Clara."

"We—that is—all his friends do," said Clara, and turned suddenly from the room.

Ellen set about putting her things in order. She saw quickly enough through the thinness of Clara's welcome and was not entirely unaware of the cause of her sudden emotion. It was with some misgiving she had agreed to come, even temporarily, under Clara's roof. True, it was only the return of the August visit; true, also, Clara herself had written pressing her to come. But Clara could not very well do otherwise, and Ellen in turn felt that to avoid Sundown Farm entirely would be to occasion local comment. She was beginning to wonder whether she had been so wise in deciding to come back[265] to the home of her childhood; the reception at the station, like a draft of foul air, was still in her lungs. In this little community she would be continually under the fierce light which beats upon an attractive widow; the friendly seclusion and impersonality of the city would be denied her in Alder Creek.

Through a window of her room she looked out upon a scene both familiar and strange. The creek where so often she had played as a child still cut its circuitous route across the corner of the farm, but its voice was silent and its shallow depression partly filled with drifted snow[266]. Away stretched the prairies, no longer prairies but the dead aftermath of the season's cultivation, not yet blanketed in their winter shrouds but covered thinly with a dirty patchwork of snow and drifted dust. The dull sky which curtained the horizon seemed an appropriate drop-piece for the still tragedy of her life.

A feeling of unsatisfied nostalgia swept over her, and she sank into a chair. Tears came to her relief. A thousand times she had told herself she must be brave, and the face she had turned to the world had been firm with courage as well as resignation, but in her private moments the ghastly loneliness and futility of it all seemed unbearable. She had hoped to escape this mood by returning to Alder Creek, and now it pressed upon her more heavily than ever. She had become aware on the short trip from the station that even Donald could be of little help. The presence of Donald, in which she always had found strength, now took on something of menace.[267]

Ellen made her stay at the Strand farm as brief as was reasonably possible. Clara treated her with studied courtesy, the others with spontaneous kindness, but she was aware that she had no part in this family

217

circle, if, indeed, it could any longer be called a circle. Fortunately the tenants of the Brown cottage had found it convenient to move on short notice; fortunately, also, the few things she had elected to save out of the magnificence of her former home arrived without delay, and the cottage was made ready for occupation.

By the third day they were able to move in. Walter went ahead with the farm truck, on which he carried Aunt Annie's trunk and her hand-made bureau (every drawer full of memories) and the few other treasures she had gathered about her. Ellen and Aunt Annie were to follow with Donald in the car. The old lady, in her best dress, looked very slim and frail. Moving again from the old farm, even into her own home, was for her an experience to stir the emotions.

She approached Clara as one dealing with a costly thing, afraid of working damage by some clumsy action. "Thank you very much, Clara, for all your kindness," she said.

Clara's cameo face softened into a smile. "Oh, that's all right, Auntie," she answered. "I did no more than my duty."

Donald clenched his teeth. Why, for once, could Clara not afford to be cordial? he wondered.

In the kitchen Mrs. Fetch put her hands on the old woman's shoulders. "It's lucky you are to have your own home to go to, Mrs. Strand. Women ain't wanted when they're too old to work their way." Sympathy might have overcome her, but angry self-pity came to her rescue. "And now I'll be havin' your room to look after, too. But maybe they'll close it up for the winter to save coal."

It was a sunny afternoon, and the car skipped over the brief four miles almost before they knew it. As they approached the little town Aunt Annie touched Donald's arm.

"I wonder if you would let me off at Clarissa's boarding place?" she asked. "I have a bit something I want to leave her."

"But Clare won't be home from her work for an hour or more."

"Then I'll just wait. Maybe she'll walk around with me when she comes home."

"Do," Ellen urged. "We'll have supper set for both of you."

The cottage, surrounded by drifted snow,[268] looked very small and snug as they stopped before it. Ellen led the way in. The door

218

opened directly into the little living-room, now set with her comfortable furniture. Walter had left a good fire going and the chill was off the air.

"You didn't bring much of your own stuff," Donald observed.

"No. It wouldn't fit here. In more ways than one. But I brought my own linen and enough of my silver and china to do me justice if I need to."

They were standing self-consciously in the centre of the little room. "Well, take off your things," Ellen said with sudden spriteliness. "You're going to stay for supper."

"Am I?"

"Of course." Then, with a little choke and her hand on his arm: "I can't let you go just yet, Donald."[269]

He laughed uneasily. "Go? One would think I was going on a journey."

"You *are* going on a journey, Donald; a long, long journey. But I had to have one hour with you before you went. That is why I sent Aunt Annie to Clare's.

"You sent her?"

"Of course. I couldn't talk to you at Clara's—I mean, at your house. I just couldn't. And there are some things I must talk about."[270]

Clumsily he came to her aid. "Business affairs?" he suggested.

"Not particularly.[271] Andrew is looking after my interests. He is putting whatever salvage there is into an endowment, and he thinks I shall have about sixty dollars a month. That, with the fifteen you insist on giving on Mother's account—and which I don't like to take—will save me from hardship. I shall live simply. I shall try to live happily."[272]

She turned toward the window, through which the low sun was pouring light without warmth. He followed here, and for a while they stood silently watching the cold death of another day.

"Sooner or later it all ends," she said. "Our little day, and then—the dark. Oh, Donald, what to do? What to do?"

"Yes, that is the question. Make the most of the day, I suppose."

"But what *is* most? Two months ago I thought I knew," she went on, as though speaking with herself. "I am afraid I almost thought I

219

would have welcomed—something like this. That is a very terrible confession, but I am afraid it's true. Now I see how impossible it all is."

"You mean we must just go on?"

"Just go on—and on. Haven't you felt that during most of our lives we move about in fog, but once in a great while, perhaps under some special emotion, the fog lifts, and we get a clear picture? It takes some great emotion to sweep incidentals away and leave only those things which really matter. Jimmie's death brought me one of those moments. It has altered all my sense of values."[273]

Donald's mind ran back through his own experiences, particularly that long drive from Winnipeg when he was reconciling himself to a sense of failure and finding in that moment, when he expected to be most miserable, a peace that passed his understanding.[274]

"When we no longer value things we are free of things," she continued, before he was able to shape his thought into words. "We catch a glimpse of Truth, and it makes us free."[275]

"To do as we please?"

"No. To do what is right."

"What *is* right?"

"Ah, there's the rub. You remember, when we were children, how sure we were? Now we wonder.[276] And yet I think a thread of truth must run[277] through it all. Donald—I don't expect ever to see Jimmie again in the flesh; ever to feel his touch on my arm, his lips on mine, or hear his voice in my ear. And yet I feel that something must survive. If not, what is the purpose of it all?"

She had taken his hand in hers; her body rested gently against his.

"Must there be a purpose?" he asked.

"Oh, surely! Life would be too utterly dreadful.[278] Perhaps it is to teach us self-control, to make the spirit master of the body. Perhaps in that way we evolve from the animal into the spiritual."

"You are quite a philosopher, Ellen," he said. "But while you profess your theory you hold my hand. Which am I to believe—your words or your fingers?"

"I know—I know." Impetuously she turned her face into his shoulder, and his arm held her close.

"Have you ever wondered," she whispered, "why the little flame of our love should live all these years when so many others have blown out?"

"Perhaps we were intended for each other from the beginning."

"Perhaps. But isn't it more likely that love is a flower which grows[279] in self-restraint? It is like something perfect in a glass, but when you are no longer willing just to admire its perfection but must break the glass to seize it—then it withers."

"You mean that[280]—ours would die, too?"

"Why not? It died between you and Clara. It died between Jimmie and me. Look about you. Oh, I know, something else, something quite fine—so fine, perhaps, that many mistake it for the original bloom[281]—may take its place. But the flower[282] is dead. Oh, Donald, I want ours to live forever!"

He did not try to argue with her,[283] but held her in his arms, wondering at the strange warfare within him. In that moment he knew she was the stronger of the two, that he would do whatever she said.

"You are taking a high stand," he managed, at length. "But you are still under the strain of a great emotion. That will pass; at least, it will soften. Then what?"[284]

"I don't know. Perhaps we can be happy; perhaps not. All I am sure of is that no other way lies happiness. It might be possible for others, but not for us. We may discard our beliefs, but we cannot discard the effects of our beliefs. It is Fate."[285]

They watched the sun sink behind the rim of the world. The snow took on the reflected glory of the sky; the evening star came out with sudden brilliance.

"There!" she said. "I think I was always a sun worshipper. Did it ever occur to you that God could have made the world without beauty, if He had been so disposed? In the morning I shall see him again. I wonder if life is like that?"

Footsteps sounded on the frosty walk, and they sprang apart. A moment later Clarissa knocked on the door.

*   *   *

Donald drove home alone with his thoughts. Ellen had been particularly bright during the evening meal and the hour or two which followed; the cloud which seemed to surround her at Sundown Farm had blown away. Fresh from her presence, he was not so unhappy as he might have expected. A great tenderness nestled within him. He thought of it as the flower which they were to keep forever young.[286]

33

Spring had come again to Sundown Farm. Alder Creek had known[287] its brief period of exaltation—brief now with the cultivation of its watershed and the destruction of forest growth along its upper reaches—and had subsided into a series of lazy pools, very blue under the sky of May, linked together with threads of brown water occasionally stirred to sudden life by the migration of suckers returning from their annual expedition to the spawning grounds. Along its grassy banks the wild duck again[288] had made her nest; plovers ran aimlessly over the mud by the water's edge; an industrious muskrat was forever plying forward and back about his business, and in the still evenings the melody of its voice could be heard through the open windows of Sundown Farm.

Donald Strand glanced at the low-hung sun and decided there was time for another round before stopping for the night. He steadied himself on the plow and gave the order to his four-horse team, who received it with almost open insurrection. That last round was always a heart-break to the horses. On the homeward stretch they could develop unsuspected resources of power and speed, but the start of another round found them in a state of almost complete exhaustion. As they dragged their heavy feet across the stubble they made it plain that, while they would work to the death at their lord's command, death stood perilously near and would certainly overtake them before they had gone half the length of another furrow.

"That's one thing about a tractor," Donald remarked to himself. "It never tries to play on your sympathies." But a crack of the whip over the big bay on the nigh side brought new life to the quartette, and presently they were straining in their collars, their heads undulating hugely to their slow and heavy stride. The long shadows which fell to the eastward exaggerated horses, plow, and rider to uncouth but humorous proportions. In Donald's ears were the creak of harness, the sluff and scrape of earth along the mouldboards, and the evening message of a meadow-lark flung bravely from a nearby post.

He[289] glanced down the mile-long furrow which lay ahead. It was a workmanlike furrow, not absolutely straight, but straight enough for practical purposes, and every inch of earth was turned. He had little patience with fancy plowing; his job was to turn the earth over, evenly and completely, with the least possible expenditure of time and labor. Near the far end, like some great corrugated beast, was the outline of Walter's tractor[290] on its homeward stretch in the opposite furrow.

The horses settled into their stride, and Donald into his reverie. That was one thing about plowing with horses; the process was so nearly automatic that one had opportunity to think. His thinking was, mostly, not a strenuous nature; it was rather a re-examination of old thoughts that an attempt to give birth to anything new. He had almost reached[291] the half-century mark, and he found his mind turning more and more to reminiscence. Strange the pleasure that could be found in calling up and living over again those days when he was wrestling his farm from the grip of the unbroken sod! Time had smoothed or effaced the hardship of those early days but the aroma of achievement still clung close to the memory. He was plowing now on what had been railway land lying between Uncle Jim's homestead and the old Farquhar farm; land which he had bought for four dollars an acre and which had paid for itself again and again[292] under his careful husbandry. Yes, he had done well with his farm, even though recent crops and prices had been disappointing; if only he had stuck to his farm he would not have had to write off so heavy a loss in his last annual statement. And yet it was not all loss. Something intangible had come into his life which could not be expressed in figures but which contributed a fuller happiness than he had known in the years of his financial success. He glanced at the big square house a mile to the eastward, its western windows now flaming fire in answer to the setting sun, and felt that perhaps this last year had been most profitable of all.

As the team plodded on and the crisp stubble crackled its remonstrance against its rude up-rooting a sudden flash of memory revealed to Donald that it was in this very field, almost at this very spot, that Clara Wilson had awaited his coming that summer evening some thirty years ago. The fact that Clara Wilson was his wife, whenever he was reminded of it, stirred in him a sort of wondering surprise. She had been Clara Strand so long it was hard for him to realize that once she had been Clara Wilson, a girl not of his own stock or family, a stranger whom he had regarded casually, with no hint in his mind of the intimacy and the play of personality which down the long years should gradually work out their destiny. It never had been like that with Ellen. Ellen had always *belonged*, but Clara had come in from the outside. Yet the memory of that night touched tender chords in his being, and as he thought of Clara Wilson, as distinguished from Clara Strand, something of his old boyish fervor and delicacy stirred within him. . . .

"Walter's tractor was passing on the other side of the land. Donald glanced across, noting with pride his son's efficiency. "Pull in at the end of the furrow," he called.

"Okay," the boy answered. "Don't stay out too late yourself."

The sun had gone down before Donald reached the end of his round. A honey-colored curtain hung across the western sky, its upper edges broken into fringes and tassels of gold and copper.

"God could have made the world without beauty if He had wanted to," Donald quoted to himself. It was a thought in which he found himself increasingly taking comfort. It was an assurance that there was a purpose and an intelligence behind what seemed to be the chaos of his life. It was a cord with which he drew together the ravelled garment of his faith.

A star or two looked out. The air became suddenly cold. Donald unhitched his team and started for home, plodding behind them in the gathering darkness.

Notes

*In addition to the changes noted below, the editor has silently stand-
ardized Stead's spelling of "grey", and used an ellipsis where Stead
on occasion used a double-dash.*

Part One

1. In the original manuscript (in vol. VI, folder 24, of the Stead Papers at the Public Archives of Canada, Ottawa), the first sentence read: "The branch-line train to Alder Creek
left Winnipeg in the early morning in 1890, as it does today."

2. This sentence was in the present tense, followed by a long descriptive passage of the
morning, and gave an account of how a lady, identified as Mrs. Barrow, put him on the
branch-line of the train and left him in the custody of the conductor. The cut removed
the sentimentality that burdened the first draft. Also the dialogue between Donald and
the conductor, simply reported in the original, makes the whole scene more alive and re-
alistic.

3. Stead have cut a paragraph describing the train and introduced in the second version.

4. None of this conversation of the three suns is in the original; the second version tells
how the conductor entertained Donald with adventures about driving and snowstorms.

5. This description was introduced only in this version.

6. Stead cut a considerable part here about someone other than his uncle being asked to
meet Donald at the station.

7. Two following sentences were cut in the final version; both stressed the pathos of
Donald's life.

8. The colloquial "uh-huh.' replaces "yes sir."

9. The original narrative justifies Donald's falling asleep; Stead's cut makes for con-
ciseness.

10. Read: "Very self-conscious, he accepted their greeting."

11. Read "yours'll be on the table in a minute."

12. A short paragraph cut here said that the time was only seven and left Donald wondering why people on the prairie went to bed early.

13. An "all right" appeared after "manage"

14. "Felt" read "reached again."

15. "But Tom" read "Tom, too."

16. The sentence originally read "once gay but now sadly faded"

17. "Soon" read "presently."

18. A long section has been omitted here in which Ellen introduced Donald to the cellar and the great bins of food, shelves loaded with jams, plus the other delicacies stored elsewhere in the house. The cut passage contained the first hint of a growing feeling of comradeship between Ellen and Donald.

19. Originally Uncle Jim ended by asking "Have a good sleep?" Also Stead cut a paragraph indicating the new respect that Donald had acquired for his Uncle Jim, impressed by his wealth (of the stores of food).

20. "Announcing dinner" read "which was very satisfactory."

21. "Breathy" read "aspirated."

22. Stead here cut two sentences about servings and how they were done.

23. The original qualified "manners" and read "table manners"; gave elaborate account of the meal, with reflections on Donald's upbringing; described the day's routine and Donald's learning the many things done on a farm; and a long description of the storm.

24. Originally Stead continued with more reflections on God and sin and the doubts that beset Donald.

25. Stead here cut a passage about the strict observance of the Sabbath in the Strand household where even reading and playing was prohibited, and about the fear of sin and the doubts that troubled Donald. Interestingly enough Ellen eased his mind by pointing out that she had been listening to the Bible every night and had found no reference to reading being sinful. It also contained the development of the growing affection between Ellen and Donald.

26. Originally simply read "the schoolhouse" without any name, which explains the absence of the second sentence from the original draft.

27. That this was Donald's first Sunday on the farm is added only in the final version.

28. Stead here cut a short conversation in which Aunt Annie wondered if the preacher would come on such a day.

29. "In" read "inside."

30. "For" read "to face".

31. The first part of this sentence originally read: "A huge stove sat near the door . . ."

32. Read "Billie Harris" instead of "Harp." Why Stead changed Harris to Harp in the final version is not known.

33. This sentence read: "Some gave coppers and some gave five-cent pieces, and some had nothing to give."

34. Read "forty-three cents."

227

35. "The feminine instinct" read "the fourth of Solomon's mysteries."

36. The adjective "homemade" was inserted only in the final version.

37. Read "Sandy Wayne," obviously and error and corrected in other places; or, Stead may have decided to change the name to Andy when revising his first draft.

38. "End it" read "finish it."

39. Originally lacked the second half of this sentence.

40. This sentence not in the original.

41. Stead cut a sentence following this injunction which read; "So, for the moment, the issue rested, but Donald and Allen felt like comrades in arms who had fought, at least, a drawn battle."

42. Stead here cut a long passage about the hospitality extended to Walter Spence, and a general account of how Donald was passing his days.

43. Originally ended: "At ten o'clock Mrs. Strand found part of a tin of coffee which had been reserved for just such an occasion and they feasted on coffee and slices of buttered bread. Donald felt that it had been the happiest evening of his life." The original led straight on to "Spring swept down . . ." and did not as here begin a new section.

44. This paragraph added only in the final version.

45. "The water took longer" read "it took the water longer."

46. Originally a full stop after "thought," a semi-colon after the "Strand farm."

47. The clause "noisy regiments of wild geese were wedging their way northward" shows only in the final draft.

48. Stead here cut a passage about Ellen and Donald which I think worth while in that it gave insight into Donald's sense of honour and sin, and an endearing portrait of Mr. Matthews, the teacher.

49. This sentence shows only in the final draft.

50. "With Jack" added only in the final version.

51. Instead of "they can play together" the second version read "he can play with Jack." The idea of Jack is altogether absent in the first draft.

52. "Revealed" read "laid on the ground."

53. Originally the sentence to included: "and about the same length."

54. Originally spelt "Gaul."

55. Originally ended the smoking episode at this point with:

> Donald did so, and in a few minutes Jimmie got up to go. "Can't stay too long," he said. "Besides your folks may be wondering where we are."
> Donald retired that night at peace with the world. He had smoked without breaking his pledge, and had learned a new word for use in a emergency.

56. Originally read "but they were almost at the house," and gave an account of the seeding and soap-making as the background against which the romance of Ellen and

228

Donald flowered. Stead cut a passage here dealing with a night spent shooting ducks and another giving a detailed description of the annual picnic.

57. Originally the narrative continued to describe Hector's ability with the cattle.

58. "Grazing as they went" inserted only in the final draft.

59. Originally read "the cattle."

60. Stead replaced in the second version a paragraph describing Hector's and Donald's comradeship with simply: "The day wore on."

61. "Lying on the grass with Hector at his side" added later.

62. Dots indicating an omission are rare in Stead. The original filled the gap with Donald lost in his daydreams (with Ellen figuring in them) and the cattle straying off but brought back by Hector without much damage.

63. "The hours" read "the afternoon," and before telling of the shadow "falling eastward," read "but at length it wore away."

64. "The reluctant herd" read "the reluctant animals."

65. "Coo-man" read "cow-man." It is not a typing error in all probability.

66. "To disturb their germinating romance" read "to see what was detaining them."

67. Stead cut the question of Donald's shoes that led to the trip with Uncle Jim compressing into two sentences what had taken two pages in the earlier draft.

68. "Which" read "that".

69. "About" before "that" inserted only later.

70. Originally this statement was followed by: "an' neither could Mr. Matthews."

71. "Alder Creek" read "The Station."

72. Originally the sentence stood in an inverted order and read: "The sun was setting as they left for home," changed in the second draft; but Stead cut a long account of the day in town with sketches of a few minor characters in the final draft.

73. Originally this was only a short paragraph but was expanded later to show Jim's reception at home. The last sentence of the original paragraph is however, unaltered. "His prayer was an emotion . . . and of great things to come."

74. "Crash" read "noise."

75. "Deafening" read "indefinable."

76. The last part of the sentence originally read "and from time to time would whip a corner free."

77. "Fussing with a lamp which was continually blowing out" read "trying with no luck to light a lamp."

78. Originally read "they" before "all.

79. Instead of "was fruitlessly shouting instructions against the clamor of the storm" originally read: "tried to shout instructions, which were lost in the roar of the storm."

80. "It" read "that" in the original.

81. The last part "We'll be fighting it out, Ma!" is not in the original.

82. The original qualified the "kettle" with "tea" before it.

83. The last sentence was inserted later; originally the sentence read: "I wounder if it's [sic] swept the whole neighborhood."

84. "Grew" read "because."

85. Originally the sentence continued with "and Tom confessed he had a hail-stone bruise where he couldn't show it."

86. This sentence not in the original.

87. The last sentence was not a sentence by itself in the original but stood in continuation with the earlier one, separated by a comma, and read; "only a broken stalk here and there trembling in the sunlight."

Part Two

1. Read "on the 24th of August, 1901."

2. "Ever and again" read "from time to time."

3. Read "masterly" before the "sunburned face."

4. "Animals" read "brutes."

5. "The skin sagged about his jaws" was inserted later.

6. "Broom-like" read "long, spreading."

7. Read "the boy" originally for "Donald."

8. "I hope to" read "I'll try to."

9. "Goes for you" read "applies to you."

10. "I'm just out of twine" read "I'll need more twine by three o'clock, and the stooking is getting behind."

11. Read "Kate" instead of the more colloquial "Katie."

12. Read "the mirror" and "exactitude" for "care."

13. "Might be" read "were."

14. "An oval face" added later.

15. "Smile" read "curve."

16. "A sculptor" read "an artist."

17. "The great day it is" was more blunty "how old you are."

18. "Scheming" read simply "wanting."

19. "Twenty" was "twenty-one."

20. Instead of "drownded" read "drowned." Similar changes were made in the remaining section.

21. Read "she knew" followed with "that a teacher must not make the mistake . . ." The intervening words were introduced in the second version.

22. This whole sentence was inserted in the second version. Originally the sentence after this also started with "For his part . . ." which was deleted when this sentence was put in.

23. "Shorter than Ellen" read "not as tall as Ellen."

24. Dash replaced semi-colon in find draft.

25. "I know" read "I am sure."

26. "I went" read "I was going."

27. "Any notice" read "a bit of attention."

28. Read "as soon as the meal was finished . . ." in the original.

29. This sentence is not in the original.

30. "Danced" read "twinkled."

31. In the original Ellen continued with "Remember the time you lay awake because you said damn," followed by a retort by Donald. In the second version "Donald" was added at the end of the sentence. In the final draft Stead deleted part and changed the rest.

32. Originally the sentence began with "When she drew away . . ."

33. "Over" was followed by "yet" in the original.

34. The last sentence read: "I guess you've been noticin' how the wind blows?" and Donald's answer read: "I've had suspicions."

35. The last sentence was added later and even the one before that in the original read "and I don't know much else" after "I'm twenty-one today."

36. In the original all the "you"s were "ye"s and the "you're"s read "yer." Stead changed the "yer" to "ye're," and to "you're" in the final draft.

37. "Done our best" read "tried to do our best."

38. Originally ended with "for you."

39. "Did na" read "didn't."

40. "Was na" read "wasn't."

41. "Could" read "might."

42. Read "Donald would have pressed."

43. The reported part has been changed. The original read: "Donald ventured on another tack."

231

44. Read "strength o' muscle an' heart 'll . . ."

45. This sentence is not in the original.

46. "Him" read "em."

47. This sentence is not in the original.

48. All the "hunder"s in this section and elsewhere read "hundred" in the original.

49. "Faces" read "mugs."

50. "Taking shape" read "focussing."

51. Originally "dropped" was followed by "himself."

52. Read "Hope I didn't keep you waiting."

53. Read more simply in the original: "if I ever do."

54. The remaining part of this section was added later. The original had only a conlcuding sentence: "Then, before he knew what had happened, she had impetuously planted her lips on his cheek, and was gone."

55. "Wheels" read "feet'."

56. "That" read "it."

57. "Even" read "and," and "itself" followed after "the trail."

58. "In earlier years" is not in the original.

59. "The creek" read "Alder Creek."

60. "Donald" read "the boy."

61. This paragraph and the one after it are not in the original.

62. "Aware of" read "aware that there was."

63. "Settlement" read "neighborhood."

64. This part of the sentence read "become as hard as it could."

65. "For yourself" read "out of it."

66. "Reins" read "lines."

67. "At that time" is not in the original.

68. "Glances" read simply "eyes."

69. Originally the epithet "daintier" stood before "shoes."

70. This sentence is not in the original.

71. The remaining part of this section was added only in the final version. All earlier versions ended with: "Should she play for this stake or wait for something bigger? At any rate Donald could not be ignored, and a little experience might do no harm."

72. All earlier versions devoted a whole section to the description of the cottage at Alder Creek and narrated Mrs. Strand's reaction and planning. This is indicative of the great compression Stead made in the final draft.

73. A complete long section narrating the wedding and other incidents of the day are omitted in the final version.

74. "Easy-going" read "generous."

75. "Black ribbons" read "furrows."

76. A somewhat detailed description that followed here was omitted in the final version.

77. This sentence is not in the original.

78. "Knew anything" read "really."

79. "Lower" read "other."

80. "Picture" read "thing."

81. "Declared" read "espoused."

82. Two philosophical sentences that followed at this point cut in the final version.

83. Originally the sentence read: "He had accepted the idea that some day he should marry, as natural if not inevitable but he had never thought of it . . ."

84. "House" read "home" in all earlier versions.

85. "One night" read "that night" in all earlier versions.

86. "Qualification" read "recommendation."

87. "And money" is not in the original.

88. "In the glow from her lamp" read simply "when he looked at it."

89. Originally read "moved out."

90. "Might be" read "could be."

91. The original had a 't' and read "woudn't." Similar changes of final consonants being dropped are introduced throughout the dialogue, and elsewhere as well.

92. "Hot water" read "warm water."

93. Read "of" instead of the more colloquial form of later versions.

94. Read "a straight question."

95. In all the earlier versions the conversation continued along the same lines as it had between Donald and his Uncle Jim earlier. Stead may have cut it in the final draft because it was repetitive.

96. "Atmosphere" read "appearance."

97. Originally the adjective "large" was used before the room as well as before the rooms upstairs.

98. "Afford better" read "build better."

99. "Little drama" was simply "talk."

100. "Yet" read "still."

101. "Soil" read "earth."

102. The original draft started with this paragraph till ". . . out to his farm," then followed a detailed account of Donald's trips for firewood when he stayed at Alder Creek. In the second version Stead cut the narrative to less than a quarter, still further in the final draft. In the original the section ended with "Sometimes he went upstairs . . ."; the following paragraph about Jimmie Wayne was the beginning of a new section.

103. This was the beginning of a new section in the original draft. Most of that section was revised but allowed to remain in the second version. In the final draft, however, Stead cut most of it. Its main line of thought was an underlining of a feeling of inferiority experienced by Donald in Jimmie's presence.

104. In the original version the subject of Donald's and Ellen's marriage was a conversation between Donald and Jimmie.

105. In the earlier versions these thoughts, more elaborately written about, had filled the earlier section.

106. What was a whole conversation between Donald and Ellen in the earlier versions was cut to a sentence in the final.

107. Many changes have been made in this paragraph in the various versions but the gist of it remains the same in all.

108. In the original there were three sections between the end of the last section and the contents of this one. In the second version they had been reduced to two but in the final version most of it has been either cut or incorporated elsewhere.

109. "Would be" read "was," and even the "would be" before "humiliation" read "was."

110. "Spotted with" is not in the original.

111. "Was resigned to Donald" read "had decided it would be Donald."

112. Part of a paragraph that followed after this was retained in an altered form.

113. Referred to only as "a dance" in this version; all the earlier ones described the preparation and the dance itself in detail. It was a party arranged by Tom and Kate.

114. "Frowning again at the little bridge of freckles which was making its re-appearance with the summer sunshine" is not in the original.

115. "Signed" read simply "answered."

116. "It" read "that."

117. Originally read "Clara agreed" at this point.

118. "Perhaps" read "sometimes I think."

119. In the original "Clara" was inserted here. Stead perhaps realized the repetition and removed it in the second version.

120. "Rather suspect" read simply "think."

121. "In smooth, cool intimacy" read very simply "outline."

122. "Picking" read "looking for."

123. In all earlier versions Stead went on to describe Clara's attempts at setting the morrow's task on the blackboard but intruded to tell the reader that her mind was not on her work.

124. "Clara stood in the schoolroom door" was put in only in the final draft. All earlier versions simply read "she sat."

125. "Her self-esteem" read "convention."

126. This sentence is not in the original. In all the earlier versions there followed dreams of matrimony and Clara comparing herself with Hester as Donald's wife.

127. In all the earlier versions "arose from her chair" followed here, cut in the final draft.

128. "On the range" is not in the original.

129. "Probability" read "verisimilitude."

130. "Strand homestead" read "Harris homestead."

131. "Another half mile" read "half-a-mile."

132. "Speeded up" read "quickened."

133. In all earlier versions the paragraph continues describing how Clara, unaware of the speed with which the horses were approaching, was in Donald's path.

134. "At her presence" read simply "at seeing her there."

135. "Control" read "actions."

136. "Wondering" read "asking himself."

137. "Brother" read "disturb."

138. Added later, originally the sentence started: "He spoke to his horses . . ."

139. "Beside the blackened earth" read more simply "alongside."

140. "Breast" read "bosom."

141. "Modest" read "yellow."

142. "If I can" was "not me serve the farm."

143. "Again" read "back."

144. "Alongside" read "up beside her."

145. "Carry" read "take."

146. All the earlier versions qualified the "cream" by adding "got it from Katie yesterday."

147. "A dash of" read simply "something."

148. "Or because of that" is not in the original.

149. "Each" reach "both."

150. All earlier versions continued with a description of the table laid out under Clara's deft care with the feminine touch quite in evidence.

151. "Smothering her freckles" is not in the original.

152. A long section was cut at this point. Evidence of revision showed that it had been considerably shortened in the second version, but in the final one Stead cut it altogether. It consisted of Clara's apologies and explanations of her conduct and ended with the confession that she had been going out with Harry Long only to arouse Donald's jealousy.

153. "The meal" added only in the final draft.

154. "But he had no words" read "and they walked as one person" in all the earlier versions. Another sentence followed but was cut in the final draft.

155. "Literal" before "Hell" is not in the original.

156. "Instant" read before "night."

157. "Is" read "to be."

158. Originally the sentence started with "On the slight raise of the prairie . . ."

159. "That" read "how."

160. "Across" read "beyond."

161. "He did it" followed after "why."

162. In all earlier versions the paragraph continued to described Donald's going to bed and falling off to sleep.

163. In all earlier versions Donald's sense of honour is underlined by the narrative voice intruding to tell us that Donald planned to make the situation plain to Hester.

164. Originally in inverse order and read "had never . . ."

165. A short paragraph in the original was cut here.

166. A sentence that emphasized the conflict in Donald's mind was cut in the final draft.

167. A full section that preceded this one and narrated how Donald disclosed his plans of marrying Clara to Hester has been cut in the final draft.

168. "Himself" read "him."

169. "The night before" read "her heart."

170. "And she sang as she dressed for her duties" is not the original.

171. "Did not go by the bridge" is not in the original.

172. Originally this sentence started with "Just as she . . ."

Part three

1. "His room" read "the room" and "right" stood before "off."

2. "The privileges of the inner circle" read "admitted to the family circle." The change from "family" to "inner" comes in the final draft.

3. "Sturdy" is not in the original.

4. "Mr. Donald Strand" read only "him."

5. "Brilliance" read "light."

6. "There was a sag to his cheeks" is not in the original.

7. This part of the sentence read: "The total was as encouraging as ever . . ."

8. "Heralded by Sundown Chieftain II" is not in the original.

9. "Reckoned" read "included."

10. "Prices" read "values."

11. "Old Man" before "Farquhar" is not in the original.

12. "The total was" read "the items came to."

13. "Allowed" read "included."

14. "Creditable" read "satisfactory."

15. The last part of the sentence read: "the contemplation of it brought him less than the satisfaction he had hoped."

16. "His unhappiness" read "his dissatisfaction."

17. "Clarissa" was "Irene." The last part of the sentence read: "I suppose her school does not reopen until September."

18. "Of course" read "too."

19. In the original the sentence ended with "so don't put it off."

20. "Hungry" read "weary."

21. The original at this point contained a few sentences on Donald's brooding and feeling hurt.

22. "From him" read "with her."

23. "The day of Tom's decision" read "read "the day of his break with Tom."

24. "Hung" read "centred" and "slackened" read "drooped."

25. Stead cut in the final verison Tom's reasons for not wishing to continue with the farm.

26. Here Stead cut additional conversation in the final draft.

27. Read: "That will take all the flavor out of her victory . . ."

28. "Observed scrupulously" read "scrupulously fulfilled."

29. The second half of this sentence is not in the original.

30. "Mechanized agriculture" read "the increased size of farms."

31. The origingal included: "which separated her room from the office."

32. In all earlier versions the section continued with Donald's reflections on the mystery of life and death.

33. "Home" read "back."

34. The original here had another sentence telling of Donald's unspoken fears about Clarissa and Walter breaking away from him as Tom had done.

35. "Sixty" read "an hour."

36. "An arm" read "a bare arm."

37. The knee exposing incident was more long-drawn-out in the first draft.

38. All earlier versions contain an account of Donald's going to Aunt Annie's room and having a short chat with her before switching off the light.

39. In the earlier versions this question is not asked. Instead there is a teasing question referring to an "anarchist" friend of hers.

40. In the earlier versions there is no new section at this point.

41. Stead made many changes in this paragraph; earlier readings are longer and more detailed though the basic arrangement is the same in all.

42. "Arms" read "disconcerting gesture."

43. "Moved" read "turned."

44. "Acknowledged" read "answered."

45. In the original "Alder Creek fair" inserted here.

46. A paragraph about Tom that followed here stands cancelled in the original itself.

47. In the original Donald's feelings about Tom and Clarissa and his realization that family ties were weakening had continued at this point, cut only in the final draft.

48. Earlier versions had a sentence stood here repeating the fact that Donald had been beaten by Clara.

49. Earlier versions had a paragraph here point enlarging on the great affection that Donald had for Tom particularly, he being the first born.

50. "And had minimized it to . . ." read "perhaps, even, from . . ."

51. "Different" read "new."

52. "Or disagreement" is not in the original.

53. "When he would not disturb his family" was inserted here in the original.

54. Many minor changes have been made in this paragraph.

55. "Week or so" read "couple o' weeks."

56. Earlier versions had an account of Donald's supervisory activities as a farmer, cut in the final draft.

57. "His hired men" read more specifically "Ned and George."

58. "Them" read "his hired men."

59. Another exchange between George and Donald in earlier versions was cut in the final draft.

60. Stead's manuscript reads "warmness" instead of "warmth." Change made by the editor.

61. "Led forth" read "led before him."

62. Stead's manuscript reads "for" here which seems to be an error. Correction made by the editor.

63. "Must" read "should be able to."

64. Stead's manuscript reads "you should worry" which seems to be incorrect. Correction from "should" to "shouldn't" has been made by the editor.

65. The prayer and the reference to Ellen's letter that follow at this point were originally placed before Aunt Annie's entry.

66. This sentence was added when the passage was shifted to its present position.

67. "Its" in all earlier versions read "it must be—yes, it is—two years . . ."

68. "Two" before "years" is found in all the earlier versions.

69. A last sentence directed towards Aunt Annie cut in the final version, as well as two paragraphs that followed and Aunt Annie's polite but negative answer.

70. The sentence began "He took the high road at an easy pace."

71. In earlier versions this sentence was longer, telling the spots where the road's indentity had not been destroyed.

72. In earlier versions Stead added that their farm had passed on to a family named Cummings, with a description of its deterioration.

73. Fred Hardy was first named Fred Harp.

74. "Machine" read "car."

75. A bantering exchange that followed here between Clarissa and Walter cut in the final draft.

76. "And her rich, ruddy hair" is not in the original. All earlier versions continued with Donald again referring to her "anarchist" friend, cut in the final draft.

77. "He" read "Donald."

78. "Or even a school teacher" is not in the original.

79. "What if" read "he knew."

80. "And bursting the bounds of the quarter-section" read "and slamming the door on the quarter-section."

81. A long section that preceded this one, found in all earlier versions, is cut here. The section narrated a visit to the cemetery, Donald's reflections on death, and Walter Spence's shaky financial position.

82. In earlier versions a long paragraph at this point deals with Lizzie and Walter Spence, cut in the final draft.

83. Earlier versions add a sentence here: "Thoughts which arose from a visit to the cemetery left him groping."

84. Earlier versions have another reference to Lizzie and Walter Spence here, cut in the final draft.

85. "Red" read "amber."

86. "The trail" read "it."

87. "His course" read "the trail." In earlier versions the sentence is also longer; Stead cut the second part in the final draft.

88. "It" read "the creek" and "ford" read "spot" in earlier versions.

89. "Little" stood before "nostalgic yearning."

90. "Once" is not in the original; "again" moved from the end of the sentence to before "could be."

91. "Reached almost" read "almost reached."

92. "Palms" read "hands."

93. "Grain" read "heads."

94. "Iron-gray" read "steel-grey."

95. "Memory" read "faith."

96. A full section preceding this one is cut in the final draft; it helped bring out the tension between Aunt Annie and Clara and between Clara and Donald.

97. "Reflecting" read "returning."

98. "Place" read "home."

99. "Subdued" read "quiet."

100. "Distinctly suppressed" read "which she made no attempt to suppress."

101. "You frightened all the policemen off the street" read "policemen were afraid to come near your car." In the sentence following this one "wide" stood before "swath."

102. The simple "he caught," read "his attention was arrested by the . . ."

103. The last two sentences not in the original.

104. The direct speech is broken at this point to insert "she said, cheerily."

105. His hands are also described as being "fat and featureless."

106. "Electric candles" read "the chandelier above" and the more sophisticated "silver and crystal" read simply "silver cutlery and plate."

107. "Off the stage" followed after "disappear."

108. The sentence started with "Donald was a little embarrassed . . ." When "Donald" was removed from the beginning the second part of the sentence was added.

109. In the original Clara had declined the offer of a cigarette, and had, on the contrary, been surprised that Ellen smoked.

110. "Offered" read "invited them to."

111. "Pleased" read "obviously pleased."

112. The reference to the billiard table is not in the original.

113. The conversation between Jimmie and Donald included Jimmie's notion of how 'easy money' was made. This part was however cut in the original itself, and the conversation introduced later in other versions.

114. The direct speech had been broken to insert "Jimmie agreed."

115. "Alder Creek Fair" read "Brandon Fair."

116. A few repetitive sentences following here were cut later.

117. "Business" after "marriages" was added only in the final draft.

118. In the original this whole argument was put very differently.

119. "Overhead" followed "stars."

120. "At the door" followed after "footsteps."

121. "Shoes" read "boots."

122. "Don't pretend to be dumb" read "Don't be dumb."

123. "He" read "Donald."

124. A sentence telling of Donald's reminiscences of the bed made for him by Ellen when he was a boy follows at this point in all earlier versions but is cut in the final draft.

125. The section, in all earlier versions, continues with Donald's nostalgic memories, cut in the final draft.

126. A couple of sentences indicating Donald's decision to make easy money are deleted in the final draft.

127. Read: "When he came back Jimmie met him on the verandah . . ."

128. "Meal" read more specifically "bacon and eggs."

129. "He" read "Jimmie."

130. In earlier versions Jimmie used this opportunity to impress upon Donald the importance of working with a well-reputed firm, cut in the final draft.

131. "Andrew" read "Frank."

132. This part of the sentence is not in the original.

133. A "that" stood instead of the dash.

134. "But he was ashamed" read simply "he was afraid."

135. "A lot" before "more" is not in the original.

136. "Tribune" is specified only in the final version. The earlier ones read simply "paper."

137. "Stores" read "shops" and "gave" read "had."

138. The reference to his baseball playing is not in the original.

139. "And the smell of wheat" is not in the original.

140. "Pointing" read "filtering."

141. "Square" read "cube."

142. The original had more memories than just this one.

143. Read "question" instead of "answer."

144. "Only" stood after "we could."

145. "Enveloped them" read "caught them both in its circling breath."

146. This paragraph stands in its present form only in the final draft. Earlier versions describe what is merely stated here. Stead has achieved compression though he allowed the last paragraph to stand more or less unchanged. The original last paragraph follows this one.

147. A complete section preceding this one cut in the final draft, narrated an incident when Jimmie and Clara went to the movies while Ellen and Donald stayed at home and talked of old days and life and happiness.

148. "Stayed" read "postponed their departure."

149. "Ripening" was qualified by "fast," cut only in the final draft, and "reluctant" read "tardy."

150. "Paid a final visit" read simply "visited."

151. "Asked" read "answered."

152. The direct speech was interrupted at this point to insert "Jimmie agreed."

153. "Here" read "at my bank."

154. "Advising" stood before "you."

155. "Astonishment" read "embarrassement" in earlier versions.

156. In the original the sentence began with "are you."

157. "Tickled by the suggestion" read "hoping, under the disguise of a modest disclaimer, for an affirmative." Many changes were made to the conversation that followed.

158. The sentence in the original was much longer.

159. "Always had" read "had always."

160. "Large" before "square" was cut only in the final draft.

161. "Greatest," obviously used after much deliberation, read "chief," revised to "great," and finally to "greatest."

162. "Explain" read "define."

163. "Personally" is not in the original.

164. "Suggestion" read "promise."

165. "With his pencil" stood after "office."

166. "Seemed" read "was absolutely."

167. All earlier versions go on to clarify that Clara was not in Donald's confidence as far as his investments and his plans for his nomination went.

168. "Business-like" read "tabulated."

169. "His wife's tones" read "Clara's voice."

170. All earlier versions have three long paragraphs here about Donald's thoughts, doubts, and misgivings, cut in the final draft.

171. "But" is followed by "he realized that."

172. "Stretching" read "crawling."

173. This part of the sentence began with "The coughing of the tractor . . ."

174. A final reiteration of "He would wait," followed here in earlier versions, is cut in the final draft.

175. Read: "Footsteps stroked through the stubble beside him."

176. Completely changed from the original.

177. Started with the narrative voice telling of the change that had come over Clara.

178. Earlier versions have a paragraph after this one describing Donald's reaction to the thought of Clara's infidelity, cut in the final draft.

179. This paragraph originally stood at the beginning of the section as part of the narrative voice making the reader aware of the situation. Earlier versions, at this point, describe Donald's good luck with the stocks, cut in the final draft.

180. Reflections on the tremendous progress made in farming continued in the paragraph but were cut in the final draft.

181. Earlier versions end here; the last sentence added in the final draft.

182. Two sections preceding this one in earlier versions, cut in the final one, observance of the Sabbath, Clara's ideas on divorce, and introduction to Karl (Clarissa's boyfriend) and his ideas on various subjects, etc.

183. "Although" read "but."

184. This sentence is not in the original.

185. "The profit-takers have been cashing in" is not in the original.

186. "Have jumped in with" read "have seized the occasion ot stage."

187. Donald's doubts about Jimme's judgement, following here in earlier versions, cut in the final draft.

188. "It beats the devil" read "It's a corker."

189. This part of the sentence read: "doing business on a pretty close margin."

190. "Make way for him" read "stand back."

191. "Tuesday" read "Wednesday."

192. "But I guess" read "hope."

193. "Great" read "obvious."

194. Many changes have been made in this sentence.

195. Read simply "He told her."

196. This sentence is not in the original; the earlier sentence continued with "dazed by her selflessness."

197. "Exhaust" read "motor."

198. "The boy" read "Walter."

199. "Respectfully" read "politely."

200. "Won't be" read "will be not" in all earlier versions.

201. This sentence started with "It was after midnight . . ."

202. "Wide and brightly-lighted" read "long and nearly empty."

203. This sentence is not in the original.

204. The offering of drinks and Donald accepting is not found in the original.

205. "This morning, I guess it is, now" was inserted at this point.

206. "Bulge" read "bump."

207. "Still" read "but."

208. Read "go home now."

209. This sentence read : "He locked the securities in a private vault opening off his office, and they went down in the elevator together." The sentence following is not in the original.

210. "Though the darkness" stood at the end of the sentence.

211. "When I want it" read simply "later."

212. The second part of the conversation consisted of instructions about parking the car.

213. "Again" read "at length."

214. "Jimmie" read "he."

215. "At length" read "presently."

216. "The boy answered." is not in the original.

217. "The" read "like a."

218. "At its upper edge" read "over it."

219. "Wedge" read "fan."

220. "Picture" read "aura."

221. "They slipped" stood at the beginning of the sentence.

222. "From him" stands at the end of the sentence in earlier versions.

223. "He lose it" read "it slip from him."

244

224. The last sentence was added only later and even parts of the direct speech have been revised from the original.

225. "The housekeeper" read "Mrs. Fetch."

226. Originally continued with "she asked, looking straight at him."

227. Originally the direct speech was interrupted to insert "she said."

228. The last sentence is not in the original.

229. "Beautiful face" read "pretty cheeks."

230. "Surely we are popular" is not in the original.

231. "Concentrated" read "miniature."

232. "We can" read "may yet be ours."

233. "Like running away" is not in the original.

234. "Dropped" read "sunk" and the second half of the sentence is not in the original.

235. The sentence started with "Her muscles . . ."

236. "Measure" read "sense."

237. "Would" read "might."

238. "Feeling" read "sense."

239. This part of the sentence read: "while he could not accept the dogma the words suggested . . ."

240. "Gratification" read "placation."

241. "Named" read "set."

242. "Clara's" read "her."

243. "For the fact" stood before "that."

244. "Concern" read "regret."

245. "A-matter" read "the matter."

246. "Fix it in the books" read "put it through as a dummy account."

247. "Fear" read "terror."

248. "Belief" read "principle of life."

249. "Very quietly" is not in the original.3

250. "Realize" read "appreciate."

251. "Erect" read "was up."

252. "Of course" read "at once."

253. "Made for you" read "made on your account."

254. "Additional money," following at this point in earlier versions, is cut in the final draft.

255. "Energy" read "honor."

245

256. "Turned" read "changed."

257. "Grew to be" read "became."

258. "Item by item" read "one by one."

259. "Quite well" read "feeling quite all right."

260. This sentence is not in the original.

261. "She feared" followed after "that."

262. "At the station" read "along the platform" and "along the platform" read "to the car."

263. "She" read "Ellen."

264. "Moist eyes" followed at this point and the conjunction used before "a courage" was "but."

265. "Come back" read "return."

266. Another sentence about the schoolhouse that stood here Stead later cut.

267. A long account of Ellen meeting Donald's children followed at this point, and a visit by Lizzie and Walter Spence: all later replaced by this paragraph.

268. "To the window levels" follows at this point in earlier versions but is cut in the final draft.

269. The conversation was along different lines until Ellen's confession that she had sent Aunt Annie to Clare's.

270. "And there are a few things to be said—just to make sure we are started on the right road."

271. Read: "To begin with, yes. But they give me little trouble."

272. A franker talk followed between Ellen and Donald about their love and Donald's unhappy marriage till the point when Ellen says "Two months ago I thought I knew."

273. Many changes have been made in the conversation that follows.

274. This paragraph is not in the original.

275. Changed considerably from the original.

276. These two sentences originally read: "I suppose environment, experience, heredity all combine in shaping the answer. You remember, when we were children, how fixed were our beliefs. Then we were sure, but now we wonder."

277. Read "must have run."

278. The sentence did not end here but continued with: "if it had not purpose." Many changes have also been made in the conversation that follows till the point "I know—I know."

279. Originally this followed with another "and grows," and the following sentence read: "The restraint can be abandoned only at peril to the flower."

280. "If we were" followed here before the dash.

281. The elaboration between the two dashes is not in the original.

282. "Flower" was qualified by "original."

283. This part sentence is the only portion of this paragraph retained as it first stood. The rest is considerably changed.

284. This speech of Donald's is changed considerably.

285. The remaining part of the manuscript is missing in the original version in folder 21.

286. The story in its original form ended here. The rest was added later, possibly when the first version was revised.

287. "Known" read "enjoyed" in the earlier version.

288. "Again" came after "had" in the earlier version.

289. "He" read "Donald" in the earlier version.

290. "Tractor" read "team" in the earlier version.

291. "Almost reached" read "passed" in the earlier version.

292. The second draft ends at this point so for the remaining pages there is only the final draft.